Chris Harrison is a journalist, editor and award-winning author. He has contributed to a variety of newspapers, magazines and websites, including *The Sydney Morning Herald*, *The Age*, *The Guardian*, *The Courier Mail*, *Sports Illustrated* and *mamamia.com.au*. His bestselling travel memoir, *Head Over Heel*, has been translated into four languages and won a 2008 Victorian Premier's Literary Award. After a decade overseas he recently returned to Sydney, where he works for News Limited. He has his pilot's licence, Sicilian connections and chronically itchy feet.

His website is www.chrisharrisonwriting.com and you can follow him on Twitter @harrisonwriter

HAPPY *Eva* AFTER

CHRIS HARRISON

ARENA
ALLEN&UNWIN

First published in 2013

Copyright © Chris Harrison 2013

All rights reserved. No part of this book may be reproduced or transmitted in any form or by any means, electronic or mechanical, including photocopying, recording or by any information storage and retrieval system, without prior permission in writing from the publisher. The Australian Copyright Act 1968 (the Act) allows a maximum of one chapter or 10 per cent of this book, whichever is the greater, to be photocopied by any educational institution for its educational purposes provided that the educational institution (or body that administers it) has given a remuneration notice to Copyright Agency Limited (CAL) under the Act.

Arena Books, an imprint of
Allen & Unwin
83 Alexander Street
Crows Nest NSW 2065
Australia
Phone: (61 2) 8425 0100
Email: info@allenandunwin.com
Web: www.allenandunwin.com

Cataloguing-in-Publication details are available
from the National Library of Australia
www.trove.nla.gov.au

ISBN 978 1 74331 763 1

Set in 12/15.5 pt Bembo by Post Pre-press Group, Australia
Printed and bound in Australia by Griffin Press

9 8 7 6 5 4 3 2 1

The paper in this book is FSC® certified. FSC® promotes environmentally responsible, socially beneficial and economically viable management of the world's forests.

To my farzer

A little learning is a dangerous thing.

Alexander Pope

1

The present continuous

In memory of Peter Stevens,
musician and dreamer,
whose favourite place was Primrose Hill.
1 February 1981 – 9 June 2007

I like this plaque on my bench for two reasons. First, it's moving. Second, its punctuation is perfect. Commas in the right places. A fine tribute to both a misfit and the non-defining relative clause. You appreciate such things when you're an English teacher. When I proposed to Sarah I paid the skywriter extra to include the question mark.

I sit here most mornings with Claude. Well, I sit, Claude walks. He is much fitter than I am, though not quite as good at crosswords. Occasionally he'll fluke an answer but our success is down to me. We've won several glorified biros in *The Times* crossword competition. They're in a drawer, somewhere.

It's the view we like: St Paul's Cathedral, the Gherkin, couples kissing under oak trees and planes descending on Heathrow, many of them carrying my students. My fucking students. Most are harmless, but I wish one in particular hadn't chosen to learn English at a particular school. She has ruined everything. Even the view. Though surely she isn't capable of murdering anything other than the English language.

It's sunny but I'm shivering and have a cough like a cobblestone road. Must be the fear – they say it can trigger ill health. Better take the day off work. I'm not presentable. Ten years I've been teaching. Ten years I've been checking that students understand my instructions. The one time I forgot could cost me everything. Unlike Peter Stevens, my gravestone will read: *Here lies the idiot who used the idiom.*

I fold my newspaper to conceal the screaming headline: BANKER FOUND DEAD.

'You must swear to say nothing,' I order Claude, whose mind is clearly elsewhere. The birds mesmerise him, flitting from tree to tree. Squirrels too, chasing each other on the trunks. 'Claude,' I repeat, 'did you understand? You mustn't get me in trouble.'

From my vantage point it feels as though I'm talking to London, but the city is moving too fast to listen. For once I'm glad of that.

A breathless jogger stumbles to the top of our hill – New Year's resolution endured until July. Theatrically, he stops his watch, doubles over, then slumps on our bench next to Claude, who growls until I clip his ear. My canine confidant wags his tail for no one. I'm sure he'd never grass.

'*Tak jdeme!*'

Claude obeys my clumsy command. For a labrador, his Czech is really coming along, as is he, faithfully down the hill at my heels. Perhaps I'll just teach my morning class. Though my students will probably stay away. Last time the forecast was 'sharp showers' they were too frightened to leave their homes.

Mine is a mother of a tongue.

2

The past simple

It was impossible to believe I'd been promoted. Me, Sebastian Pink, perennial underachiever, in charge of interviewing students at a London language school. It didn't mean the end of lesson plans and leaky whiteboard markers; the rest of the week I would teach as normal. But on Mondays I was officially the placement officer, assessing in which class to place the tongue-tied new arrivals. For the first time I had a title beyond 'only child' and the names I'd been called at school, which weren't the kinds of credits you'd emblazon across your CV.

No doubt it was a reward for my staying power. Unlike countless colleagues who had come and gone, for ten years I'd been safeguarding against split infinitives at The Future Perfect in Primrose Hill. As an English teacher I was the definite article, at least that's what my wife Sarah said, before lamenting the fact that my pay packet was a singular noun.

I could perhaps have earned a little more at one of the chain schools like Easy English (oxymoron, in my opinion), but I was fond of the smaller class sizes (and the broken coffee machine which the principal still hadn't realised returned your money afterwards) to be found at The Future Perfect, although Sarah said it was simply the path of least resistance, and she might have been right. Converted from a Victorian terrace house in Fitzroy Street NW1, the ten-classroom college nurtured the Queen's English in surroundings that were quaint, quirky and quintessentially English.

In my new role I was replacing Malcolm – MA in linguistics, daughter at Cambridge and encyclopaedic knowledge of Shakespeare's plays – whose fling with a Japanese student was broadcast, quite literally, around the school. The extracurricular couple had conjugated more than verbs in the language laboratory and Katsumi's oriental tush had inadvertently touched the master record button on the teacher's desk. Their lunchtime liaison was subsequently played to a bemused but aroused group of intermediate students expecting to hear an audiobook called *My Kind of Holiday*, which many thought it was. But it was Malcolm who was sent packing, 'retired early' to a lonely life spent pulling the drinks trolley ever nearer and correcting the grammar of people on telly.

It didn't take long as placement officer to realise that Malcolm was perhaps better off. Mondays consisted of welcoming, registering, grading and orientating twenty or so anxious foreigners, from teenagers to victims of a mid-life crisis, who spluttered responses to a string of monotonous questions designed to test their grammatical accuracy, their conversational fluency and the extent of their vocabulary.

The word in the staffroom was that I had been recommended for the post by Rhonda, the school principal, a no-nonsense Lancashire spinster whose views on English Language Teaching (ELT in the trade) one either swore by or swore at. Until now

I had belonged to the former. Rhonda was a stickler for grammatical accuracy. When, one frigid Monday, she had arrived to find *Cocaine I love you* graffitied on the front wall of the school, rather than wash it off she raced to the nearest hardware store, bought a bottle of spray paint and added the comma after *Cocaine*.

My dubious new job was even more repetitive than teaching, my pay remained the same, and to Sarah's and my mother's surprise I didn't get an office. I conducted my interviews in one of the classrooms, gazing out the window and across the street to where W.B. Yeats had lived as a boy, contemplating his poem 'When You Are Old'. With advanced students I could at least stray from the questions and conduct a conversation. But with beginners, well, I got more sense from Claude.

'Welcome to The Future Perfect. My name's Sebastian. Is this your first visit to London?'

He was sixteen, French, and covered in pimples. Of course it was his first visit to London.

'Ahh . . . *oui*, yes.'

'And what are your first impressions of Primrose Hill?'

'Man . . . er . . . 'ow you say – *travailler*?'

'Work.'

'And woman push ze baby and 'er wear ze big sunglass.'

He was quite an observer. Let's see if he's got the past simple.

'And when did you arrive?'

'Zis morning.'

They rarely take the bait. Let's try again.

'And what did you do yesterday?'

'Yesterday I . . . er . . . go to ze restaurant to 'ave a launch.'

Hmm, no past tense. Can't stick him in an intermediate class. What about the present tenses? Let's see if he's got that third-person 's' which they all forget and which keeps the school afloat.

'Can you tell me what David Beckham does?'

''E play foodball.'

Nope.

'So tell me about your family.'

'My fuzzer is a liar and my muzzer is an arse.'

I'd been teaching too long to raise an eyebrow at what many would consider a startling revelation.

'I see. And how long has your *father* been a *lawyer*?'

I stressed the words he had mispronounced. Tricks of the trade.

'Er . . . for per'aps twenty year.'

'And your *mother* – how long has she been a *nurse*?'

I'm hoping he's got the present perfect continuous.

'Er . . .'

Prompting.

'She has been . . .'

'For per'aps ze same.'

He can't take a hint. I'll give him one last chance.

'Do you have any brothers and sisters?'

'Yes – a bruzzer.'

'And what does he do?'

''E is a bonker in ze city.'

The policeman in *'Allo 'Allo!* wasn't an exaggeration.

'And how long has he been a bonker? Sorry – *banker*.'

Occupational hazard.

'Five year.'

'Which bank?'

'Deutsche Bank.'

He was a high-flying bonker. Time to check adverbs of frequency.

'It says here you go to school in Paris. Tell me about your daily routine. What do you *usually* do in the morning?'

'Er . . . ze first sing I do in ze morning is open my arse.'

What, with his eyes closed? He must make quite a mess.

And on it went for five or so minutes. He had a cat. He wanted to be a liar like his father. His girlfriend was called Amelie. He couldn't wait to visit Madame Tussauds. His favourite film was *Mission Impossible.* He wanted to learn English 'for job' . . .

'Thank you, Jean-Paul. From tomorrow you will be in classroom eleven. I'll see you a little later for the orientation tour.'

I stamped his form PRE-INTERMEDIATE, signed my name for the umpteenth time, then called out a somewhat lethargic, 'Next!'

The name on her student card read Doughnut Porn, uncommon for London but the Jenny Jones of Thailand. Google her, however, and I don't believe you'd find the shy young woman sitting before me, perched on her chair, fidgeting slightly, hoping to impress in her second tongue. Then again, maybe you would.

Apart from her name, the interview was routine until I probed Doughnut's knowledge of the future tense. Mine might have been predictable, but what did her future hold?

'And what will you do this afternoon, Doughnut?'

A question you don't ask every day, graced by an equally esoteric response.

'Er . . .' She thought for a moment before consulting her electronic dictionary. All the Asian students have them. It makes life difficult for teachers whose spelling is suspect because their best efforts on the whiteboard are immediately cross-referenced. 'Dentist pull my dickhead tooth.'

An English teacher's ear is tuned to a different frequency and can detect clarity where others would hear only static. Doughnut, however, had mine beat.

'Sorry, could you repeat that please?'

She studied her small screen carefully.

'Dentist pull my *dickhead* tooth.'

I tried not to laugh.

'Could I see your dictionary, please?'

She spun it around obediently.

'*Decayed*. The dentist pull your *decayed* tooth.'

Maybe she'd eaten too many doughnuts.

'Is it painful?' I inquired.

'Yes – painful.'

'How long has it been painful?'

A chance for her to show off her present perfect.

'Two weeks.'

Ouch! Perhaps *dickhead* was a better adjective after all.

Intermediate.

'Next!'

In a cramped English classroom I spent my morning with the world. With an Italian water polo player called Lorenzo Calamaro. With a Brazilian model, Fernanda Silva. (I steered her clear of Frank's class. Her looks would trigger his stutter.) With a Polish au pair raising a wealthy Londoner's children. With an Arsenal fullback. With twenty Argentinean school kids. With Spanish newlyweds on an eccentric honeymoon. With a Japanese interior designer, a Russian photographer, a South Korean medical student, a Colombian architect, an Iranian doctor, a Ukrainian fencing coach, a Portuguese optometrist, a Swiss housewife . . .

Some had interesting stories, but most didn't have the vocabulary to recount anything too enthralling, at least not intentionally. Their delightfully naïve mistakes were my job's redeeming feature. At The Future Perfect a plumber fixes plums, the past of 'split' is 'splat' and, at Christmas parties, transvestite Japanese shepherds watch their frocks by night.

At the conclusion of their interviews I helped the new arrivals get their bearings. Many had only arrived in labyrinthine London that morning. After banking their cheques, the principal constantly reminded us how traumatic that must be. Audrey, our accommodations officer, directed students to their host families: ageing Londoners whose grown-up children had left behind money-spinning spare rooms. I suggested ways to make the students' time in Blighty run smoothly. Straightforward stuff such as look to the right when crossing the street, 'supper' means 'dinner', you must be eighteen to drink in pubs, don't bother trying to open a bank account . . . That sort of thing. I also told the Italians that the English expected them to queue.

Most importantly, I ensured they knew the way to school. The majority were staying nearby, so the beginners walked, the intermediates arrived *by* foot and the advanced students arrived *on* foot. Those coming from further afield took the Northern line to either Chalk Farm or Camden Town. Others took the number 31 bus up Adelaide Road and alighted, as one advanced student put it, 'where piercings stop and prams begin'.

I began my orientation tour on the top floor of the school, showing the students every feature of The Future Perfect. It reminded me of my real estate agency days, except I now had twenty potential buyers, all of whom had already paid their deposit.

Before the house was converted into a school in the early eighties, its loft space would have been home to a family of mice and forgotten family knick-knacks. Now it was home to a family of mice and classrooms one and two. Few students complained. The rodents rarely revealed themselves. And when they did they provided valuable vocabulary practice.

Teacher: 'What's that?'
Students: 'Mouse.'
Teacher: 'Plural?'
Students: 'Mice.'

Teaching English is made easier with real-life examples.

The leaky roof in classroom two was also a handy prompt, particularly the ingenious remedy on the floor in the middle of the room.

Teacher: 'What's that?'
Japanese student: 'Fishing box.'
Teacher: 'Good but not quite.'
Italian student: '*Contenitore.*'

Teacher: 'In English?'

Italian student: 'Contenitor?'

Teacher: 'Keep trying.'

German student: 'Container.'

Teacher: 'We're getting there.'

Mexican student: 'Bucket.'

Teacher: 'Brilliant!'

Time to go downstairs.

The third floor was home to the IT lounge, a flattering title for three dusty computers and a TV – although the latter was flat-screen, technically, because someone had made off with the picture tube. The standing joke at school was that it was easier to find a mouse in the loft than in the IT lounge. I rushed students past Luddite Lounge as quickly as I could; on my first guided tour as placement officer I had been forced to explain the meaning of an obscene outburst from Walter, bald head and handlebar moustache, who we found slapping a computer monitor with the palm of his hand and shouting, in exemplary English, 'Your mother, dear boy, is a whore!'

Student: 'What's that?'

Teacher: 'Our head of IT.'

Those who understood thought I was joking. And in essence I was, given that Walter – before a regrettable incident at another school – was without doubt the most gifted English teacher a student could hope to find.

Also on the third floor were classrooms three to six, bright and spacious compared to those in the loft and with far less fauna and a lower risk of flood. All the teachers wanted these rooms. The students were more relaxed and you could conduct your class without banging your head on a beam, which wasn't the kind of verb that wanted a real-life example.

The second floor housed the cafeteria, run by Robert, our resident chef. He was no Gordon Ramsay but he liked to think he was contributing to the students' cultural experience by serving up cheap and cheerful English fare: fish and chips, shepherd's pie, toad in the hole and so on. Our longest-serving member of staff, Robert was almost fired on one occasion for launching a saucepan at an Italian who declared mushy peas a crime against 'umanity and threatened to report Robert to the EU.

Classrooms seven to ten were on the first floor, along with the staffroom – a student-free zone. The most luminous room in the school (excuse the real estate agent adjective; old habits die hard), it had recently been refurbished from an IKEA catalogue but was messily decorated with indelible markers, dog-eared textbooks, a disobedient photocopier and a kitchenette in need of a clean. Above the sink was a noticeboard proudly bearing the school's motto, *Trim, Taught and Terrific*, partially obscured by a baby photo from a member of staff on maternity leave and a postcard from a teacher who'd emigrated to Oz.

My orientation tour concluded on the ground floor, where I pointed out Rhonda's office before assembling the students in the foyer of the school which, like their English, was under renovation. The principal's tropical fish tank added a touch of life and colour to the spot cloths and ladders cluttering up the entrance. Rhonda couldn't find an English builder so she'd offered the contract to some Polish students who received free lessons in exchange for their labour. Though beginners, they would surely be fluent by the time the foyer was finished.

After the tour, students gathered in the rear courtyard. The outdoor space was cleverly paved with bi-colour bricks so that, looking down from the classrooms, you could read the school's name. The principal insisted that the painstaking feature created a 'super' last impression to a student's first day, as long as they overlooked the cigarette butts between the bricks. We did have a caretaker who was supposed to pick the butts up, but he was so poorly paid he used to smoke them instead.

While the students snacked on finger food Robert had prepared – Scotch eggs, crisps and Coca-Cola – I gave out their textbooks and checked they knew which classroom to go to the following morning. When I then left them on the cobblestones to make new friends, they darted for compatriots and the security of mother tongues so quickly it felt as though I'd detained them against their will. For The Future Perfect's new recruits it had been a daunting day.

That was my Monday as placement officer. My every Monday as placement officer. For someone whose only skill was The English Language it was disturbing to think I had misinterpreted the term 'promotion'.

3

Conjugate

Call centres fix ninety per cent of faulty electrical products by asking if the appliance is plugged in properly. Fertility clinics do likewise, although they rephrase the question.

Having passed forty and at the peak of her profession, Sarah was obsessed with getting pregnant – a verb mistakenly passive, in my opinion, given the activity required to achieve it. My wilting rose had tried everything from casting folic acid across her porridge to doing headstands after sex, hoping to coax my spark in the direction of her plugs.

Our love life had become industrial but without the revolution. Romance had gone and taken spontaneity with it – par for the course when you stop 'making love' and start 'trying for a baby'. I'd come home from The Future Perfect to find her naked, primed and strategically splayed on the bed, thermometer poking out and pillow propping up target parts. 'I'm ovulating at this precise moment,' she'd declare. 'Jump on, Jack Rabbit. I want every last drop.'

Foreplay consisted of putting down my briefcase. I wasn't granted time to untie my laces, let alone take off my shoes. Sarah wished to create a life but was herself somewhat dead; unerotically still, as though one of her many books on the subject suggested sperm swim better in calmer waters. Her breasts and mouth had become redundant. She was a contraption I entered, like a scrum machine for a rugby player. I closed my eyes and conceived the following morning's lesson on auxiliary verbs.

We anticipated Sarah's period like prisoners awaiting trial. A few days before sentencing she would march into Boots and buy a pregnancy test. I suggested that waiting for a natural verdict might be less traumatic, but my opinion was ignored – I had served my purpose by packing the scrum. My wife then locked herself in the bathroom and painstakingly aimed for the sensor the way a jump-jet hovers above an aircraft carrier. Claude and I held our breaths as the plastic jury pondered. Silence. Only one line again. They should fashion a toothbrush on the other end so the contraption serves more than a split-second purpose.

Our failure to multiply was harder on Sarah than it was on me. She had checked her fertility soon after deciding on starting a family. I begged her to leave something in life to destiny but commercial real estate agency managers can be methodical to say the least. When given a gloved thumbs-up she looked expectantly at me and ordered a deposit. It was done with her signature brand of brusque humour, her acetone affection, but in truth she always did have trouble separating life from work.

After six months of siphoning my sperm with no result, Sarah began to question its quality. This was, once again, put playfully yet directly: at the breakfast table one morning she peered over *Property Week*, suggested my pistol was firing blanks and told me it was time to analyse the gunpowder. Sarah often employed metaphors when referring to my genitals. I welcomed it as a trace of creativity in a woman whose life revolved around stamp duty and square metres, or inches in this case. Facts and figures were the tools of her trade. And dates.

'I've made an appointment for you to see the GP tomorrow at four.'

I swallowed Marmite toast.

'I'm teaching.'

'Get Fer-Frank to do some of that cover he owes you.'

We had an unwritten hierarchy in our ground-floor flat: Claude obeyed me; I obeyed Sarah. It hadn't always been that way. We used to share decisions. Until her fixation with adding to the family had subtracted from my capacity to have a say.

I felt relieved when the doctor informed me I couldn't mate for three days, although I told Sarah he'd said six. My gunpowder needed to be as potent as possible for the fertility test the following week. (More cover for Frank.) I was given a plastic vial and told I had forty-five minutes to get my sample to the hospital – this would be a test of both seed and speed. With my car in for service that meant fondling my fountain either on the bus or at the hospital. I valued my freedom, so plumped for the latter.

Other than accompanying Sarah to A&E after a skylight in a loft conversion of a house she was showing collapsed on her head, I had managed to avoid hospitals since donating my appendix to science as a child. (The woman I called my mother once had a facelift but that was in a private clinic.) As such, I had blissfully forgotten the requisite flower and balloon stall at the entrance, the vending machines, the confusing signage, the shiny lino corridors and, worst of all, the smell of the sick. Conjuring an erection in such a setting was going to be an even greater feat than getting Sarah pregnant.

Life as a language teacher had taught me to plan ahead, so I first located the microbiology department to save searching for it later when the stopwatch would be ticking. Bizarrely, there was no bathroom on that floor, so I went downstairs and found the cleanest toilet cubicle with adequate elbow room and a functional lock on the door.

The most exciting aspect of masturbation is the plethora of partners within arm's reach. After the sexual persecution of recent months I hoped Sarah would forgive my fantasising a more casual companion. But no one seemed keen to join me in that grimy cubicle. I closed my eyes and pictured Kylie singing 'Locomotion'. Nothing. Kylie singing 'Better the Devil You Know'. Still nothing. Kylie singing the *Neighbours* theme tune. As flaccid as mozzarella. Maybe the kiosk sold dirty magazines . . .

I must confess that I had been quite looking forward to my return to adolescence and hadn't expected to need both hands. I simply couldn't get started. (It crossed my mind that I was at least in the right place to consult a doctor about the problem.) Then I remembered the snapshot of Sarah in my wallet and, as a last resort, pulled her out, placed her lovingly on the cistern, and ten minutes later the dormant volcano was close to erupting. Is there better proof of a healthy marriage?

When my eyes began to glaze over I paused to unscrew the cap on the vial, revealing a reclusive opening of about two centimetres diameter – the natural urge to close my eyes was out of the question. Sarah's metaphor was momentarily appropriate as I aimed my engorged gun at the tiny target. Was I seeing things or did my wife's eyes roll in the photo as, once again, I strayed off target in the bathroom?

Despite a sign declaring the bathroom to be cleaned at regular intervals, I made the messy discovery that there was no toilet paper. Sperm fast expiring, I was left with no alternative than to mop up with my morning paper; for the first time I wished I read the *Daily Star* rather than *The Times*. Still to do the crossword, I chose the front page pessimism on terrorism and global warming. Did Sarah really wish to procreate?

Humiliated, I skulked upstairs and flagged down a lab assistant.

'Excuse me,' I said softly, hoping not to attract the attention of patients in the queue for blood tests. 'My GP told me to leave this with a member of staff so that it would go straight in the fridge.'

'Well then I suggest you find a member of staff,' said the middle-aged woman squinting at my vial.

'Oh, sorry, but you're wearing Crocs.'

'So?'

'I thought all hospital staff . . . Never mind.'

I found a seat outside the microbiology lab's double doors and waited for someone with a name badge to appear. Several minutes later a buxom blonde with medium heels, half glasses, a clipboard and a white coat pushed through the doors. Had I seen her ten minutes earlier, filling my vial would have been simpler.

'Excuse me,' I tried again. 'Do you work here?'

'Well, I wouldn't wear this white coat as a fashion choice,' she replied. 'How can I help you?'

'I just need to leave this sample.'

Thankfully the woman recognised the container and didn't need an explanation of its contents. She plucked a biro from her left breast pocket.

'What time did you do it?'

As I constantly said to my students, the verb 'do' has myriad meanings.

'Five minutes ago,' I admitted, realising she knew I had done it on the premises, though thankfully she didn't ask where.

'And how long was it since your last ejaculation?'

The blood test queue turned its collective head.

'Five days.'

I had fled before she'd finished scribbling on the sticker.

On the bus home, wringing my wrist and reading the remainder of my paper, I realised I had forgotten the photo of

Sarah on the cistern. The next person unlucky enough to use that cubicle would do so under the sunburnt scrutiny of my bride on a beach in Corfu. I prayed they didn't then drop in to her real estate agency.

■

I say *her* agency but it also used to be *mine,* or at least *ours.* I was twenty-eight, thin as a breadstick, a trainee leasing agent. She was twenty-nine, stout as a truffle, and the same. I'd fled Rugby for the city. She'd gone nowhere, though not for long. We started on the same day. We started in the same branch: *Fla*ttery in Regent's Park. A six-desk office with a water machine and a map on the wall with red thumbtacks for sales and blue for rentals. The window was adorned with photos of the better properties on our books, most of them already sold or let, though customers had to step inside to learn that. A street directory, a clump of keys and a standard-issue Mini. Thirty viewings a week and the boss was your best friend. We discovered that together and shared a rookie smile.

A loosener at the nearby Queens Head & Artichoke became a habit. The knot in my tie had slackened by six and we both enjoyed a drink, which slackened it further still. Though conversation sparkled, we knew we had prospects when silence weighed nothing. I gazed at her plump, pale hands – delightful dough. She folded my tie and fed it to my pocket. We both smoked. You still could. It was quickly agreed who was the Queen's head and who was the artichoke.

She was shorter than me but more driven – something of a dynamo. Her steel-grey eyes seemed severe at first but softened when focused upon you. Her brown hair was dyed blonde, her fingernails painted red, and she wore rouge to mask a small acne scar on her left cheek. Compared to me, however, she was beautiful. We'd only been together a few weeks when she described me as a renovator's dream. I had a crooked nose from falling off my bicycle as a boy, ears like the FA Cup and a maze of hair so unkempt it resembled an unloved thatched roof on a period property we couldn't shift. I supposed that meant I had character.

We made love in most of our properties, agreeing that shaking the foundations was as good as a full structural survey. We even mated in our Minis, like two fond sardines in their tin. Sexually we were suited because we were both rather hopeless at it. The first time I undressed with the light on she choked on her cigarette smoke and gasped, 'Buyer beware!' I liked her honest tongue. She soon had the freehold on my heart.

Sarah was promoted to sales and given a key to the branch, though her diligence was still mixed with abandon back then. Beer in my bloodstream, house wine in hers, we'd return to work while the rest of London was settling down to a property show. We made love in the blind spot of the agency's CCTV cameras. She straddled me with those thoroughbred thighs – that way she could keep an eye out for the cleaner; already she thought of everything. I thought of nothing as I nested among her breasts. Saliva glistened in the tinge of high street neon. She wanted to manage the branch. She sure could manage me.

That Valentine's Day, I found her name badge in the coffee room before work and daubed I LOVE in Tippex next to her name. She arrived late for the only time in her life and hurriedly clipped my confession to the jacket of her black business suit. Her first customer pointed it out and I LOVE SARAH glared across at me, pretending to be busy changing my desk calendar to 14 February 1995.

When I changed my calendar to Valentine's Day the following year, Sarah was the assistant manager. When I changed it a year later, she was the boss. Despite leaving me in her professional wake, she still had a soft spot for me. I never asked why in case she changed her mind.

After two years as a leasing agent I felt sure I had driven my Matchbox car around the world without leaving London, and that *Flattery's* motto – *We'll Get You Everywhere* – was as big a fib as most of our advertising copy. Life was unvaried, made of lead; indeed, the only thing that changed was the date on my desk calendar.

My heart just wasn't nourished by the titillating Zen of real estate, and Sarah's seemed to harden the more time she spent therein. When, to impress the big wigs, she raised my weekly quota of viewings from thirty to fifty, I felt somewhat gazumped. We had one final fling in the blind spot and a skinful at the pub. The agency was Sarah's. She had won it fair and square.

Sarah supported me while I drifted. Edited my short CV. I moved in to her Chalk Farm flat where I watched *Letters and Numbers* on her large-screen TV, let the postman into the building, spilled Earl Grey on the crossword and patted my dopey dalmatian, Bullseye, with my unshod foot. I was old before my time, but there were worse ways to strangle the weekdays, such as showing people where to live rather than telling them where to go.

Despite my 'lack of industry' (Sarah's management-speak for lounging around), I made a household contribution. Dinner was on the table without fail when she finally came home from work, after which we snuggled up on the sofa to watch the property shows that used to be on while we were indulging in 'private viewings'. I can't think why I watched them. My professional interest in the industry had waned and my real estate portfolio consisted of a shed on the Hampstead Heath allotment in which Sarah's father had lost interest and given to me. Its renovation options were limited, although I did put a pool in almost every time it rained.

Sarah's widowed mum, Janette, was the only interruption to my day. She'd invent an excuse to drop by and then far outstay her welcome. I think she needed help with the crossword. She'd complain about everything from my lack of ambition to Bullseye's hair clogging the carpet. Sarah sided with her mum. Said it had become essential since her dad died. But her mum and I were at loggerheads. Funnily enough, the first time I compared Janette to the barbed garter Opus Dei members wear to remind them of sufferance coincided with the first night I slept at the allotment. It wasn't too uncomfortable. Bullseye kept me warm.

The sex was regular, I fought with her mum and we watched telly most evenings. Marriage was the next logical step. On a three-star trip to Cornwall I blew the bulk of my savings on an engagement ring and a skywriter.

'Without a question mark,' I explained to the pilot, '"marry me" is the imperative rather than a request.'

'Question marks cost extra,' explained the piston-engine Cupid.

I hoped he crashed when he was through.

Sarah's response to my costly proposal was not what I had hoped for.

'Why don't you teach?' she asked as I hugged her on the damp hillside. Despite the cold she had removed her shoes to feel the grass between nail-varnished toes. When you spend your life in an office you must maximise rare outings, whatever the weather.

'Sorry?' I replied.

'Only you would make that plane put a question mark. You're a grammatical snob. Why don't you teach?'

A consequence of my lonely childhood was an addiction to books and their constituent parts.

'That's answering a question with a question. Not cricket. I want an answer.'

'I'm serious, Seb. You're good with people – other than my mother and most of my friends. And you always correct their English.'

'*You're always correcting* their English. The present continuous is better to emphasise a vice or bad habit.'

'I rest my case,' said Sarah, returning her gaze to the sky, where my proposal had deformed and looked more like 'merry mes'.

'Will you marry me if I teach?'

'I will.'

I kissed her. Her lips provided welcome warmth.

We returned to our hotel with me believing I had somehow committed to more than Sarah.

We married in Islington and honeymooned on Corfu. Janette babysat Bullseye. Kicked him with her slippers, no doubt. Sarah returned to work with a tan. I turned pale when I learned the cost of my CELTA course (Certificate in English Language Teaching to Adults). Eleven hundred pounds! The Greeks had my last drachma. So Sarah paid. Said it was my wedding present. No point asking my parents, who'd recently spent their surplus pennies on a summer pad in Provence ('we've got our retirement to think of') and now had more houses than children, which I supposed was just as well.

We weren't close. We'd never been close. And I had been somewhat disowned after fleeing to London and showing no interest in the family accounting business, an ironic term given my mother all but forewent a family to nurture the business. I was breastfed by the buxom shelves of my local library. At least my parents had the money to pay late fees. From time to time my mother tried to juggle both me and her career, but she consistently forgot to pick me up after work and often left me in the company of Enid Blyton by the freshly painted gate of my posh primary school.

When she did finally turn up she never thought to ask why my tie had been cut, my chin grazed and my hat stolen again.

But it was no bother to buy me another. Why she'd wanted me I'll never know. In the end she handed me over to a nanny – my third mother. Had anyone found me endearing enough to bestow a nickname upon, Pass the Parcel might have been apt.

Just as long as that parcel wasn't passed to my father. He'd have dropped it. Not through carelessness but through a lack of interest in the contents. Apparently he'd been involved at the start. I remember a framed photo on the mantlepiece of him holding me as a baby. But it was poorly cropped and slightly out of focus, as though catching him in that parental pose was akin to photographing a Formula 1 car.

He worked and played golf, worked and played golf, worked and played golf . . . At my mother's insistence he took me to the country club one Sunday and let me rake the bunkers after he'd hacked his way out. When I subsequently used the swear words I'd heard during that hacking, my mother clipped me around the ear and sent me to my room.

When my father was at home he still indulged in his preferred pastime, as our long corridor provided putting practice. He'd aim for various parts of our snoozy red setter. 'The tip of his tail to win the Masters,' my father would announce. He found it funny. I found it slightly sadistic, particularly when he missed and hit poor Duke in the testicles, or what would have been his testicles if they hadn't had him 'fixed'.

Three decades later, my father still working and playing golf, I passed the CELTA and landed an interview at a language school near Oxford Circus.

'Looks like they miss you at the real estate agency,' observed the principal, reading Sarah's sparkling reference (signed in her maiden name – Crompton – of course). 'Why did you leave?'

'I wanted to teach.'

'So why the two-year gap?'

'I was training.'

'The CELTA course takes a month!'

'I shopped around.'

If he penalised drifters and second-starters his staffroom would be empty.

My students were mainly Asian, far too busy mispronouncing to notice the fear with which I stood up the front and toiled to untie their tongues. I tried but was wasting my time. The Asian mouth is constructed differently. No matter how strong Hiroshi was on paper, his teacher would always hail from Lugby rather than Rugby. No wonder they can't play it.

My nerves passed with the days, my confidence grew with the weeks, my lesson plans disappeared within months. I went from sheepishly entering the classroom knowing every phase of the lesson by heart to breezing in with a hangover and a vague idea. And Hiroshi didn't suffer. He was going to the horselacing on the weekend whether I stayed up all night preparing or scribbled a few frantic notes before class.

I enjoyed the job at first, or at least certain aspects. The students told me I was a good teacher so I told them they were good students. I possessed something they wanted and they looked up to me as though my knowledge of English had been painstakingly acquired rather than picked up in the course of my life along with flat feet and piles. I had never been admired.

But the job weighed after a while and was unvaried despite the range of levels. I grew tired of seeing South Koreans fly to London without the third-person 's', spend two months and two thousand pounds at the school and still fly home without it. 'You don't pay excess baggage to take the "s" home,' I told them. But they always forgot it, no matter how often I reminded them.

I moved to The Future Perfect to be closer to the flat, though I didn't say that at the interview. Primrose Hill was a far prettier and more sedate place to work than Oxford Circus. You could open a window without a bus entering the room, and my new school had 'celeb spotting' on its social calendar rather than just karaoke nights and a weekend in Bath. I taught my first class the same afternoon as my interview. Ten years later I was part of the furniture.

Sarah, in the meantime, had been promoted to national manager and was working fifteen-hour days at company headquarters in Holborn. On the rare occasion we did spend an evening together we'd either watch TV or she'd do Sudoku while I solved the crossword, or what was left of the crossword after morning walks with Claude. Bullseye was dead and buried at my allotment; yes, against the rules, but it was my fennel he was fertilising. I simply didn't get Sudoku. What feeble high is the reward for putting the numbers 1 to 9 in the right order time and time again?

Our paths and pastimes had separated. Sarah had stuck with property while I found refuge in words; I had run to them as a child and was doing so again as an adult. Teaching English, however basic, meant I was at least surrounded by kindred spirits who could help with 2 across or 6 down, which compensated for the fact I had a monotonous job that only ever earned me enough money to be broke. Sarah's annual salary was five times mine, though she too was always skint. Like many of my students, she only knew one verb – to spend.

On a four-star trip to the Lake District Sarah kissed me for the first time since Christmas. Again with those warm lips. A serrated westerly ruffled Lake Windermere. Rowing boats jerked at their moorings and ducks declined to take off.

Dyed blonde hair flew in Sarah's face. Strands in her mouth as she spoke.

'Seb, I've been thinking . . . I want to have a baby.'

'Sorry?' I replied, raising my ears from my coat.

'Do I need to write my proposal in the sky?'

'Is it a proposal?'

'I'm forty-one. It's now or never. I want to have a baby.'

'I thought your job was your baby.'

'Don't cast me in your mother's mould – I want a real baby.'

'Do you have time for a real baby?'

'I'll make time.'

'Are you sure you won't pay someone else to make time?'

'Someone else. Who someone else?'

'I don't know – a silly au pair.'

'What's wrong with a silly au pair?'

'Why have children if you want someone else to bring them up?'

'If I promise to make time and not hire a silly au pair, will you have a baby with me?'

I gazed at the wild water. Harnessed the strength of the wind.

'I will.'

We returned to the hotel wondering who had made the bigger commitment, and who had told the truth.

■

The unadorned brown envelope looked like trouble. I was no longer home all day to let the postman into the building, but with the hours Sarah was working I was still first to collect the post. I'd paid my tax on time. Had they discovered Bullseye's body at the allotment? The letterhead jogged my memory: NHS.

Mr Sebastian Pink, D.O.B 2/2/72, was perfectly fertile. His sperm sample contained over two million active sperm. It sounded like enough.

I ate dinner, finished the crossword, walked Claude and went to bed, leaving the letter on the kitchen table. When Sarah got home she woke me from a dream about steam trains by pawing at my pyjamas.

'What the hell are you doing?' I asked hazily. 'We were just passing Waterloo.'

She arranged her pillows, stripped and lay down.

'Jump on, Jack Rabbit. I want every last drop.'

4

The third person

Porridge. Opera house. Foreskin. Shoe . . . My cryptic Monday was coming along well. A ripening spring morning on Primrose Hill. Joggers panting. A pram or two. Claude putting the cocker in a spaniel among infant dandelions. Me on our bench, slumped slightly, jacket undone, surveying each clue and eyeing London for the answer. It was a sacred start. I would have stayed all day.

Despite wavering enthusiasm about our decision to start a family, based on my own parentage and Sarah's marriage to her career first and me second, I had spent a wet weekend in bed, trying to give the real estate agent a different kind of deposit. A clue in my Sunday crossword described how I felt: *Tired adder in distress (7)* – DRAINED.

Somewhat spookily, crossword clues often summed up my life and were more accurate than the horoscope, which I never bothered to read. Last Friday, 12 down had perfectly described Claude: *Alloy turns out to be dependable (6)* – *LOYAL*. And the day

I met Sarah, I solved: *Catch a girl with ring (6)* – LASSO. These days the rope was somewhat frayed.

Eight o'clock. Twelve degrees. Londoners scampered – above, in and under their city. Almost time for me to move too, though my commute was more sedate. Drop Claude home then stroll to work: down Chalk Farm Road, traverse the railway at Bridge Approach, then crisscross through Primrose Hill, that Mediterranean crumb in a cosmopolitan loaf. I even worked in what sounded like a crossword clue.

My life was empty. My grid was full. Except for one: *An old friend is a gem (4)*. Pesky clue like a random cloud obscuring the sun. There was always one. Often the easiest. Gnawing away. Bedevilling your day. Compilers knew it and charged a pound per minute for the solutions hotline. I never called. A pound per minute for a four-letter word provoked several expletives of equal length. *An old friend is a gem. An old friend is a gem.* Sometimes the answer is right in front of your eyes.

The black Range Rover pulled up outside the school just as I arrived on foot from the opposite direction. With tinted windows, the only illumination of the monochrome monstrosity were flashes of sunshine on alloy wheels and yellow private number plates – T1MS. Even the windscreen was tinted, which I thought was illegal unless you're the prime minister and don't want the public taking pot shots. The rich never cease to amaze me: buying showy rollers to be seen, then darkening the windows not to be. How inconvenient to be posh.

With an air of sinister celebrity it was the kind of car that demanded attention. Perhaps some Premier League footballer was tired of not understanding his coach and had come to learn English. Perhaps he'd even brought the coach. But why did the car linger, engine alive, outside the school? Was it dropping off or picking up?

Front seat silhouettes appeared to unite before passenger-side shadow retreated abruptly, though driver dallied. The car ticked over silently, justifying its noisy price. Still no door opened. Still no announcement of who was within. Then, like a spy blowing its cover or a tight-lipped star allowing a scoop, the passenger-side window descended slightly, shy of halfway, permitting a plume of cigarette smoke to escape.

An old friend is a gem.

I wasn't one for gossip, for prying, but the quotidian of my life, the ennui of my existence, perhaps pricked my tired antennae. I entered the school and climbed the stairs to a first-floor classroom from which I had a better view into the Range Rover, over the passenger's left shoulder into the space between the two occupants. It was a peepshow of sorts, through car window rather than keyhole, a censored mosaic of movement. With the adrenaline of shame I spied blonde hair (in stark contrast to the black window beheading her), the pale brow of a beautiful young woman, a gear lever, plush leather interior, a flash-looking phone by the handbrake, and a man's trousered leg . . .

Footsteps in the creaky corridor! I retreated from the window and cleared my throat. A Japanese student nodded subserviently as he walked past the room. I forced a smile, put down on a desk the tatty leather satchel Sarah had bought me on my first day as a teacher, then closed the door to the classroom in which I would soon be interviewing students. My old coat didn't want to come off but eventually I freed my hand from the torn seam inside the left arm and tossed it over the back of a chair. I lost a fortune in loose change down the lining of the pockets. I rattled when I walked.

Denying the distraction outside, I arranged the desks for the interviews, but within seconds I was back at the window, forehead against the cool pane of glass which my warm breath began to cloud. Unlike the clues in my crossword, this time the pieces of the puzzle were visual. The man's hand came into view, protruding from a crisp cotton business shirt complete with cufflink. He sure put my old coat to shame. The passenger raised her lips to the gap in the window to release another precise plume of smoke. Was she not allowed to smoke in the car? In the man's hand a bonsai box, perhaps velvet, which he offered but the girl shook her head and refused it. The box then reappeared open and this time was accepted, though it disappeared from view before I could spy its contents.

Husband and wife? Father and daughter? Lovers? Was the fact they had stopped outside the school a random coincidence or was she a student? My morning was growing more cryptic by the minute.

His palm appeared, open, horizontal, beckoning her to give the box back. Her own hand, vertical, implied protest, but he snatched it playfully — or was it forcefully? A few seconds later she leant his way, the back of her grey dress in view. She stayed in that stretched position for a few moments before leaning even further towards him, her head now surely near his lap. Then she sat back abruptly and tossed her cigarette out my peephole before sliding it effortlessly shut, sealing the car like a zip.

As though the lens cap had been applied to binoculars I jolted my head back and focused on more familiar sights outside the school. Students filed into the building below me — some in groups, others solitary. For many it was their nerve-racking first day, for most merely a continuation of their course. When the bell rang I was still at the window, watching the car, pondering its occupants, but when a student knocked on the door my Monday turned its usual shade of mundane. It's a sad and slightly twisted scenario: in my students' eyes I was interesting and experienced in life; in mine, well, when you're imagining the lives of others, what does it say about your own?

■

'Welcome to The Future Perfect. My name's Sebastian. Is this your first visit to London?'

There were eighteen new arrivals. I could have quizzed them in my sleep. Almost had on one occasion.

'Yes,' replied Didier ('Call me Didi'), twenty-nine, from Berlin, spectacles tight on the bridge of his nose.

'What are your first impressions?'

'I luff London,' he said confidently. 'It's a boiling mug.'

My furrowed brow disappointed him.

'I beg your pardon. It's a what?'

'A . . . *boiling* . . . *mug*?' he said speculatively.

I suppressed a smile. One of few highlights in the interview process was when advanced students attempted to flaunt their idioms.

'Do you mean *a melting pot*?'

'*Scheiße!* Yes – a melting pot.' He slapped his leg. Hard.

'Don't worry,' I reassured him. 'It was a brave attempt.'

I glanced out the window at shy sunshine. *An old friend is a gem. An old friend is a gem.* Words in a washing machine. A boiling mug of my own.

'And what did you do last night, Didi?'

With a name like Didi I expected him to be on a first-name basis with the past tense.

'My girlfriend and I vent to a French restaurant.'

'Was the food good?'

'Yes, dare ver many moth-vatering dishes.'

I let it go. His grammar was smooth, despite the moths.

'What was your favourite dish?'

'Definitely der dessert. I had der tiramisu and my girlfriend became a chocolate mousse.'

This time I intervened, for the sake of his girlfriend as much as his English.

'Try again, Didi. You had the tiramisu and your girlfriend . . .'

'Became . . .'

'No.'

His glasses rose as he contorted his face. Then they dropped, both spectacles and penny.

'Ah, right, yes . . . my girlfriend *got* der chocolate mousse.'

'Got' in English equals *'bekam'* in German, so Didi's translating brain had chosen 'became', a concept known as 'false friends'. A knowledge of other tongues makes for a better English teacher. I was limited to the most common mistakes and the Greek I'd picked up during our honeymoon on Corfu.

'Well done, Didi. From tomorrow you will be in room nine. Next!'

An old friend is a gem.

Ludmila's chest arrived before she did. Hippopotamus boobs, suffocating jelly, imprisoned by a purple bra. Fakes, I believe, like the fur trim on her handbag. The silicone siren flaunted far more than idioms and had spent a small fortune to look cheap. Perfume and tobacco were locked in battle, a ring adorned each finger, pink lipstick applied thick, violet eye shadow (to match the bra?), yellow teeth, skirt above the knee and shirt transparent, like the woman within.

'Welcome to The Future Perfect. My name's Sebastian. Is this your first visit to London?'

'Yes.'

'What are your first impressions?'

'You are lonely.'

'Of London.'

'More varm than Kief.'

She smiled. At least that was natural. Almost sweet. She might have been attractive had she not tried to be.

'And what did you do last night, Ludmila?'

I shuddered to think but had to ask.

'I did nothink. Der same as tonight.'

I ignored the hint.

'What about last weekend?'

'I vent to cinema. I luff cinema.'

'What did you see?'

'*Pirates of the Caribbean*. I luff dis film. Did you see it?'

No present perfect but a strong (and no doubt colourful) past.

'No, *I haven't seen it.*'

'Is dog's billocks.'

'Dog's *bollocks*,' I corrected.

'Can you repeat?'

I lowered my voice. The principal roamed the corridors. On one occasion she just happened to be passing my door when my entire class was chanting 'choke the bishop' in full voice. They hear it. They want to use it. They might as well pronounce it properly.

'Dog's *bollocks*,' I said softly.

'Dog's *bollocks*,' she repeated. '*Pirates of the Caribbean* is dog's bollocks.'

She was actually a good student, give or take a definite article.

'I luff all film viz Johnny Depp,' she continued. 'I think he is gentleman. Like English gentleman.'

'Except when he's trashing hotel rooms.'

'Vot means?'

'Nothing. Sorry.'

I had forgotten my next question. Perhaps I couldn't do it in my sleep. *An old friend is a gem.*

'You are gentleman?' inquired Ludmila, crossing her legs, her skirt riding high, presenting the muscle and meat of her thigh.

'I am married gentleman,' I replied, thumbing my wedding ring.

'I like to get married.'

'I'm sure you will.'

'I like to get married viz English gentleman. Not Ukraine men. He is angry.'

'Why is he angry?'

'Because I don't vant to marry him.'

I laughed. She didn't care.

'And do you have a job, Ludmila?'

'Not actually.'

'What job would you like to do?'

'I vood like to be film star actress. I luff cinema.' She leant forward. My eyes widened. 'Do you like cinema? Vee could go to cinema. Vee could sit in back row.'

I laughed again. 'I'm short-sighted.'

'Vot means?'

I scribbled on her student card, then cut the interview short.

'It means, Ludmila, that from tomorrow you will be in room two.'

She was intermediate, but I was teaching intermediate, so I put her with Fer-Frank's beginners.

'Next!'

One by one they entered. One by one they left. The nervous, the overconfident, the reticent, the visa-hunters. I gleaned their life stories, then dispatched them to the school's classrooms like a heart pumping blood to a body. Ten weeks as placement officer and that heart was close to cardiac arrest. Even teaching was beginning to drag. The privilege of meeting people from different countries, of having the wide world in one poky room, grew tedious after a while, despite the likes of Ludmila offering to vandalise the status quo.

Every new face was different. Every new face was the same. I told my students, many of whom were mixing with foreigners for the first time, not to stereotype, then did so myself. It was impossible to deny trends. The Italians spoke about food and the lack of bidets in Britain. The Japanese spoke about gadgets. The Brazilians about God. The Swiss knew how to be superior, the Germans uncompromising, the French aloof . . .

Occasionally I'd learn an interesting fact, such as in Japan you can't swim in a public pool if you've got a tattoo as it's a sign of the Mafia. (David Beckham wore a wetsuit apparently.) In China you can't visit an internet café if you're under eighteen. In South Korea you're considered one year old when you're born. Johnny Depp starred in *Pirates of the Caribbean* . . . Essential titbits.

I'd tell Sarah that helping people better themselves and their lives was far more rewarding than selling million-pound properties or advising a sheikh which inner-city apartment to purchase, though at times I would have loved to try it. To rediscover stimulation. To make easy money rather than struggle to make sense. Nothing could alter the direction of my day. Nothing could alter the direction of my life. Mysterious Range Rovers and troublesome crossword clues were as exciting as it got. *An old friend is a gem. An old friend is a gem.*

When Eva from the Czech Republic edged into the room I was as threadbare as the carpet. My shirt was untucked, my shoes unpolished, my eyebrows untrimmed, my hair uncombed, my faithful blue pullover had a hole at the elbow, the contents of my pockets were an empty wallet, a set of keys to a flat I didn't own and a crossword grid with four squares unfilled. Despite resembling a scarecrow, I satisfied the school's dress code because I never wore jeans, a loophole from which I knew that one day I would hang.

Shameless Ludmila had looked no further than my citizenship. Shy Eva looked no further than the floor.

'Welcome to The Future Perfect. My name's Sebastian. Is this your first visit to London?'

'No.'

She was different already.

'You've been here before?'

'Er . . . no.'

Very different.

'Is this your second time in London?'

'No, I vont say . . . I here for bit time now. From November. I not here from yesterday.'

'I understand.'

Eva stared at her plain leather shoes. I remember them well as they were almost scruffier than mine. Unlike Ludmila, she spurned make-up, yet something was masked, some shroud of sadness. She denied her beauty and other people's vain attempts. Her fingernails were unpainted, her fingers unadorned. Shoulder-length blonde hair was pulled back in a ponytail. An ankle-length grey dress was loose-fitting, denying curves, wintry for the time of year. A hooded Puma tracksuit top completed the patchwork of unglamorous garments. Yet she was beautiful.

When Eva finally raised her head to hand me her student card I glimpsed a forlorn face with flawless skin and sapphire eyes that avoided my own. They were moist, as though she had recently been laughing or crying. I couldn't tell which. And though they dominated her face they led elsewhere, to a story or stories untold. Her one blemish was a lilac bruise on her neck, barely visible in the shadow of her hood. Was it a love bite? I couldn't discern. Perhaps the hood was an attempt to conceal it. Her only decoration ran across the blemish: a silver chain pulled taut by a pendant, a tiny prism of colour. Perhaps an opal. Yes, an opal. It was impossible. An OPAL!

An old friend is a gem – OPAL.

My sigh alarmed her, enduring like an erotic release. Then goosebumps. (Sudoku can't give you goosebumps!) Embarrassed, I gulped my cold coffee, grimaced, then looked at Eva. She was the last piece in my puzzle, and left me without a clue.

She shifted on her chair. Her skin was flawless, her cheeks dimpled, her teeth as white as a cumulonimbus. Even her eyelashes were blonde. Pure blonde. Honest at the root. While her grey dress was like a sack, like a curtain across a stage, withholding clues from a man no longer adept at deciphering them.

Walter, our technophobic head of IT, broke the uncomfortable silence by abusing a computer in the room next door. He reminded me of Basil Fawlty giving his red Morris Minor a 'damn good thrashing'.

I pulled my crossword from my pocket and filled in the final four squares.

'Vot you do?' asked Eva, pink creases on her perfect forehead.

'I'm finishing the crossword.'

'Is rude!'

Her first forceful utterance betrayed the nicotine on her breath.

'You did it for me.'

'I no understand.'

I pointed to her pendant, which she covered with her hand.

'That was the answer – *opal*. I couldn't get it. Then I saw yours.'

Her cheeks reddened as she tucked the semi-precious stone (not really a 'gem' – compiler's mistake) under the collar of her dowdy dress.

'Is not mine,' she said, almost by way of apology.

'Why not yours?'

I was forgetting myself.

'Yes . . . is mine . . . but not by me. Prissent?'

'Present.'

'Yes.'

I hesitated but couldn't resist.

'Who from?'

Eva's face fell as she scrutinised the carpet once again. The pieces of more than my crossword puzzle were falling into place.

'From bruzzer,' she said plaintively.

I folded my crossword and returned it to my pocket.

'From your brother in the Czech Republic?'

Such sadness on her face – the emotional weight of a lie.

'I no understand.'

'It doesn't matter.'

The opal was stunning but I didn't dare say so. I had once told a South Korean girl that I liked her earrings and the following day she presented them to me gift-wrapped, despite the fact they clashed rather heavily with my two-day stubble and faithful blue pullover. In South Korea, explained Walter in the pub later, if you say you like something it means you want it and they feel obliged to give it to you. He had no one. He knew everything.

The floorboards creaked in the classroom above. I returned my attention to the present, and to Eva's linguistic grasp of the past.

'And what did you do last night, Eva?'

'I look for baby.' She saw my confusion and self-corrected. 'No – I look *after* baby.'

I flipped her student card. Read from the back. Sure enough, Eva was one of north London's army of au pairs. Five pounds an hour away from slavery. Pushing prams and changing nappies for the chance to learn my language. It explained the sadness, though not the shyness.

'Tell me about your host family.'

'Zey live in Humpstead.'

'Nice house?'

'Big house. More big, er . . . Czech president.'

I smiled at the unexpected comparison.

'How many children do you look for . . . sorry, after?'

'One.'

'Boy or girl?'

'Boy.'

'How old?

'Two.'

'What's his name?'

'Zoos.'

'Zoos?'

'Is Greece name. God.'

'Oh – Zeus.'

'Okay.'

I rolled my eyes at immodest new-age parents. What the hell was wrong with Walter? The name, I mean. I could hear through the wall what was actually wrong with Walter. This time it was the photocopier whose ancestry was under attack.

'And what do Zeus's parents do?' Apart from eating his siblings, I thought, amusing myself with Greek mythology. ELT can be a lonely pastime, particularly when your teenage students get their rocks off on *Pirates of the Caribbean*.

'Zey job.'

'What kind of jobs, Eva?'

English blood. Czech stone.

'She doctor.'

'And the husband?'

She scratched her neck.

'He bank.'

She seemed irritable at my mention of the man, who sounded like something of a hot-shot, the kind of guy who wore crisp cotton business shirts and drove . . . I stood and walked to the window. Vacant street where the Range Rover had been.

'What's his name?'

'Who?'

'Your boss.'

Eighteen degrees outside. The third degree inside. I felt sorry for Eva, who believed my questions were designed to probe her level of English rather than her private life. And usually they were.

She scratched her neck again. Appeared hesitant.

'Boss name Tim.'

The Range Rover's number plate – T1MS. My smile was thin and self-satisfied. I turned and looked at Eva: blonde hair, grey dress (before she had put on the tracksuit top), nicotine on her breath . . . Jolly nice of her boss to drop her off on her first day at school, and jolly nicer of him to give her a gift to mark the occasion.

Eva sat at her desk quietly, obediently, head slightly bowed, staring straight ahead like a prisoner in the dock.

I was unsure what to do with my revelation and so shifted my eyes back outside. Suddenly I noticed a man at the window of a house on the opposite side of the street, next to W.B. Yeats' former home. A ghostly presence, half hidden behind a curtain, he was on the second floor, higher up than me; perhaps that's why I hadn't seen him sooner. Alarm when I realised he was watching me. I stepped back. Had he been there all morning? Elderly and well dressed with silver hair the colour of wisdom, he seemed serene and gentle: the kind of man I hoped my father might be, the kind of man I hoped I would become.

What would he say to me, my father, given the morning's goings-on? Probably to mind my own business – I was an English teacher, not a private investigator. Time to interview Eva rather than interrogate her. Time to do the job my father would never know I did, unless it was him watching from the window on the sunny side of the street.

With the weight of my own past upon me, I returned to my chair and sat down, moving on from Eva's present and turning to her future.

'So, let's see, um . . . what job would you like to do when you . . . ?' I trailed off. 'Grow up' sounded inappropriate and I'd forgotten how I usually phrased it. It was a tricky area. According to her student card Eva was twenty-five, although female students often lied about their age.

'I not know. Arkhetek?'

'Architect.'

'Okay.'

She was indifferent to new vocabulary, which I found strange given she was prepared to wipe up Zeus's foul-smelling thunderbolts for the chance to hear some.

'Sounds exciting. You must enjoy being in London. Lots of

interesting buildings: St Paul's Cathedral, Big Ben, Westminster Abb—'

'Zis old,' she interrupted, her timid voice strengthening. 'I like new arkhetek. Guggenham. Jerkin building.'

Finally some wind in her sails.

'Ah yes, the *Gherkin*,' I said, though I preferred Eva's pronunciation given it was brimming with bankers. 'One of my favourites. Very . . . well, I don't know – conical.'

Like a fool I made the shape with my hands. Very nearly drew it on the whiteboard. Force of habit.

'Okay.'

I brushed the hair from my eyes. Was she smiling at my discomfort?

'Or housevife,' she volunteered.

'Sorry?'

'I like housevife.'

'Oh, right. For a job, you mean.'

'In Czech Republic like job. Is good job.'

'Not a very well-paid job. Not that I—'

'Chiltren pay wiz love, no money.'

I smiled at her quirky suggestion, or was it an observation?

Her shyness returned.

'So you'd like to get married?' A nervous pause. Well, nervous on my part. On hers, I couldn't tell. She popped in and out of her shell like a schizophrenic snail. 'If you'd like to be a housewife, you'd like to get married, wouldn't you?'

Eva ignored the question as though she realised it was not routine, that yes and no answers were no good to a man supposedly interested in the outer reaches of her vocabulary. Instead, and for the first time, she turned the inquiry to me, though it had suffered for its rebound.

'You marry?'

'Yes.'

'Haf you chiltren?'

'Er, no, but my wife wants to start a family.'

Eva frowned. 'And you?'

'Well, of course, I do too . . .' I tapped the table. She waited patiently. 'It's just that sometimes I get cold feet.'

Her brow creased again. Five lines like a musical score.

'Chiltren good,' she said, 'but London people no haf time so I haf job.'

'I've got time. I just don't think I'm cut out to be a father.'

'Cut? Where cut?'

'No, sorry, I mean I don't think I would be a good father.' I was forgetting to grade my language – the golden rule in ELT. I was distracted by the mystery before me. The girl who didn't want to be beautiful.

'Vy sink no good farzer?'

I scratched my stubble, eyed the window and squinted at the light as though the answer to Eva's question lay in the distance. For the first time as placement officer I had switched roles, with a student asking questions and me lost for answers.

'I, er, well, I wasn't close to my father so I don't have an example to follow. And I have no experience of caring for children.'

'Experience?'

'I babysat a friend's child once but I've no experience of babies. Changing nappies, vomiting, sleepless nights . . . That sort of fun and games.' Eva seemed intrigued, though she may just have been trying to understand. 'It's not like other jobs where you get to practise beforehand. There are no courses to find out if you'd make a good father or not. Perhaps if there were I wouldn't be so worried.' I shifted on my chair and looked towards the window, remembering the mystery man in the house opposite. 'And perhaps if my own life had been different . . .'

'To be farzer like paper I see in café.'

'Sorry?'

'Like paper in café,' repeated Eva, sketching a square in the air with her fingers as though playing charades.

'I'm sorry but I don't know what you mean.'

She seemed to be recalling a memory, or how best to word that memory.

'Argh,' she sighed, frustrated, shaking her hands as though conjuring the concept. 'Paper in café. In window ... er ... yes!' Her eyes lit up. She clicked her fingers. '*No experience to be necessary*!'

For the first time she smiled, though the smile was stifled as soon as it appeared.

'No experience necessary,' I corrected. 'And it's a *sign* in the window, not a *paper*.' This was, after all, an English school. And I needed to remind her who was doing the teaching.

'Yes,' she continued, ignoring my correction. 'To be farzer no about experience. To be farzer about love.'

I felt my cheeks redden. This really was a role reversal.

'Well, I ... I wouldn't ...'

'But I sink you good farzer,' interrupted Eva.

'How could you possibly know that?'

It sounded rude. I hadn't meant it to sound rude.

Eva indicated the hole in my pullover. Flesh where wool should have been.

'No good to love and care you, perhaps good to love and care other.'

Confusing, yet crystal clear.

'I'm not sure if that's an insult or a vote of confidence.'

'Vot means?'

The bell startled the building.

'It means, Eva, that from tomorrow you will be in room six.'

She was a beginner, but I didn't want Fer-Frank's stutter confusing her so I squeezed her in with my intermediates.

'Next!'

5

Embedding

Our neighbours made love at the same time each morning. I could have set my clock by their raunchy routine. Such was the athleticism of their affection for each other that they managed to shake my bedside lamp, something Sarah and I failed to do despite being on the same side of the wall. If I listened hard I could decipher the woman's pleas: 'Higher . . . Lower . . . Hammer it in!' Were she not gasping her list of instructions I would have sworn she was helping him hang a painting.

Sarah slept through our erotic alarm clock but it always woke me, or certain parts of me. She only stirred on that particular Sunday when Claude noticed I was awake and bounced into the bedroom to lick my face.

'Sebastian, what's that noise?' she inquired vaguely.

'Just our neighbours plumping each other's pillows.'

Sarah stretched, sat up and pulled the quilt high. Claude jumped on the bed and curled at my feet, knowing he'd get a kick if he tried the other side. After yawning and wiping the sleep from our eyes we had no choice other than to listen to the lovemaking.

'Gosh, they sound like wildebeest,' said Sarah. 'Did we ever make that much noise?'

'Possibly,' I replied. 'I suppose you don't really notice the noise when you're making it.'

My wife leant over and teased the top button of my striped pyjamas.

'Want to try and out-groan them?'

I freed my feet from beneath Claude and threw off the quilt.

'Mind if I make a cup of tea first?'

When I returned from the kitchen with two mugs and three biscuits Sarah was reading *Property Week* and Claude was pruning his paws. The neighbours were spent. Wind and rain at the window. Sunday morning was back on track.

It was too blowy and wet to walk Claude at either Primrose Hill or the allotment, so I sat up in bed and marked some writing homework. Ludmila's mention of 'English gentleman' had prompted me to ask my class if England was populated by gentlefolk or not. Half a page. Due on Friday. The results were intriguing and one in particular, penned by a South Korean student, I simply had to share with Sarah, who put down her industry magazine and painted her fingernails as I read:

Gentlemen's Country
By Yoon Pong

Most people say England is Gentlemen's country. And also they think Englishs are very kind and sympathetic etc. When I arrived here in United Kingdom of England I was so surprised and disappointed. Specially horrible teenagers with hood. When I was travelling to Oxford I saw some group of teenager – the most dangerous in England. And then I and they went pass each other. The problem began that time. A girl in the group hit my arm and laughed. It was absurd so I said to her 'What the fxxx are you doing? Do you wanna fxxx with me?' With my smile. Eventually they sweared and went their way.

I hate two kinds of English person, first teenager with hood and second is twenties with white van. After travelling to Oxford, no! It was before. Yeah, I remember clearly because that day I went to Princess of Wales pub first time. Anyway, I and my friend were going to pub. We were waiting for bus. But bus didn't come, just little freaky white van. I hadn't known them before. Anyway they came to us and spoke swearing. 'Hey fxxxing Asian guy,' screamed to us. My friend didn't wanna quarrel but I said them 'Shut the fxxx up, fxxxing horrible unemployed! Come on fxxxers. Why are you escaping?' I growled to them. But they already went away. So I just went to Princess of Wales and drink beer. It was tasty!

As I said, many people say England is Gentlemen's country. I didn't write good things, but most of people are very kind (maybe). If you wanna travel to England, I'd recommend. But don't forget, be careful about teenager with hood and twenties with white van. If you haven't problem with them, England is one of best country of the world.

PS Sorry Sebastian, next time I'll use more tense like you ask. Have a good weekend. Yoon Pong.

Sarah laughed. Even Claude appeared to be grinning, though that may have been because he had polished his testicles into such a shine that he could admire his own reflection. The Pink family was a happy family, despite the fact it didn't have as many members as Sarah would have liked.

Unfortunately the feel-good moment didn't last. If I'm honest, it was my fault.

'That nail polish stinks. Do you have to do it in bed?'
'You let your dirty dog on the bed.'
'*Our* dirty dog.'

'So you admit he's dirty?'

'Claude's not dirty. Look at his loganberries – as shiny as the sun on a puddle.'

Silence as Sarah contemplated the image. 'Do you have to be vulgar first thing in the morning?'

'You were the one who wanted to out-groan the neighbours.'

Sarah dipped her brush while I took a red pen to Yoon Pong's prose.

'I can think of someone else to put on that list of people to avoid,' said Sarah.

'Who?'

'You.'

'That's below the belt. I'm a cake-and-crosswords man. A gentle creature compared to the racist hoodies who clashed with Yoon Pong.'

'And Walter. In fact, most of your colleagues should go on the list.'

'Thank you, Sarah Schindler.'

She stuck out her tongue, playful yet defensive. The teasing had always been harmless between us. But something had shifted since we'd started trying for a baby. We were uptight and anxious, lending a harsh edge to comments that might previously have been taken as affectionate banter.

'Why should Walter go on the list?'

'Because he has a one-track mind.'

'Only because no trains ever arrive at his station. And what's wrong with the rest of my colleagues?'

'They're linguistic snobs and grammar bullies that think if you don't speak English properly you are thick.'

'*Who* think.'

'What?'

'Linguistic snobs and grammar bullies *who* think if you don't speak English prop—'

'Oh, bugger off, Sebastian.' A sour glance. 'My grammar okay there?'

'Watertight.'

'Whoopee.'

Further silence. Necessary rest before digging a deeper hole.

'And your property pals are pillars of society, are they?'

'What's that got to do with it?'

'I'm simply saying that I'd put several of your bricks-and-mortar mates on Yoon Pong's list before I put Walter and co. I think we could even find room for your mother if we looked hard enough.'

'Thin ice, Sebastian.'

'Look, Sarah, we wouldn't be having this pointless conversation if it wasn't Walter's barbecue this afternoon.'

'I'm not coming.'

'You probably won't have to. The weather's foul. I expect it'll be cancelled.'

'Good. Might save Walter another Anti-Social Behaviour Order.'

Walter's spring knees-up was an annual event which had met a premature end the previous year. Eyes rolling around in his bald head, our drunken host tried to flaunt his knowledge of French by claiming the word 'barbecue' derived from *barbe à queue*, meaning 'whiskers to tail', or 'beard to bum' as he preferred it. Walter bared his own examples of both to provide a practical demonstration of his theoretical knowledge. The neighbours had these big bay windows. The Old Bill had these little handcuffs.

I threw Yoon Pong's homework on the floor. (I'd given him an A and suggested he send it to the *Daily Mail*.)

'Sarah, sweetie?'

'What?'

'I'm sorry.'

'What for?'

'For putting your mother on Yoon Pong's list.'
I interpreted her silence as 'apology accepted'.
'Have you finished painting your nails?'
She held up ten scarlet fingers.
'Are you ovulating?'
She took her diary from her bedside table – clumsily, as her claws were still drying – opened the diary, eyed the roof, performed a mathematical equation.
'No.'
I rubbed her leg with one of my occasionally cold feet. The earth moved under Claude.
'Want to tangle anyway?'
She blew on her nails.
I shed my stripy socks.
'Out!'
Tail between his legs, my labrador left the room.
Sarah peeled back the covers. We hung a familiar painting. Her blonde hair was a lie. The bedside lamp stood still.

∎

Only Sarah was upset when the sun came out. Modern-day meteorologists would have some fancy term but the wind simply blew the rain away. I opened the curtains to reveal stunning spring sunshine, squinted like a prisoner released from solitary confinement, then wondered where the hell I'd left my sunglasses at the end of last summer, if in fact I owned a pair. There wasn't a cloud in the blinding blue sky; indeed, the only evidence it had been raining all morning was the damp garden grass and Claude by the door with his lead in his mouth.

Walter lived in Hampstead (or Humpstead as Eva pronounced it) in a house he had inherited from his late parents. He couldn't afford its upkeep on a teacher's wage, so slowly but surely the house had begun to resemble its sole occupant: weather-beaten and wild with an eccentric front hedge. The only hedge Walter pruned was his propeller-like moustache, which afforded him the nickname 'Clear for Take-off'.

Sarah climbed reluctantly from the car, Claude cocked his leg on Walter's lopsided letterbox, and I tugged at the damp clog of mail inside. Judging by some of the postmarks, Walter hadn't collected it for several weeks. ('Think about it,' he said later, 'how much good news comes in the post?') The bricks of Walter's front path were hazardous and askew, surging weeds disfiguring their order like teenage teeth in need of dentistry. No point knocking on the old front door – the key was in the lock.

We followed the hum of voices to the overgrown rear garden, where a mossy wooden table had been laid for twelve – two more than last year if you didn't count the police officers. Who were these mystery guests? Walter had said nothing about newcomers at school during the week. And he usually told me everything, and more.

The usual suspects were already in attendance and had forgiven the host for last year's 'flop'. (Walter disliked that description since it was caused by his impromptu strip.) Fer-Frank lounged in a hammock hung precariously between the bold branch of an oak and Walter's washing line. My colleagues Clarissa, Tiffany and Peter milled around a murky pond, frowning at the gagging goldfish and wondering whether to call the RSPCA. My other colleague, Samuel, had brought a Mexican student he was seeing.

Samuel was tall and handsome with designer stubble and muscles that flexed when he wrote on the whiteboard. As a result his female students were more gifted at propositions than prepositions. Ying from Japan offered him an 'all the body' Chinese massage, Parisian Antoinette cut him a key to her host family's house, and Viktoria from Uzbekistan sent him her underwear with a maladroit missive: *I want you to taking them off with your tooth.* He showed Rhonda the note and she made him correct it and hand it back. I should have taught when I was single rather than wasting time as a real estate agent. Few customers stroll into Knight Frank and hand their knickers to the leasing agent.

Sarah placed the Greek salad she had made in the centre of the wonky table, withdrawing her hands slowly in case the bowl moved. Claude chewed a bone by the veggie patch. I poured a glass of chardonnay and joined Walter by the ancient barbecue. Against the back shed leant a rusty roller-mower which hadn't moved since last year, unlike the weeds devouring it. Bees bothered the wisteria. A wind chime betrayed the breeze.

The conversation was standard fare for a gathering of grammar bullies for whom a misplaced apostrophe could trigger an aneurism. The Queen's English was in danger of extinction and we were its only hope. On weekdays we took our frustrations with the evolution of language out on our students. On weekends we moaned about those we couldn't save.

'I deplore this new abbreviated SMS language,' said Rhonda. 'What's it called?'

'Text-speak,' said Walter, almost spitting the word.

'It's robotic and misleading,' added Samuel. 'A friend of mine the other day wrote "see you Saturday" as "CU", and I thought it was the beginning of the word "cunt"!'

Rhonda flinched. Samuel noticed and duly apologised.

'D-does it really take that l-long to write the words "see you"?' said Frank. 'It's not the M-Magna Carta.'

'Yes, but young people don't have time these days, Frank,' explained Walter. 'They're all too busy inking their skin and voting on reality TV.'

Sarah usually tolerated my colleagues for my sake, but on this occasion she appeared to be struggling.

'I have more of a problem with the misuse of "like",' said Clarissa, who had left the goldfish to their fate and joined us around the table. '"And I was, like, so happy."'

'It's fundamentally wrong,' said Rhonda. 'People actually become similes when they say they are "like, so happy".'

'Couldn't agree more,' said Peter, scoring brownie points with the boss. 'But better that than "I'm *so* going to enjoy this". You can't put "so" before a gerund.'

Sarah's glass was empty. I don't think she would have protested otherwise.

'Why don't any of you work in secondary schools where you might actually make a difference? Forgive me for saying so, but most of your students aren't proficient enough in English to make the kind of mistakes which cause you such angst!'

The wind chimes detected the chill in the air.

'Yoohoo – sorry we're late,' called an overdressed young woman preceding a more casually clad man into the garden. 'Glen had to stop in Archway to tell a kebab shop owner there was a grammatical error in his sign.'

Sarah and the woman rolled their eyes simultaneously.

'Aha, there you are,' said Walter, remembering he was host. 'Right – ladies and gentlemen, this is Glen and Margaret. Glen and Margaret, these are ladies and gentlemen.'

We were flattered.

'What did the sign say?' asked Clarissa, skipping the 'pleased to meet you'.

'"Probably best kebab in UK",' quoted Glen.

'Think I know it,' said Walter. 'Grotty little shop by the tube station?'

'That's the one,' replied Glen. 'Could use a good clean and a couple of definite articles.'

We laughed in chorus. Sarah and Margaret simply did not understand. Words were our life, our addiction and affliction.

'And what did the kebab shop owner say?' my wife inquired.

Glen pretended he hadn't heard.

'Yes, what did the fellow say to you, darling?' insisted Margaret.

'Buy kebab or fuck off,' admitted Glen.

Sarah and Margaret laughed simultaneously. It appeared the odd ones out had got even.

M&S crisps were passed around, another cork exited another wine bottle, assorted swamps of hummus appeared, most of which resembled Walter's pond. Margaret and Glen made themselves comfortable at the table while Walter poured them generous glasses. It was revealed that he and Glen were former colleagues from Walter's previous school in Kilburn, from which he had been fired for giving students wildly inappropriate teaching materials, including Shakespeare in a beginner's class. Rather than 'to be', he taught 'to be or not to be'.

'It was then that I strayed into IT,' announced Walter.

Some might say Rhonda was herself performing *A Comedy of Errors* when she employed him, though I would argue she was simply kind-hearted. Exhibit A: Fer-Frank. A language teacher with a stutter is the equivalent of a pope with Tourette's.

'And where's Jack?' asked Walter, happy to change the subject. 'Did you decide not to bring the little bundle of joy?'

'Piroska's fetching him from the car,' replied Margaret. 'I expect they'll be along soon.'

As if on cue, Margaret and Glen's Hungarian au pair trudged into the garden, burdened like a pack horse under a kindergarten of toys, bottles of baby formula *and* pinot grigio, bags containing nappies and towels, plus a dummy in her mouth and baby Jack in a papoose. We watched the perspiring Piroska stumble towards us as though she were attempting some sort of record for carrying the most items the furthest distance, and we couldn't lend a hand lest we invalidate that attempt. Margaret finally lightened her load when the pack horse lost its step and veered perilously towards the pond. She did what any sensitive person would have done in such a situation – she plucked the dummy from Piroska's mouth.

'Where's the steriliser?' Margaret barked at Piroska, who was slowly emerging from under her portable pile.

'I sorry,' replied Piroska, 'I forgot it at home.'

'Can one *forget* something at home?' asked Walter. 'I believe that's a Germanism – *Ich habe es zu Hause vergessen*. In English we would more likely *leave* something at home, wouldn't we?'

Margaret shot Walter a look of pity.

'Would it be permissible to boil the dummy in water,' she inquired, 'or do they only do that in Berlin as well?'

The wind chimes again.

'I'll get a saucepan,' volunteered Walter, heading for the kitchen.

'I'll give you a hand,' I said, following him inside.

It had clearly been some time since Walter had washed up. The sink was buried under a concertina of dirty dishes, the majority of them stained with tomato ketchup. Walter tweaked his moustache and watched Piroska from the kitchen window, while I banged about his cupboards in search of a saucepan.

'I say, Sebastian,' he began, 'I didn't realise Hungarian girls were quite so beautiful. We don't get many at school, do we? They probably can't afford it.' He moved aside as I scoured the cupboard he'd been blocking. 'Cracking arse. She ticks all the boxes and adds a few of her own.'

'Keep your hands where I can see them, Walter.'

'If I'd known she was coming I'd have tidied up a bit.'

'And baked a cake.'

Walter's chuckle became a cough.

'That's rubbish,' I continued. 'You wouldn't tidy up if Her Majesty the Queen dropped by for a bacon sarnie.'

The clatter of unused baking trays.

'I really should hire someone to take care of that mess. I've been thinking of getting an au pair myself.'

'You haven't got any children.'

'So?'

'It's pretty much mandatory.'

'That's not the impression I got from a website I was browsing the other day. What was it? Au pair world dot com? Some of the photos the hopefuls were posting suggested *they* intended to do the breastfeeding. Think they were confusing wet nurse with au pair.'

'What were you doing visiting au pair world dot com?'

'I told you: I'm considering home help.'

'You need a cleaner – an elderly lady with a gammy leg.'

'I need an au pair – a Hungarian nymphomaniac with impertinent breasts. No London home is complete without one.' He sipped his wine. 'An au pair is like a tennis racquet in the umbrella bin by the front door. Standard issue. They should sell them at Habitat.'

'I've got several in my intermediate class at the moment.'

'Really – tennis racquets?'

I rolled my eyes.

'Au pairs.'

'Any lookers?'

'Just one, but I get the impression she'd prefer not to be.'

'Care to elaborate?'

I gave up on the cupboards and tried the pantry. The host of the year lit another cigarette.

'She's a new arrival. And unlike most of the other female students, she wears the dowdiest clothes and pays no attention to appearance. It's as though she's striving to be plain when she's actually anything but.'

'A female who strives to be plain . . . Does such a female exist?'

'Aren't you forgetting your ex-girlfriend, Walter?'

'She had no alternative. There's quite a difference. Tell me more.'

'There isn't any more. I've simply got a new au pair in my class who is stunning but shy.'

'Sounds delicious. What's her name?'

'Eva.'

'The first woman. "Giver of life". Don't eat the apple if she brings one for her teacher.'

I laughed at his wisecrack.

'Why do you read so much into names?'

'My ex-girlfriend was Alice M. Bent. Were she a crossword clue she'd be "Malice".'

I gave up on the pantry and contemplated the sink.

'Use the gloves, dear boy.'

I rummaged through the rubble and located a saucepan – same vintage as the lawnmower. I held my breath. Scrubbed it clean.

'I must say you're going to great lengths for little Jack,' said Walter. 'You'd make a good father, Sebastian. I suggest you and Sarah get on the springs right away. Then you can lend me your au pair on weekends.'

'We're one step ahead of you, believe me.'

'So that's why Sarah is so tetchy.'

I snatched his cigarette and fouled my lungs.

'Don't be a dummy,' I replied. 'Now let's go and sterilise one.'

Walter put the saucepan between the onions and the steaks and boiled Jack's silencer on the barbecue. When the saucepan had cooled he offered its contents to Margaret, who motioned with her wineglass towards Piroska. In his puerile way, Walter was right: when it came to the extent of the au pair's duties, looking after the baby was the tip of the iceberg. She was dispatched back and forth to Margaret's Mercedes to fetch cigarettes, sunglasses and wine. Her boss didn't allow her to eat at the table; instead she was cast a crucified sausage and told to take it inside – with Jack, of course. I couldn't help thinking that Claude had a better cut of meat at the bottom of the garden. Despite protests from most, Piroska cleared the table and served dessert. For one horrible moment I thought she was going to be ordered to do Walter's washing-up. And for her maximum effort she received the minimum wage. Was the opportunity to learn a second language worth such a servile first job? I felt sorry for her. I felt sorry for Jack. I felt sorry for Eva, wherever she was.

Our stomachs were full, our wine bottles empty. It was gone five but the breeze had dropped, the sun was still strong and the lingering light was that divine mellow magic which turns England to paradise a few weeks a year. Samuel's Mexican girlfriend, Chantico, had stripped down to her knickers (or *diph*-thong, as Walter quipped) and was sunbathing near the pond. Walter was perched beside her, stroking his moustache and asking the significance of her various tattoos. Fer-Frank had returned to his hammock, the old oak creaking under the weight of his lunch. Claude was dreaming under the table while the rest of us were slumped in our chairs, turning slowly with the sun like chickens on a spit. There was little else to do – we had finished the wine and the grass was far too ungroomed for croquet.

'Can I hold Jack?' asked Sarah.

''Course you can,' replied Margaret.

She nodded at Piroska, who deposited the baby in my wife's lap, something I was finding difficult to do. Sarah held Jack clumsily yet caringly. Dislodged his sunhat as she slid her arm behind his neck to support his lolling head. She had no experience of newborns. Her younger sister Jessica had a baby daughter but she had been born after Jessica (or the Jester as Sarah called her) emigrated to New Zealand with her Kiwi husband. Sarah sent gifts for birthdays and Christmas but was yet to be anything more to the little girl than a name on a card. Her mother had been to visit and brought back a photo which Sarah kept on the kitchen fridge, beneath a magnet from a wine club which read: *Life's too short to drink bad wine.*

'Does he sleep well at night?' inquired Sarah.

Margaret looked at Piroska, who answered for her.

'Slip okay. Sick sometime. Cry a lot.'

'Has he started smiling?'

'Yes – he haf beautiful smile.'

'How old is he now?'

'Four months,' declared Margaret. Finally one she knew.

Chantico had run out of tattoos and Walter returned to find Jack lying semi-snugly in Sarah's arms.

'What a handsome chap,' he said, patting the newborn's head as though he'd mistaken him for Claude. 'He's your photocopy, Margaret. He's even got your first nose.'

Suppressed laughter. Even Glen sniggered.

'Gootcheegootcheegoo,' said Sarah, coaxing an infant smile.

'I say,' declared Walter, 'you're a natural, Sarah. When are you and Seb going to spawn?'

The bastard couldn't cook but he sure could stir the pot.

Sarah carefully handed Jack back to Piroska.

'You're not clucky yet, are you, sweetheart?' I said, hoping to stifle the conversation and protect Sarah's privacy, even if I had let the cat out of the bag earlier with Walter.

'No, not yet,' lied Sarah. 'Too many liquids coming out of too many places,' she added, feigning a shiver.

I had forgotten how well she could protect herself.

'How old are you?' asked Margaret.

'Forty-one,' replied Sarah.

'Mustn't hang about,' advised Walter. 'Best-before date fast approaching.'

'Shut up, Walter,' said Rhonda, who shared Sarah's age.

Walter raised his hands – his standard signal that he was finished making people feel uncomfortable. Surprisingly, Sarah continued the conversation, dropping me in it better than Walter ever could.

'We've talked about it briefly, but my Neanderthal husband is worried about me going back to work rather than bringing up the baby.'

And I had tried to protect her.

'That's why God invented au pairs,' proclaimed Margaret. 'I was back at work six weeks after Jack was born.'

'What work do you do?' inquired Rhonda.

Margaret tucked a stray strand of hair behind her ear. Her husband fished a miniscule insect from his wine.

'I'm the CFO at an advertising house.'

Other than the fact she wore high heels to a barbecue, her resemblance to Sarah had me slightly spooked.

'Don't you feel as though you're missing out on Jack's development?' inquired Peter. 'Wouldn't you rather stay home with him?'

'What – and go back to work to find a man at my desk who wants two sugars in his coffee? Not a chance. I've worked my stockings off to get where I am. Plus we're about to take over a smaller agency. I've got to steer the ship.'

'I thought maternity leave was more generous these days,' said Samuel, a surprise contributor, whose only hitherto interest in the women's movement was how they swayed their hips.

'Y-yeah,' added Frank. 'The B-B-BBC keeps going on about e-qu-qu-quality of the sexes.'

'Don't believe it,' replied Margaret. 'Women are doing well in middle management, but go upstairs to the rooms with a view and you'll still find men with photos of their family and golf calendars on their desks. This may be the twenty-first century but a woman still has to choose between having a family and having a career.'

'Isn't having children fulfilling?' asked Clarissa, whose husband's job in Stockholm was currently stopping her from multiplying.

'Only if those children have enough food to eat,' replied Margaret.

'Glen works,' I suggested.

'Glen earns peanuts,' retorted Glen.

'Can't they eat peanuts?' quipped Walter, to scattered sniggers and stern glances.

'I tried to convince Margaret to stay at home for a time,' added Glen. 'Then I realised we couldn't afford it on my teaching wage.'

'So if I earned more . . . sorry, if Glen earned more,' I asked Margaret, 'and the law protected your rights at work a little better, would you be happy to stay home with Jack?'

The CFO eyed her son, who had puked on Piroska's shoulder. She fingered a diamond earring. 'Naturally,' she squeaked.

'Filthy little fucker!' erupted Walter.

'What the hell?' cried Glen.

Our sunburnt host pointed to the bottom of the garden where a squirrel scurried nimbly across the top of a tightrope fence.

'What's wrong with squirrels?' asked Glen.

'Rats with good PR,' scowled Walter, striding off down the garden, followed closely by Claude.

'My turn to hold Jack,' declared clucky Clarissa.

Piroska obediently handed him over. My colleague studied the newborn's face.

'He's got lovely eyes, Margaret. Yours or Glen's?'

'Piroska's,' whispered Frank from his slow-swinging stupor in the hammock.

Cue the wind chimes.

'I beg your pardon?' said Margaret.

'Nothing,' intervened Samuel. 'He's pickled. He didn't mean it.'

'No,' said Frank, 'I meant the p-postman.'

More scattered sniggers.

'That's an old one,' said Rhonda.

'S-so's the postman,' said Frank.

When trouble starts at Walter's, you expect Walter to be involved. On this occasion, Your Honour, I can confirm he was elsewhere.

'That's in pretty poor taste,' complained Glen.

'S-sorry,' Frank warbled, 'but you've g-got to admit Piroska does everything else.'

With Frank still chuckling, Margaret rose in a most dignified manner, removed her gold-armed Gucci glasses, visited the barbecue, armed herself with a carving knife, smiled pleasantly at her audience, strolled towards the oak tree and sliced at the rope supporting Frank's perch.

Too boozed to beg, Frank thrashed about in the hammock like a fly trapped in a cobweb. Then he fell to earth. A sickening thud.

Frank was a big chap – tall and overweight. Those ambulance boys asked what he'd been doing in the hammock in the first place. He suffered severe concussion and a broken collarbone, though when he telephoned the school on Monday to report his injuries, Rhonda didn't believe it was him on the line because his stutter had vanished. Nor did it return.

It wasn't all silver linings, however. On the drive home in the car Sarah added Frank to Yoon Pong's blacklist. One by one the staff of The Future Perfect were being disgraced. Usually it's the students who lack discipline.

Police last year. Ambulance this year. I suggested Walter book the fire brigade in advance for next year's bash.

6

/Óbligáysh'n/

Pandemonium in the staffroom. Normal for ten to nine. A matter of minutes to curtain call and panicky actors still learning their lines. Lessons being patched together, textbooks hunted down, teachers cursing photocopiers and audio cassettes being wound to the appropriate place, or thereabouts. That familiar feeling of 'I may need to improvise'. A second's calm. A sip of coffee. Then the bell and a unified moan.

I waited until five past to give the stragglers time, then collected my thoughts and materials before trudging upstairs to room six. Teaching English was like riding a bicycle, though at times my tyres were flat. To pump them up I stopped by the bathroom, splashed my face with cold water, stretched a smile, closed my eyes and filled my lungs with a lingering breath. That was the beginning of my pre-class checklist, which wasn't part of the CELTA course but in my opinion should be.

Pre-class Checklist
(In order of importance)
1) Flies firmly fastened.
2) Wash face with cold water and, after washing hands, ensure that water hasn't splashed on trousers as it will appear sinister and students won't give benefit of doubt, they'll simply Facebook (if that's a verb) their friends to say their teacher is incontinent.
3) Nostrils clear of snot.
4) Teeth clear of food debris.
5) Check for bad breath by blowing into cupped hand.
6) Ensure marker pens haven't leaked in pockets, particularly trouser pockets.
7) Check for newspaper print on face (if recently been doing crossword).
8) Ensure Walter hasn't stuck any juvenile post-it notes on your back.

Teaching is a performance. Actors are under scrutiny. Stages at The Future Perfect were small to say the least. I stood outside my theatre and absorbed my audience's staccato chat. My hand choked the door handle. An actor waiting in the wings. Waiting for Godot. To teach or not to teach? That was the question I asked myself every morning at nine o'clock.

I turned the knob.

'Good morning, everyone!'

'Good morning, Teacher!'

A triumphant spring morning. Birdsong in the courtyard. Sunshine in the room. Freshly cut grass on the breeze from Primrose Hill.

'Who can tell me what the weather's like today?'

'Rubbish,' replied Giuseppe.

'Sorry?'

'Rubbish,' repeated the Italian.

'Hmm . . . does everyone agree?'

'No,' said Doughnut. 'Is sunny.'

'Very good. Everyone – *sunny*.'

In unison. '*Sunny*.'

'Why did you say it was rubbish, Giuseppe?'

'I am a-sorry. Udder teacher say dis di only word I need for England weder.'

'Everyone – *cynical*.'

In unison. '*Cynical*.'

'How to spell?' asked Doughnut.

I wrote it on the board.

'Pronunciation spelling,' demanded Jean-Paul.

I wrote /sínnik'l/ on the board.

I sat down. Teaching is about building rapport. If you sit, you're one of them, although Giuseppe was one of a kind. I scattered my things. Found the attendance log. Looked over at Eva – legs crossed, arms folded, keeping herself to herself, dressed in blue cargo pants and that same hooded tomboy top several sizes too big. The prettiest girl in my class paid the least attention to her appearance.

'Okay: Giuseppe – yes. Doughnut – yes. Jean-Paul – yes. Fernanda?'

'Yes.'

The Brazilian model was also a model student. She'd breezed through pre-intermediate and was now distracting the males in my intermediate class.

'Sibylla?'

'Yes.'

My Dutch student. Top of the class. Meek, modest and not entirely comfortable with her unofficial nickname – Clever Clogs.

'Agnes?'

'Yes.'

A surly Swede from Stockholm. Religious fanatic. I once told the class that the past participle page in the textbook was their 'bible' for irregular past tenses and she asked me not to call it that for religious reasons.

'Yoon Pong?'

'Yes.'

'Lee?'

'Yes.'

Two South Korean handfuls.

'Ludmila? . . . LUDMILA?!'

'Yes.'

My look at her face was hijacked by her bouncy-castle breasts.

'I thought they were in a different class? Sorry . . . I thought *you* were in a different class?'

'I changed,' she replied, eyes beaming. 'Are you flattened?'

'*Flattered*.'

'Are you?'

Saved by a knock at the door.

'Come in!'

Breathless and lame, Kazuki from Osaka entered the stuffy room.

'Solly for late,' he stammered. 'I fall down stair and twist my uncle.'

I heard all sorts of awkward excuses for arriving late, though my favourite was still the Chinese student who tried to buy a tube ticket to Mind the Gap.

'Natalina?'

'Yes.'

'Ulrica?'

'Yes.'

Polish and German au pairs.

'Goodness,' I declared, 'a full complement. Have I forgotten anyone?'

65

The class looked at Eva, who reluctantly raised her hand.

'Ah, yes – Eva. Silly me.'

Eva had managed to attend my class for almost a week without divulging any personal information other than the fact she was in the wrong room, something she managed to do without uttering a word. Though I hadn't seen her boss bring her to school again, and despite my personal pledge not to pry into her private life, she was intriguing me more each day. Her face was always downcast, her eyes were always red, her mind was always elsewhere, her clothes were always unfeminine and sometimes dirty and dishevelled. I was desperate to learn more about her, so that morning's warm-up game was the ELT icebreaker called Find the Lie.

I stood to give instructions.

'Okay, everyone writes three sentences about themselves. Two must be true. One must be false. Then we will read out our sentences and the class will ask questions to discover which is the false statement. Does everyone understand?'

A cordon of lukewarm nods.

'How many sentences do you write?'

'Three.'

'How many must be true?'

'Two.'

'How many must be false?'

'One.'

Ensuring they get it is half the job.

While they penned their brief biographies, I wandered the room to make sure they were following orders – 'monitoring', it's called in the trade. English teachers are highly skilled at reading over people's shoulders. (I never need buy a newspaper when travelling on the tube, though other passengers sometimes object when I help them with the crossword.) My sneak preview gave me a chance to ascertain whose sentences were hieroglyphics and whose would be understood by the majority of the class. The exercise was designed to relax the students and loosen their tongues for the rest of the lesson, so phrases containing untaught grammar, or attempts at untaught grammar, were best left alone.

'Lee,' I said, 'would you like to go first?'

He bowed his head, which meant 'yes'.

I had seen the South Korean's sentences and deemed them a safe start. He rose and read monotonously from his spiral-bound notebook.

'I love dog. I was soldier in army. I have been to England.'

Competent grammar, if light on articles, and that third sentence was hardly a red herring given the location of our little game. Still, we were rolling.

'Vot means "soldier"?' asked Ulrica.

I marched on the spot and presented imaginary arms. Teaching is a performance, remember.

'Everyone – *soldier*.'

In unison. '*Soldier*.'

'How to spell?' asked Doughnut.

I wrote it on the board.

'Pronunciation spelling,' demanded Jean-Paul.

I wrote /sṓljər/ on the board.

The students had a test every month. The teacher had a test every minute.

'Okay, now let's ask questions to see which one is false.'

A pause as ten attorneys prepared to interrogate the accused.

'Have you dog?' inquired Fernanda.

'Yes,' replied Lee.

'How olt is dog?' asked Ludmila.

Lee's eyes shot to the ceiling – a giveaway to say the least.

'Ah . . . about seven,' he replied cautiously.

'Is zis seven dog jears or seven 'uman jears?' asked Jean-Paul.

Lee looked confused. I didn't blame him.

'Don't worry,' I told him. 'Next question.'

Objection sustained, you might say.

'Vot is name of dog?' asked Natalina.

'Dinner!' interrupted Giuseppe.

Jean-Paul and Natalina laughed.

'Excuse me, Giuseppe,' I said, no longer one of them, 'please don't make fun of Lee.'

'Is okay,' said Lee. 'He right. Is lie. I honest write "I love *to eat dog*".'

Agnes winced. The Swede clearly didn't eat dog meat.

'What is a-wrong wid spaghetti?' asked Giuseppe.

The Italian wasn't keen on it either.

'So you don't have a dog?' I asked, making a mental note never to bring Claude in for show-and-tell.

'Yes – my father have,' replied Lee.

'Does he eat dog?' asked Natalina.

'Dey all eat dog,' interrupted Giuseppe.

'Shut fuck up, spaghetti man,' yelled Yoon Pong, lending credibility to the dialogue in his homework.

My ploy to learn more about Eva seemed to have derailed slightly, though it had certainly loosened their tongues.

'Quiet, everyone!' I shouted, loosening my own. 'In this classroom it is not permitted to swear or to attack someone on the basis of their culture or religion.'

'What means?' said the class in chorus.

I wrote it on the board. Gave an explanation. Thankfully Jean-Paul didn't ask for the phonetic spelling.

'Okay,' I continued, weary already. 'Let's try again. Who wants to go next?'

'I go,' declared Ludmila.

I hadn't seen her sentences for fear she might think I was monitoring something else, but after the incident with Lee I no longer felt fit to judge.

Ludmila sprang to her feet and, remarkably, kept her balance.

'I play piano. I haf been in earthquake. I vont to be film star actress.'

'Good sentences,' I said, relieved.

'Vot means "earthquake"?' asked Ulrica.

I pretended the floor was moving, which Sarah would no doubt have construed as an attempt to dance, then cowered under my desk and shook my materials to the floor.

'Everyone – *earthquake*.'

In unison. '*Earthquake.*'

'How to spell?' asked Doughnut.

I wrote it on the board.

'Pronunciation spelling,' demanded Jean-Paul.

I wrote /érthkwayk/ on the board.

'Okay, let's find which one is false.'

'How . . . long . . . have . . . you . . . been . . . playingthepiano?' asked Sibylla, taking the present perfect continuous for a slow but skilful spin.

'Since I was twelve,' replied Ludmila convincingly.

'What is earthquake like?' asked Yoon Pong, without an expletive for once.

'Terrible!' exclaimed Ludmila. 'You don't know if to grab your cat, your passport or your mother.'

The interrogation stalled as we contemplated the unusual choice.

'What about Ludmila's third sentence?' I prompted.

'Have you ever been in a film?' asked Sibylla.

'Yes,' replied Ludmila.

'What kind of film?' asked Kazuki.

Dangerous territory – I kept an eye on Giuseppe.

'A short film my ex-boyfriend made . . .'

'Okay, let's guess!'

'. . . about corrupt election in Kief.'

I wiped my brow.

'Okay, let's guess,' I said more calmly. 'Who thinks Ludmila plays the piano?'

Twelve hands were raised, including mine.

'Who thinks she has been in an earthquake?'

Four hands shot up.

'Who thinks she wants to be an actress?'

Seven hands in the air, including mine.

'I vin!' exclaimed Ludmila. 'I never play piano in ever my life!'

The top-heavy Ukrainian had easily duped her classmates. I had to admit she would make a good film star actress.

After the anxiety caused by Lee and Ludmila's examples, I considered binning the game and beginning the grammar. Find the Lie was less stressful at lower levels, where students didn't have the vocabulary to spark scandal. The last time I'd played was with a group of beginners, who had flushed out the fib among innocuous fare such as: *I have female sister. My father very tall. My family have tree cars* (which I assumed had environmentally friendly emissions). The second sentence was the lie, in case you are wondering; his father actually very short. It was hardly scintillating, but at least no one was doing porn or eating their pets.

Despite the morning's hiccups, I decided to press on. The timid Czech enigma had sat on her secrets too long.

'Time for one more,' I announced. 'Hmm, let's see, who hasn't had a turn?' (I didn't want her to think I was picking on her.) 'How about . . . ?' (Eva was practically hiding under her desk; perhaps she thought the earthquake was still a threat.) 'Eva? Would you like a turn?'

Colour stained her cheeks.

'Come on, you've been Secret Squirrel over there. Let's hear your three sentences.'

'What means "seclet"?' inquired Kazuki.

'A *secret* is something Eva doesn't want us to know.'

'How to spell?' asked Doughnut.

I wrote it on the board.

'Pronunciation spelling,' demanded Jean-Paul.

I wrote /séekrit/ on the board.

'And vot means "squirrel"?' said Natalina.

'A rat with good PR' would have been a bridge too far.

I looked into the courtyard for a live example (although they hadn't returned since Walter fired his slingshot from the canteen window), then did my best to draw a squirrel on the board. Teachers often have to portray new vocabulary, especially at low levels, but they are not artists and rudimentary sketches can be, well, rude. I once tried to draw a tap on the board. When the students sniggered I rushed to add water, which only made things worse. I quickly wiped it off, though my students' smiles were indelible. On this occasion, fortunately, my subject's bushy tail made things simpler.

'There we are,' said Michelangelo, finishing the Sistine Chapel. 'Everyone – *squirrel*.'

In unison. '*Squirrel*.'

'How to spell?' asked Doughnut.

I wrote it on the board.

'Pronunciation spelling,' demanded Jean-Paul.

I wrote /skwírrəl/ on the board.

'I confused,' declared Kazuki. 'Why squilel have something he don't want me to know?'

Occasionally, just occasionally, I thought I should have stayed in real estate.

Eva probably hoped the diversion had spared her. If anything, it had made me more determined.

'Right, where were we?' I said. 'Ah, yes – please read your three sentences, Eva.'

She uncrossed her legs slowly, stood, cleared her throat, eyed her notebook. Her fringe touched her eyelashes and twitched when she blinked. Ponytail again but looser, messier, more relaxed. The opal remained but the blemish on her neck had vanished; love bite after all. Why then was she so sad? Whose teeth were at her neck? Only a fool would think three shallow sentences might shed light on a mystery so deep.

She held up her notebook.

'I au pair,' she whispered.

Damn – knew that already.

'I enjoy to gamble.'

I almost laughed at her obvious lie. Blatantly out of character. Apart from the love bite she seemed more suited to a convent than a casino.

'I good at crossword.'

Eva acknowledged my surprised grin by returning it. I hadn't expected her sentences to be playful, much less a private joke.

'What means crossword?' asked Lee.

Eager to keep the spotlight on Eva, I flashed an example from my paper, before writing the word and its pronunciation on the board. When I turned back to the class, however, she was already back in her seat.

'Hang on, Secret Squirrel, we haven't finished,' I said, motioning for Eva to stand, an instruction she reluctantly obeyed. 'Okay,' I roused the court, 'let's find which one is false.'

'How long have you been an au pair?' asked Sibylla.

'What means "au pair"?' said Kazuki.

Sibylla closed her eyes, perhaps so as not to roll them. She was too good for the others. Balancing levels in group classes is almost impossible.

'Means "servant",' spat Ulrica.

Giuseppe and Jean-Paul sniggered.

'How olt your chiltren are?' inquired Natalina.

'Two,' replied Eva.

'Ah, you lucky,' said Ulrica. 'My boys twelve and nine. PlayStation all the day. Brain like bomb. It make them so aggressive.'

We were veering off course again. For some reason I didn't brake.

'Aggressive normal for England chiltren,' added Natalina. 'Mine scream at parents: *I hate you. I kill you.* He throw shoe. Parents just ignore him. He monster and they ignore him. They should beat him.'

'You mean *smack*,' I interrupted. 'Everyone – *smack*.'

I wrote it on the board. Did the funny spelling. The class ignored me – piqued by the nanny confessions.

'But in England is against law to smack,' continued Ulrica.

'No, can smack but can't leave bruise,' advised Natalina.

'How to do zis?' asked Ulrica.

The students turned their heads as though watching a tennis match.

'Use phone book,' suggested Natalina. 'Like police in Poland. Hit hard and no bruise. Never.'

'Must never to smack chiltren,' declared Eva, participating finally, if not on the intended topic.

'Why not?' asked Natalina. 'My parents smack me and I fine.'

Moot points – both if children should be smacked and Natalina's mental health. I was interested in neither. Eva was escaping again.

'Okay, let's get back to Eva's three sentences. How about some more questions?'

'Vot is your host family like?' asked Ulrica.

Eva's expression changed abruptly. Her body language was more fluent than her English. Clouds in her eyes as she contemplated the carpet. I could see she was uncomfortable and rushed to protect her. My concern was professional. Perhaps even paternal. I sensed in her a mystery that needed to be solved.

'Let's move on. What about Eva's second sentence?'

'I don't remember it,' said Giuseppe.

'She enjoys gambling,' I reminded him.

I was partial to a punt myself. In fact, I once considered crossing a greyhound with a dachshund so it might win the photo finish.

'What kind of gambling you like?' asked Fernanda.

Eva searched the ceiling for words. The roof of a language school gets a bigger workout than the whiteboard.

'Card, horse, casino . . . anythink,' she replied finally.

'Are you ahead?' I asked, although I wasn't supposed to be playing.

'Vot means?'

'Have you won more than you've lost?'

'Vid gamblink?'

I nodded.

She shrugged her shoulders – surprisingly broad, though that may have been the effect of the hooded top she was wearing.

'I hope, but . . . pff, maybe not.'

'Vot is best you ever vin?' asked Ludmila, clearly excited by the topic.

Eva eyed the ceiling again, inventing a figure no doubt.

'Five thousands.' The students were wide-eyed. 'Koruna,' Eva assured them. 'No big here.'

'Vot is vorst you ever lose?' asked Ludmila.

Eva looked out the window this time. The class waited patiently. I wished they hung off my every word like that.

'One time, poker in Prague, I lose car.'

I laughed aloud. It was over the top. She would make a terrible film star actress.

'You lost a car?!' exclaimed Sibylla, who could suspend disbelief better than I could.

'Shit car,' insisted Eva. 'Škoda.'

Even Ludmila looked shocked, concerned it might be true.

'A car is big lose,' said Lee.

'No,' replied Eva, 'I like valk.'

Her sense of humour was unexpected and made her sadness more difficult to fathom.

'What about Eva's third sentence?' I coaxed.

'I don't remember it,' said Giuseppe.

'She's good at crosswords,' I replied.

'Can you do Czech crossword?' asked Sibylla.

'Yes,' replied Eva.

'Can you do English crossword?' asked Ludmila.

Eva looked at me. Fingered her opal. Smiled cheekily.

'Easy,' she replied.

I had sensed she needed my help, though she could clearly fend for herself. I may have been her teacher, but she was teaching me a lesson.

'Let's vote,' I declared. 'Who thinks Eva is an au pair?'

Twelve hands in the air.

'Who thinks she likes gambling?'

Eleven hands in the air.

'Who thinks she's good at crosswords?'

One hand in the air.

The class thought I'd been fooled. For once they may have been right.

'Okay, Eva, which one of your sentences was false?'

She squinted and lowered her head as though expecting a bomb to explode.

'Can you repeat?' she asked timidly.

Patience is a virtue, particularly for a language teacher.

'Which one of your sentences was false?'

She ducked her head even lower.

'False?' she repeated.

'Not true,' I explained.

She shrugged her shoulders.

'All true.'

The class groaned in unison. Eva looked frantically about her as though some imaginary tide was rising.

'One of your sentences was supposed to be false,' I reminded her.

'Oh, *sakra*,' she replied. 'No understand.'

I should have realised there and then that Eva didn't play by the rules, but teachers have a habit of learning the hard way.

7

Habitual actions

Walter raised his glass. A clink as it met mine. Then his usual verbose toast: *To dogs' ears and the will o' the wisp; to keenness, and light, and the speed of a horse.* Elbows up. Ambrosia down. A shared sigh as our workday drifted into the slow lane.

After an arduous stint 'down the mines and yours', as Walter quipped, the Princess of Wales was a suitably mellow establishment to plunder a pint, compare crosswords and iron the creases out of our day. Mouth-wateringly close to the school (though its proximity was negated by the fact I almost always ducked home to pick up Claude), and comprising the corner of the same row of terraces, the pub was our pick among five on offer in Primrose Hill because music appeared to have been barred. We used to patronise the Queens, higher up in the posh postcode, but left when they put in a telly.

A cigarette machine was the only modern marauder in a public house which celebrated the past. Cluttered walls were a mosaic of crooked pictures, including Walter's favourite, *The Warrior's Return* – the subject of which, he suggested, was a language teacher. The windowsills were laden with ornaments as bygone as some of the barflies, the tables were wooden and worn, the chairs creaked agreeably when you sat on them, and the sound was that endangered purr levitated by loose tongues and lively chat. While the rest of humanity was striving for progress on the other side of the double front door, and making such a clatter in the process, we dusty regulars at the Princess of Wales were savouring times when conversation was king.

Walter felt ancient in modern surroundings and believed a chair should be as old as the arse upon it. After an ELT conference in the city I once dragged him into a branch of the slick and shiny chain All Bar One, where his moustache began to wilt and he misplaced his thirst for the first time since puberty. He faked an asthma attack to escape but regained his breath when returned to the Princess's palliative embrace. 'They had numbers painted on the tables!' he lamented to our landlord. 'I felt like a fucking prisoner of war.'

I liked the cobweb layout of our local, with the bar at the centre and scattered seating around. The barman was our spider, we his trapped insects, succumbing slowly to stings and small poison doses. After being accosted with questions at school all day it was a relief when Tony didn't need to ask what we wanted. Spitfire was our pleasure – the 'bottle' of Britain. Walter's nickname, Clear for Take-off, grew more appropriate with each sip.

Dogs were permitted provided they were on a lead. I didn't need one; my command was Claude's lead. Tony let him in regardless and quipped that I had a ropey voice. Walter said it was his best joke after his prices.

Always the same faces by the table near the window: Alf Garnett types with hunched shoulders and straight talk, watching Fitzroy Street, drinking bitter and being it, towards the government, towards the council, technology, the price of a pint . . . They were unable to cope with the pace at which the world was moving. They belonged to the past. In them we saw our future.

We sat in one of two triangular nooks at the rear of the pub, where old books gathered dust, unread, except by Walter. He had the habit of plucking one from the shelf at random each afternoon and reading aloud the back-cover blurb with thespian aplomb. I found it tedious, but if I complained about Walter's annoying quirks I would have had no one to tolerate my own.

That afternoon he pulled *The Common Millionaire* by Robert Heller, primed his pipes with Spitfire, then delivered the lines with an air of profundity:

> *This is the age of the common millionaire. Not only because all millionaires – unlike the gilded aristocrats of earlier days – are common men, but also because making a million is far easier these days. One prime reason is inflation, which has made it four times easier to make the magic seven digits.*

Walter sipped his drink. Sniffed the musty pages. Peered over half-glasses to ensure I was listening.

> *That's only partly why there are so many millionaires around. The age of the common millionaire has seen a multiplication of methods for amassing undue riches, and Robert Heller lists the twenty-four most popular means.*

'I'm confident ELT will be among them,' added Walter as an aside.

Remember: any fool can make a million, which is why many of them have. The ranks of the rich are full of the untalented, the uninspired and the unmemorable.

Walter flipped the fading hardback in his hand, pondered the front cover and then tossed it on the table; his every movement was ceremonious, deserving an audience of more than one man and his dog.

'What utter mange,' declared the orator.

'Don't be so sure,' I countered. 'Some of Sarah's property pals are millionaires and I wouldn't describe any of them as talented or inspiring.'

'So is Sarah a millionaire?'

'If she sold the flat and cashed in all her shoes.'

Walter laughed, coughed, referenced an early page.

'But our good friend Mr Heller was writing in 1974, when real estate was about having a roof over your head rather than a buy-to-let variable tracker loan to value asset release equity ping pong splish splosh splash.'

'What's your point?'

Walter returned the tome to the shelf.

'My point, dear boy, is that property development won't be on Heller's list because this book belongs to less rapacious times, when people bought houses to have a roof over their head rather than dinner party conversation, and real estate agencies served their customers rather than their greedy selves.'

We sipped in unison when we agreed on something.

'Well, when Heller writes an updated edition he'll be sure to include real estate,' I suggested. 'There are probably forty-eight ways to make a million now, though I'll bet sitting in the Princess of Wales every afternoon isn't one of them.'

Walter sat back, frowned, appeared offended.

'We're just letting the air out of our tyres.'

'Which is why we're going nowhere.'

'Well *Hell*er can go to *hell*,' declared Walter. 'Who needs money?' he asked rhetorically. 'As long as you've got your . . .' His cough interrupted his cliché, though I'm fairly sure he was going to say 'health'.

'These days money is health,' I proclaimed.

'And don't I know it,' affirmed Walter. 'I went to the dentist last week and he said every time he looks in my mouth he sees his next Caribbean cruise.'

I smiled confidently; Sarah booked me in for regular check-ups.

'People can no longer afford to be poor.'

'Old-fashioned values will triumph.'

'The planet's spinning faster, Walter, and old-fashioned values are losing their grip. Sarah's agency raked in record profits last year thanks to hundred per cent mortgages peddled to people who can't repay them. Not an old-fashioned value in sight.'

'They're on a hiding to nothing. Along with the banks they're in bed with. It will end in expensive tears.'

'What would you know about banking?'

'It's not banking, it's human nature. Too much of a good thing leaves one wanting less, as Basil Fawlty said.' Walter drained his glass with gusto. 'Apart from Spitfire, of course. Your shout, dear boy. My plane's been shot down.'

Claude whimpered in dream sleep, his snout on my shoe.

'You get these,' I said. 'I don't want to wake him.'

Walter leant back and looked under the table at my lazy labrador.

'I wonder what he's dreaming about?'

'Twenty-four ways to make a million beef Schmackos.'

Walter laughed, coughed, strode to the bar, ordered two more drinks then smoked outside while they arrived. I watched him on the footpath, pacing back and forth like an expectant father, a cloud of grey rising at regular intervals. An attractive Argentinean student passed by. She knew his face from school. Walter smiled nervously, waved, watched her bottom disappear. Loneliness and drink make a man's eyes honest.

'I've got good news,' he announced as he returned with the next round. 'I've almost finished preparing Monday's teacher-training session for the interactive whiteboard. It's been causing me sleepless nights but I think I've established how the fucker works and I'm fairly confident I can explain it to you all, though what's wrong with using chalk has me beat.'

'I suggest you don't use that as your opening remark.'

He put my beer in front of me. Sat down and sucked his.

'Why do they have to complicate things, Seb? I can't see the point of this contraption beyond making it difficult to do what teachers were already doing with ease.'

'I'd scrap that line too.'

'Seriously, other than the blow-up doll, I can't see the point of certain inventions. They don't solve problems and they don't make humanity happier.' From his pocket Walter fished his mobile phone – a brick of a thing, a modern antique. 'A friend was showing off his iPhone to me the other day. He pressed a thousand buttons. Waited a thousand minutes. "This is the inbuilt GPS," he boasted. "In a few seconds it will tell me where I am."'

'Didn't he know where he was?'

'Apparently not.'

'Where was he?'

'At my place.'

'So he knew where he was.'

'You'd assume so.'

'So why was he looking up his location?'

'That was my question.'

'What was his answer?'

'He didn't appear to have one.'

'Did his phone have a camera?'

'Seven megapixies.'

'*Pixels.*'

'As you wish.'

'So if he was lost he could have taken a photo of where he was, and then that would have helped him find his location.'

'It's that sort of logic that sells those things.'

'Or he could have just asked you where he was.'

'I wouldn't have been able to tell him.'

'Why not?'

'I don't have an iPhone.'

We laughed and tipped our drinks, delighted with the journey we had taken without leaving our chairs. When Sarah asked what it was I saw in Walter, I tried unsuccessfully to sell her such conversations.

It was approaching six and the springtime light was fading. Suits crowded the Princess as though anticipating her arrival. They slow-sipped their evening elixir while chronicling their paths to it. A placid crowd – rarely any trouble beyond a difference of opinion on the politics of the day. Walter browsed his Tory *Telegraph* and rolled the next smoke. My pocket beeped and woke Claude in the process.

'A text from Sarah,' I announced.

'What's it say?' asked Walter.

Nothing was sacred.

'*Will be home late. Hope to catch a Jack Rabbit when I get there.*'

'A Jack Rabbit?!'

'Long story.'

'I'll get another round.'

He stood and checked his zip (a former teaching habit), stumbled outside, smoked a cigarette, chatted with a few regulars, returned with two more pints and some nuts, then continued the conversation as though he hadn't moved.

'You see what I mean about pointless inventions? That text from Sarah – instant communication, but only of bad news.'

'It's not exactly "news" that she'll be home late.'

Walter smiled sympathetically.

'So that's why you're not yourself. All that talk about going nowhere and money being king.'

'It's nothing, really.'

'I'll tell Tony to keep them coming. I think we're here for the long haul.'

'There's really nothing wrong.'

'Spit it out, Seb. A problem shared is a problem solved.'

'Halved.'

'Oh, leave off – I'm not one of your students.'

I raised my elbow to cool my mouth.

'Could we change the subject? Why don't you dazzle me with interactive whiteboards?'

'What's happened between you and Sarah?'

'Nothing.'

'Is Jack Rabbit tired of lettuce?'

I regretted sharing Sarah's text. Cold beer had a habit of putting me in hot water.

'Jack Rabbit's diet is no concern of yours.'

'Really? So why isn't he looking forward to an evening gorging himself on rocket?'

I put down my bottle, then lost it.

'For fuck's sake, can we please stop talking in rabbit metaphors?!'

A middle-aged couple, the sort with theatre tickets, turned to look at us. Walter waved their way while clawing open a pistachio.

'Fine,' he replied softly. 'I'll get to the point if you will.'

He was undressing me like the nut.

I took an enduring sip as though it were truth serum.

'Alright, here's your scoop: Sarah and I have been trying for a baby since, well, for quite some time. My heart and my head have been locked in battle at times, though I've been doing my bit to hit the jackpot. But after meeting Margaret at your barbecue I'm convinced it wouldn't work out because in Margaret I saw Sarah and in Sarah I saw Margaret.'

Walter pursed his lips. 'Now there's a double-page spread.'

'Sounds as though you're the rabbit in need of rocket.'

The couple looked around again.

'And you're a lucky bastard,' said Walter.

An unexpected twist. Even Claude raised his head.

'Why am I lucky?'

He thought for a moment. Put down his drink.

'Because you have problems I'd love to have. Sarah will never be as shallow as Margaret. Perhaps at times she works too hard but she loves you despite your faults and wants to have your children.' He closed his eyes on a memory he didn't have. 'Dear God, what I would give . . .' He trailed off. Regained his thoughts. 'Deep down you like your job and your job likes you. Your students worship you and the wolf's never sniffed at your door. That's why you're lucky, Sebastian Pink.' He lifted his bottle and refuelled. 'I, on the other hand, look as though they've already performed the autopsy. I am loved by no one except my morning hangover and I have a grand total of three friends and no children I know about.' I assumed I was one of the three. 'Franz Kafka said man's greatest achievement is to have a family. All I have achieved is an empty house and a deep distrust of each passing day. As you point out, dear boy, the planet's spinning faster and I'm losing my grip. When I fall off, that's it – no trace I stopped by other than the books my father gave me, which the vultures will buy for copper coins at Oxfam, and probably never read.' Rather than crick their necks, the couple had turned their chairs. 'So hop on home, Jack Rabbit, and dig till you strike gold.'

There was silence, the aftermath of an avalanche, then Walter performed his usual magic act of making his drink disappear.

'I'm really sorry, Walter.'

He avoided my eyes.

'You're all I've got, Sebastian. I know it's a cliché but you're the son I never had. I don't want you to say that to someone someday.'

If only he knew the truth. If only Sarah knew the truth.

'Why don't we change the subject? How's that new hammock of yours?'

He contemplated the wise old books on the shelves before delivering a truth to be found in many of them.

'Choices, dear boy. This irreversible thing called life is about choices. The luck is to be found in making the right ones.'

I sat forward in my chair.

'The luck is having a father who helps you make the right ones.'

'And that's where you'd come in. I've already told you you'd make a first-rate father.'

'Perhaps, but if Sarah and I have a baby I'm convinced some Polish girl will be its surrogate mother.'

He grimaced and exhaled vehemently, lips vibrating like those of a horse.

'Fucking nonsense! Not forever! Just until it's through with projectile vomiting. Then you and Sarah can take over when it goes to university, though that's where many rediscover such behaviour.' He smiled at his observation. Flashed his dentist's next Caribbean cruise.

'It would make me a father but might ruin my marriage.'

'Sounds as though it's struggling already. Perhaps kids will put it back on track. Make the marriage evolve.'

'That's not the right reason to have them.'

'Neither is not having them because you might get a little helping hand at the start.'

I peeled a pistachio. The shell fell on Claude but didn't unsettle him. He was used to finding crisps and other nibbles in his coat. As, indeed, was I.

'I couldn't have an au pair living with us.'

'Why not, dear boy? Too tempting?'

'It would feel like exploitation – paying a pittance for someone to bring up your most prized possession.'

'Worked for you.'

I snorted.

'Did it?'

Walter's face contorted with confusion.

'Anyway, why are you suddenly advocating the rights of au pairs? Does this concern that new student of yours? What's her name – Lolita?'

'Eva.'

He reclined in his chair. Waited for me to talk.

'I'm worried about her, that's all. Something's not quite right and I can't put my finger on it.'

'Have you asked nicely?'

I ignored the joke, though it was good to have him back.

'Sebastian, you're a man of the world . . . Well, of Middle England. Haven't you ever asked yourself why Eva might deny her beauty?'

'What do you mean?'

'You've had other au pairs in your class. You must know what happens to some of them behind closed doors.'

'They work like slaves.'

'After they've knocked off.'

'They study English and visit Madame Tussauds, if they can afford the admission fee.'

Walter put down his bottle and moved his chair closer to mine. He glared at the couple, who turned back to their own lives.

'Let me put it this way, Seb. Have you heard the one about the little boy talking to his sister in their St John's Wood home?'

I shook my head.

'They're playing in the garden and the little boy asks: "How many penises has Daddy got?" "One," replies his sister. "Wrong!" says the little boy. "Daddy has two penises – one to wee out of and one to clean the au pair's teeth when Mummy has gone to bed."'

Walter sat back. Watched for my reaction like a doctor who has delivered a blow.

'The love bite on her neck.'

'Hardly in her job description.'

My mind raced.

'I suspected there might be something going on. I even saw him give her a gift. But that doesn't explain her sadness, or why she tries to deny her beauty.'

'It does if she's not a willing participant.'

The silent wake of another avalanche.

'What the hell are you saying, Walter?'

He sat back and assumed an authoritative tone – the doctor was now backing up his theory with fact.

'Such situations are rare but not unknown to au pairs. A few months ago Rhonda had to intervene on behalf of a Polish student of Clarissa's. The brother of the man whose children the au pair cared for was turning up every evening and putting the hard word on the girl. Rhonda shifted her to another family. But it was the girl who complained. Different set of circumstances.'

I clenched my jaw. Cast my mind back.

'I saw her protest in the car.'

'In the car?'

'Her boss's car. Outside the school.'

Walter's smirk was mischievous.

'Sounds as though Sebastian has been snooping.'

'She refused the opal at first and I think tried to escape a kiss.'

'The opal? A kiss? You *are* up to speed.'

'Well, I was a long way away. And the windows were tinted. But I saw their silhouettes. And she put the tracksuit top on afterwards to try and cover her neck.'

'My, my – you're a regular Poirot.' Walter tipped his already empty bottle to his lips, chasing that last reclusive drop. 'Sounds as though you're hot on the trail, dear boy.'

'The trail? The trail of what?'

'I'll leave you to do the math, as they say.'

'I'm no good with numbers.'

He tabled his drink.

'So find the words.'

My drinking companion checked his watch and declared himself late for his evening electronics class. Rhonda made him attend. He was lucky to have such an understanding boss, and lucky that a language school can survive with misfiring machines.

Sarah's text gave me no reason to head home just yet, so with Claude for company I made for our bench atop Primrose Hill. I thought of the bench as a bookend – where my workday started and finished. Though it belonged to Peter Stevens rather than me, when I saw someone else sitting on it I felt as though they'd broken into my house.

It was dark and the park was deserted but for a squirrel here and there, zany shadows zigzagging like a balloon expelling its air. The moon was veiled by wisps of cloud as whimsical as Walter's cigarette smoke. Claude cleaned his paws while I watched the blinking city, a sinister silhouette that refused to relinquish my wife. I wondered how many of Robert Heller's twenty-four ways to make a million were good for the institution of marriage. A car alarm wailed in the distance. Would she come home if her child were waiting?

I pulled the first of two bottles of take-away Spitfire from my jacket pocket, thrust it towards the night sky and borrowed Walter's line: *To dogs' ears and the will o' the wisp; to keenness, and light, and the speed of a horse.* Claude turned his head away as I took a solitary sip.

I thought of Eva. Of Tim. Of Walter's shocking suggestion.

I spoke to the city.

'The trail of what?'

8

Passive

I sunk into her like a candle into a cake, her wet warmth rushing through me. Soft squelch and silken spasm, a velveteen path to oblivion. Her legs locked around my back. My head buried blind in her neck. Arms beneath her, hands raising her, fingers in the glow of the flame. Surrendering groans as the love whip lashes. Staccato cries as the soft skin stretches. The vice tightens. The voice strengthens. The whip quickens. The sweat glistens. We thrash as though it's a struggle, as though one of us must concede, then the knot unravels and we collapse . . .

Banging on the wall.

'Keep it down, will ya?!' shouted our hypocritical neighbour.

I opened my eyes and saw that my wife was taking liberties with a certain part of me that could be awake while the rest of me was asleep.

'Sarah?' I raised my head off my pillow. 'Sarah?! What the hell are you doing?'

She dismounted, grabbed the quilt with those painted

fingernails and pulled it to her throat as though *I* was the intruder.

'Alright. Calm down. I just thought your sperm might be less stressed if you were asleep.'

I propped myself up on my elbows, confused by familiar surroundings. Sarah reached for a bedside copy of *Property Week* and plumped her pillows as though nothing had happened. Claude ambled in to investigate, jumped up on the bed, flapped his tail and curled at my feet. It was, in those respects, a typical Saturday, barring my eccentric alarm clock.

I adjusted my pyjamas and acknowledged my hangover with a groan. My head was pounding and my eyes protested against the light penetrating the curtain. I slumped back on my mattress, coughed, sneezed, farted . . .

'That's quite a concert,' said Sarah.

'You were the one playing the organ.'

She feigned shame. A cute expression.

'We out-groaned the neighbours for once. We should do it more often when you're asleep.'

'As long as you don't expect me to be on top.'

Sarah smirked, opened her magazine and spoke while reading.

'You sure were sleeping deeply. Mind telling me where you were last night? You weren't here when I got in.'

'Well at least now you know how it feels.'

She touched my chest. Turned tender.

'I'm sorry, Seb, but work's manic. We're putting together a *massive* project and if it goes to plan I could get quite a commission.'

I scratched Claude's ear with my foot.

'I know it's a cliché, sweetheart, but isn't there more to life than money?'

She sighed, lowered her magazine and raised her eyes to the roof.

'It's called a nest egg, Seb.'

'Well, we're fine as far as the nest goes.'

'I was trying to take care of the *egg* bit but you woke up.'

'Forgive me for not being able to make a baby in my sleep.'

'You can't make a baby while you're awake!'

I smiled. Acquiesced. I never was one to deny the truth. This was the banter that strangely bound us together. The gloves might have been off yet we were in the same corner.

'So,' continued Sarah with a slight change of tone, 'where were you last night?'

'Oh, just my usual double date with Walter and the Princess.'

'And then?'

I massaged my temples to buy time.

'I, er, must have fallen asleep on Primrose Hill.'

Sarah sat forward and turned towards me.

'What?! You fell asleep in the park?'

'Well . . . dozed off.'

'Great – I have a husband who sleeps on park benches. You must have looked like the town drunk.'

'No, *he* was at his electronics class.'

'And with cow-eyed Claude for company. You must have looked like a team of beggars. Did you find any coins in your cap when you woke up?'

'It's Primrose Hill, sweetheart; they write out cheques.'

She laughed. Wonderful to make her laugh. Nothing raucous. No mouth open, no head back. Just one stifled but genuine giggle. I closed my eyes and remembered our relationship's early days: sharing a sleeping bag on a camping trip to Wales; a bee stinging my bum as we made love on a picnic rug at Great Yarmouth; nibbling her ear in the Queen's Head and Artichoke and pretending to accidentally swallow her diamond earring. Though neither of us were exuberant creatures, in our own way we were mad about each other. But nowadays it seemed we were increasingly mad at each other. The phrasal verbs had shifted slightly yet significantly. Did all marriages slide that way or just ours? Infertility was surely the source of the strain. It seemed appropriate that I was a teacher of idioms given the only thing I was familiar with breeding was contempt.

'So why did you fall asleep?' asked Sarah. 'Did you drink too much with Walter?'

'Perhaps one or two more than usual.'

She sat back against her stack of pillows and turned a page of her magazine. It made a comforting sound.

'Were you celebrating something?'

'Hardly.'

'So why the extra drinks?'

'Oh, you know, Friday night . . . Plus we were discussing a problem student of mine.'

The sound of another page turning, too quickly for it to have been read.

'Don't you just move problem students to another class?'

'She shouldn't be in my class in the first place.'

'Why?'

'She was . . . er . . . incorrectly graded.'

Sarah lowered her magazine and looked my way.

'Don't *you* grade the students these days?'

'Well, yes, but . . .'

'Sounds like it was your mistake then.'

'Sounds *as though* it was your mistake then.'

'You're not grading me, Sebastian.'

I freed my leg from beneath Claude, sat up in bed and reached for the multi-storey stack of paper beside my bed: crosswords, students' homework, third-hand Graham Greene from Cancer Research. Sarah began patting at her face with cotton wool and one of the many lotions she kept by the bed. Her hair was restrained by an elastic, and one of the straps of her black silk nightdress had fallen from her shoulder.

'Well, go on then,' prompted Sarah. 'I'm listening.'

I took a few sheets of paper from the homework pile.

'Listening?'

'To the story of your problem student.'

I rearranged my pillows and sat up straight. Grimaced as my headache throbbed.

'It's not a classroom or learning issue. And as her teacher I probably shouldn't get involved. But . . .'

'But . . . ?'

'But I think she's having problems with her host family.'

'Like what?'

'*Such as.*'

'Just tell me.'

I folded the sheet over the top of the quilt.

'She's an au pair and I think, well, Walter thinks her boss might be making advances she has difficulty denying.'

'Why does Walter think that?'

'Oh, he's seen things.'

'*Seen things* . . . Like wha— Such as?'

I blew her a kiss.

She screwed up her nose.

'So, what has Walter seen?'

'He's seen the boss giving her presents, them kissing in the car, a love bite on her neck . . . that sort of strife.'

Sarah's eyes narrowed for a moment.

'Perhaps they're having an affair.'

'Perhaps. But Walter doesn't think she's a willing participant.'

'Why would he think that?'

'Because the student seems very sad and, er, Walter saw her trying to avoid the man's gifts and advances.'

I shifted my gaze in case my lying eyes gave me away.

'Sounds as though Walter has been snooping.'

'Walter has his defects but I trust him. He says it's happened to other au pairs. And the student's behaviour in class is consistent with everything he says.'

'So you agree with Walter?'

'Not often, but in this case, yes, I think so.'

Sarah paused her beauty routine.

'That's ghastly, Seb. You have to do something.'

'What can I do?'

'Get her out of there!'

'How?'

'I don't know, but do something.'

'Such as?'

'Can't you talk to Rhonda?'

'Not unless the student asks me to. It's really none of my business.'

Sarah put her cotton wool and bottle of lotion on her bedside table, before turning purposefully towards me.

'Sebastian, sometimes in life you have to make things happen rather than stand back and watch things happen. Some people can't ask for help, not because they lack the words but because they lack the courage.'

I brushed my wife's arm with my hand.

'I love you, Sarah. Perhaps I haven't said it enough lately, but I love you.'

She smiled, leant over and kissed me on the cheek.

'That's good, because my mother's dropping by this morning.'

I didn't dare groan, despite the excuse of my hangover.

I settled back with some student compositions and a red pen. After their amusing take on the topic of English society, I had asked my class what they thought of our food. Somewhat predictably, Yoon Pong's efforts proved the perfect starter, a thousand times more appetising than *Property Week*.

'Listen to this, Sarah.'

She reached for her lotion and cotton balls.

England Food
By Yoon Pong

England cousin (cuisine?) is famous and generally known as shit, the worst thing you eat in your life, unless you eat soap or sand. That's why there are full of foreign food restaurants in England. Its really difficult to find England restaurant in England. I think pub is England restaurant. My host family street look like Tieland or India, without wheelbarrow car (rickshaw?). Englishs look away from their own food because it isn't delicious. No! All they have are junk food like fish and chips which is their pride. And I notice they eat potato a lot. Potato everything. There is reason why they don't develop food like other nations: I think that the weather is not good for growing craps (crops?).

England food for me is not fantastic. I just feed it in. My instinct refuse but I not listen. But I like English breakfast. That's all I like. It's not special but addictive. So, in conclusion, just don't eat England food if you can. I wouldn't recommend to my friends, except friends I hate a lot.

Sarah laughed aloud. Even Claude seemed to be smiling; the skin in his mouth had a habit of drying and sticking to his bottom teeth. Once again my South Korean student had brought the Pink family closer together. I gave the foul-mouthed Cupid a B+ and suggested he send it to Jamie Oliver.

'Speaking of food,' said Sarah, as I moved on to Doughnut's take on the same topic, 'I hope you get over your hangover in time for Margaret's dinner party this evening.'

'Whose dinner party?'

'Margaret's. Don't tell me you've forgotten.'

'I knew nothing to forget.'

'I left you a note on the fridge.'

We were seeing so little of each other.

'You mean Margaret from Walter's barbecue? Margaret the mother of the year? I didn't even know you'd kept in touch.'

'It's all networking, Seb.'

'You mean she's your friend because she's professionally useful.'

'She's sending a few clients my way. Companies need office space. But we get on well besides work. We did lunch together at Je Ne Sais Quoi.'

Why had it been necessary to name the restaurant? I wouldn't have named the restaurant. It wasn't Sarah as much as the circles in which she moved and the company she kept.

'Can't you go on your own? I haven't got the head for it.'

'Glen will be there, don't forget. You can correct signs together.'

'Please, Sarah. My joints ache. I think I'm coming down with something.'

'Well you will sleep on park benches.'

'I'm serious, sweetheart, the lurgy's taking hold. I coughed something up earlier and the tissue walked away on its own.'

'Don't be disgusting. But please come. And there'll be people we don't know, so for God's sake don't correct their English.'

I changed Yoon Pong's B+ to an A. It was, after all, possible to have friends you hate a lot.

I desperately needed a bath to try to drown my hangover, but as I pulled back the covers to crawl to the bathroom my wife placed her hand on my arm.

'Seb, we need to discuss something.'

'Can't it wait? I feel like a plane crash.'

'No, it can't. Unless we want to lose all hope of having children.'

My cough was so jagged and dramatic that Claude jumped from the bed. Thank heavens it was Saturday; who knows what unpleasant words I might have elicited if stood in front of a class that morning?

'Please, darling, another time.'

'But that's just it – there *is* no more time. I'm off to Dubai next week and if we're going to adopt we've got to get the ball rolling.'

I jerked my head in her direction.

'Adopt?'

'I'm starting to think it's our only option.'

I returned my students' homework to the pile. Sat up and faced Sarah.

'When did you think of adoption?'

'Margaret suggested it.'

'Well why don't you adopt Margaret's baby? She doesn't seem to want it.'

'You're so cynical.'

'Look, Sarah, I thought we'd discussed this. I don't think you've got time for children. You're addicted to work. Look at your magazine!'

'What *about* my magazine?'

'You should read books, Sarah. The lives of people are in books.'

'Well *my* life is in this magazine. It keeps me abreast of what's going on in my industry.' She rolled it up. Whacked me playfully on the head. 'And it's better to hit you with.'

I shielded myself with my pillow.

'Can't you turn work off just for a few moments? What's wrong with *Grazia* or *Marie Claire*?'

'You mark your students' homework in bed. You talk to me about your students' problems.'

We sat in silence. It had started to rain.

'I'm sorry, Sarah. I don't want to argue with you. But it seems to me we've been squabbling ever since we decided to start a family.'

Sarah gazed at a painting of a fishing boat we had bought while on holiday in Cornwall. Over time it had gone wonky in its frame.

'Do you love me, Seb?'

'I just told you I love you, even if you're rarely around for me to love.'

'It would change if we had children. I know it would. I've made enough money to build a nest. Now I want to fill it.'

'That's commendable and responsible. But I really don't want to adopt.'

'Why not?'

I fluffed my pillows, lay back down and closed my eyes.

'I just don't. It's either ours or it's not meant to be.'

'But there are so many children out there who need loving homes. Perhaps we can't have children for a reason. Perhaps we're meant to love a baby who's already born rather than give birth ourselves.'

'Beautiful sentiments, Sarah. But it's not the same sort of love.'

'What would you know about it?'

A teardrop of rain collected at the top of the window. I watched its slow descent. Sarah had described such a happy childhood on our early dates. Fun-filled family anecdotes revolving around her and her sister Jessica. Dad fixing bicycles, Mum sewing badges onto picnic rugs, the Easter Bunny leaving flour footprints in the garden and Santa Claus sneaking down the chimney. What was I supposed to do after meeting that chipper cast of characters? Write some villains into the fairytale?

It wasn't to compete that I chose not to tell the truth about my family, my real family, if 'family' was the term for it. Perhaps my mother had a valid reason for the difficult choice she made; at least I hope it was a difficult choice. No, it wasn't about competing with Sarah's rosy upbringing that I chose to lie initially about mine. It was about being worthy of the attention of someone who placed value in what family could provide, emotionally rather than materialistically, at least back then.

My life had begun with rejection and my adolescence had made a habit of it. Sarah had broken the chain. I was making the unchartered journey to someone's heart and hoped not to be turned away. It was wrong not to tell her, but fear can make you do the wrong thing. Perhaps that rang true for my mother as well as for her son. And I told myself that I could always tell Sarah later, if it lasted, when she loved me enough to forgive. But each time I summoned the courage I feared rejection once again, not because of what I had lied about, but because I had then lied for so long.

The raindrop had reached the bottom of the pane.

'Sebastian?' repeated Sarah, 'what would you know about adoption?'

'I'm allowed an opinion based on instinct.'

'An opinion based on instinct? What on earth does that mean?'

'It means what it means. I don't want to adopt. Anyway, why can't we try IVF?'

She had found a way into my arms, though we lay as straight as the stripes on my pyjamas.

'I'd feel like a science experiment – the drugs, the tests, the stress. And our baby would be conceived in a clinic.'

'So? Walter was conceived in a cupboard.'

'Please don't try to be funny, although that does explain a lot.'

I turned towards her, pulling her close and kissing her forehead.

'Look, millions of women do IVF. It can't be all that bad.'

'And good luck to them. But not this woman.'

'Why?'

'I'm forty-one, Sebastian. There's no guarantee IVF will work, and if I lose any more time I'll be less suitable if not ineligible for adoption. The clock is ticking – both the biological one and the cheap Chinese thing on your wrist.'

'So adoption's the easy way out.'

'I just think there are lots of unloved children we could help.'

'And I think we should try IVF first.'

'It's *my* body.'

'It's *our* baby.'

Each olive branch snapped. We needed Yoon Pong again.

'Or,' said Sarah, hand heading south, 'we could keep trying.'
'Please don't, I need a bath.'

Her thoroughbred thighs were across me, searching for the saddle. A hand went down to help . . . prickly at first, then smooth. She consumed me slowly, like a snake swallowing prey. She threw her head back, placed her hands on my thighs, thumped and grinded with clumsy force. I held on to the paisley duvet, hoping our last olive branch didn't snap. As she closed her eyes and trembled, her *Property Week* fell to the floor.

■

Piroska opened the stained-glass front door, lowering her head like a servant as we squeaked past on the polished cedar floor. Margaret was putting on Mahler and Glen was in the garden with baby Jack. We were the first to arrive and, I hoped, first to leave. 'Love-leee!' chirped Margaret when she saw us, rushing over to air-kiss our cheeks. I found Glen's humid handshake more the stuff of Cricklewood.

The weather had brightened and a table for six had been laid in the conservatory. The glass room spied on the garden, which looked in better shape than me. The lawn was mown, the hedge was trimmed, the birdbath cupped a posh puddle. There was even a mossy Venus de Milo; I wondered if Piroska had severed the arms hoping for a voodoo effect on her boss.

'My dog's in the car,' I said to Margaret. 'He's perfectly happy to stay there but would you mind if I brought him in?'

Our host looked quizzically at Sarah, as though my wife had failed to mention the quadruped guest when they'd made plans at Je Ne Sais Quoi.

'Well, I suppose so,' she replied reluctantly. 'If you must.'

Margaret showed Sarah the rest of the house, including several original artworks which had been purchased as investments. I carried Claude through to the garden so that his paws wouldn't scratch the cedar. When baby Jack saw my dog, his face lit up as though one of his toys had come to life.

'Just don't let him piss on the Venus,' whispered Glen. 'She paid excess baggage from Athens.'

'Really?'

'No, that's just what she tells the neighbours. She got it from Homebase.'

I accepted the wineglass Glen thrust in my hand and didn't bother to say 'when' as he poured. Jack was pinned into a swanky bouncer, his seatbelt fastened as though the chair could do nought to a hundred in less than six seconds. I knelt beside him and tickled his foot.

'They don't call them bassinets anymore,' volunteered Glen. 'Not fancy enough.'

'What do they call them?'

'Well, this here is the Coco Plexistyle Baby Lounger.'

I wolf-whistled.

'It's a beauty.'

Glen raised his glass in silent toast.

'When you become a parent, your vocabulary expands as rapidly as the baby's.'

The chair rocked as Jack kicked his legs.

'He's a content little fellow,' I observed. 'He looks like you.' My host smiled. 'I hope you've forgiven my colleague for his drunken remarks at Walter's barbecue.'

Glen's first sip was even longer than mine, though his didn't wash down an aspirin.

'You mean suggesting Jack looked like Piroska?'

The aspirin lodged in my throat. More wine cleared the blockage.

'Well . . . yes.'

'It was all in jest,' said Glen, sipping further. 'And besides, he could do worse.'

I looked up at the conservatory windows, wondering if they had spied a goddess of love in the house as well as the garden.

Tennis balls popped like corks behind the hedge. We only saw the lobs. Each rally had its own rhythm. Players squabbled over the score.

Glen noticed my interest and explained.

'There are two courts,' he said. 'I've often thought of trimming the hedge so I can watch but I prefer to follow the points by ear.' I helped myself to a bowl of pistachios. 'It's a musical battle,' he continued. 'A pizzicato pop for an ace, staccato for a baseline exchange, largo for a lob, accelerando as a player attacks, and when the pops are prestissimo I know they are volleying at the net.' It was, I think it's fair to say, as eccentric a hobby as trainspotting. 'On one occasion,' he went on, 'I followed an entire match and when it was over I went and asked the players the score and I was only one game out.' Perhaps more eccentric than trainspotting. 'I know it's sad, but I often sit out here with a drink and listen to the lexicon of the game. The language of ball sports is fascinating. Cricket particularly, but tennis, too.'

We sat on the grass and waited, peeling pistachios and our ears. Jack pawed a shape on his activity bar and Claude licked his paw by the birdbath.

POP . . . pop . . . pop . . . pop . . . pop, pop, pop-pop . . . POP!

'Just long!'

'Caught the line, I think!'

'I'm standing right on it!'

'Play two!'

We sipped in unison and awaited the replay.

POP . . . pop . . . pop-pop . . . pop . . . pop . . . pop-pop-pop . . . POP!

'Hard luck – just wide!'

'Not again?'

''Fraid so!'

'*Oh, for fuck's sake!*'

I cringed at the expletive and eyed Jack.

'Of course,' said Glen sotto voce, 'I may not find it as fascinating when Bubs here is of an impressionable age.'

Glen was a small man, unassuming, with a sprinkle of freckles on his forehead. His clothes were smart and fashionable; I assumed Margaret had influenced his wardrobe, and Piroska had ironed it. I wondered how long ago his and Margaret's lives had exploded into different directions like a firework at the outer reaches of its flight. Was Jack an effort to reunite them?

'*Bend the knees on the volley, Barbara!*'

'What's fatherhood like?' I asked, taking Glen slightly by surprise.

He swirled his wine in his glass without snobbery.

'Wonderful,' he replied, placing his palm against his son's rosy cheek. 'I just wish we could spend more time with him.'

'London's so expensive.'

'Try adding day care to the list. Seventy pounds a day! An au pair is much cheaper.'

I stared into my wine, one ear on the Wimbledon hopefuls.

'Not keen on finding out about fatherhood for yourself?' asked Glen.

'Of course, but . . . well, it's complicated.'

'Say no more. I shouldn't have asked.'

He swirled his wine again.

'We've been trying for ages but I don't think it's meant to be.'

It felt good to tell the truth for once. Confiding in those peripheral to your life is somehow easier than in those close to it.

'*Fine shot! Textbook tennis!*'

We laughed. I coughed. Glen patted me on the back.

'Tell me something,' I said, lowering my voice, 'would you adopt if you couldn't have your own?'

'That's a tough one,' he said, looking skyward. Puffs of white punctuated a stretch of blue like commas in a sentence. 'I must confess I enjoy it when someone says my son looks like me. Perhaps that's why I bristled at Walter's when your colleague said what he said.'

I thought of Piroska at Walter's barbecue, of her broad range of duties. I thought of Eva, of her complicated plight and my decision to help.

'Tell me something else: if Piroska wanted to find another job, what would she need to do?'

Glen appeared puzzled by the question, which he answered with shrugged shoulders initially.

'Give us a few weeks' notice and she could leave. But it's not as simple as that. They get attached to the children. In a way they become their own. And the children spend more time with them than with their mothers, so it's a delicate relationship to interrupt.'

I emptied my glass, perhaps to numb the professional in me.

'I have this student, you see . . .'

'Yoohoo!' called Margaret from the conservatory, gold bling on the wrist of the hand she was waving. 'Come along for a flute of fizz overlooking the lawn!'

'My wife's friends have arrived,' announced Glen, clearly feeling the need to distinguish. 'Best go and say hello.'

Piroska dutifully came to collect her ward and she and Glen shared the weight of his bassinet, or whatever it was called. When the au pair turned her ankle on a tennis ball that had strayed from the courts (followed closely by a cry of '*oh, pooh!*') Glen rushed to her aid before remembering himself, turning serious all of a sudden and limply suggesting she be more careful in future.

Margaret took extra care of the introductions, finding it necessary to include a brief résumé with each name.

'John Tilson, hedge fund manager at Magnum Money, and Jennifer Pembroke, chief economist at Deloitte, this is Sarah

Pink, née Crompton, managing director of *Flat*tery, and husband Steven, English language teacher and owner of the labrador by the wandering jew.'

'Um,' braved Glen, 'it's Sebastian.'

'Oh, sorry,' said Margaret. 'How rude of me – the dog's name is Sebastian.'

Sarah smiled sympathetically but didn't feel the need to save me from scorn. Cheeks were kissed and hands shaken. Claude had made the stray ball his own.

'Piroska!' cried Margaret. 'A bottle of Blanc de Blancs and six flutes.' As she ushered us into the garden she donned her Gucci glasses. I recognised them from Walter's barbecue – she had taken them off to cut down Frank. 'Remember to check the lamb,' she instructed, when Piroska emerged with the posh plonk.

Margaret was taking out her jealousy of her husband's temptation on the source of that temptation, and guileless Glen was finding it tricky to cover his tracks, eyeing the Hungarian help as she poured the French champagne. Margaret's rush to return to work meant letting another woman into both the house and the parental relationship, and Glen, deprived of his wife, was distancing her even further. It seemed a suburban stalemate and everyone was innocent and to blame, except for Jack, little Jack, who would probably suffer it most. I wondered what similarities there were between Piroska and Glen and Eva and Tim; though Piroska, I had to admit, seemed perfectly happy in the house.

'*Salute*,' mispronounced Margaret, turning her attempt at an Italian toast into something more military. Then she latched onto John's arm and administered the sedative: 'So how's business?'

'Booming,' replied John, tweaking the collar of his Savile Row shirt. 'We've just taken over ISS and our foray into Singapore futures is exceeding even optimistic expectation. Plus we're into our new Canary Wharf offices and they are chic with a capital "s". There's a helipad on the roof and a swimming pool on the fourteenth floor.'

'Vice-versa would have made things more interesting,' quipped Glen.

Margaret glared at her husband. I hoped ISS didn't stand for the International Spelling Society. Chic with a capital 's'?!

POP!

More champagne.

POP . . . POP!

Champagne tennis.

'What about you, Jenny darling?' continued Margaret. 'I thought of you during the BPL share float.'

'That's sweet of you,' replied Jenny, whose pinstripe blazer made her appear taller than nature intended. 'We stuck our necks out a little but the subsequent Morgan merger justified our stance.'

It was gobbledygook.

'*Let! Second serve!*'

'What's hot, Sarah?' asked John.

I presumed he was referring to the finger food Piroska was parading.

'Property is still gold,' my wife replied. 'There can't possibly be a slump while so many people are praying for one.'

My mistake.

Glen leant forward and whispered in my ear in a tired tone, 'And the footsie did a whatsie on the carpet.'

I didn't dare laugh.

Weather-wise it was a lovely evening: lasting warmth, lingering daylight and the gentlest breeze drifting through wide bay windows, soft enough for shirtsleeves, strong enough to carry the scent of lavender from the garden into the house. Though we moved to the conservatory for dinner, the topic of conversation stayed put: *derivatives, liquidity, securities, arbitrage* . . . If only my students' vocabularies could grow as fast as mine did that evening. I was tempted to ask John for the phonetic spelling of each word but feared that Margaret would slice me up like the lamb.

'I hear you're off to Dubai next week?' John prompted Sarah.

'Yes,' she replied, dabbing her mouth with an embroidered serviette, 'we're thinking of investing in a new-build seven-star resort in the shape of a prawn and I'm going out there to take a look with our international risk-management team.'

John raised his eyebrows, impressed. Then he reached for his wineglass while removing some lamb from his teeth with his tongue.

'Jenny and I have just come back from there. We stayed at the Burj Al Arab.'

'What shape's that?' asked Glen.

'A sail,' replied Jenny, not noticing that a mockingbird had flown in from the garden.

'Play two. I wasn't ready!'

'Magnum are trading heavily in that region at the moment,' continued John. 'Here's my card. I'd love to talk further with you on that prawn project.'

Sarah appeared uncomfortable. Stole a sip of her Château Laroque.

'Um, well, I wouldn't be able to discuss . . .'

'Enough said,' John assured her. 'But here's my card anyway.'

John handed Sarah the crisp cut of paper. His six-storey watch caught the cuff of his sleeve.

'Who are you flying to Dubai with?' asked Margaret.

'Emirates,' replied Sarah. 'On the new Airbus.'

'We're flying with them first class to New York next week,' bragged Jenny. She sat straight, newsreader straight. 'Bit of business, then on to Antigua. Staying at the new six-star Reflection. Apparently it's got an underwater restaurant.'

'I stayed in a hotel in LA recently that had an interactive

bathroom with a waterproof LCD screen and broadband access so you could do business in the bath,' said Margaret.

'Jack often does his business in the bath,' put in Glen.

Margaret's glare lines risked permanency.

The finer things in life, misspelled and mispronounced, was the topic of conversation for the remainder of the meal. Perhaps I was hostile towards it because of my hangover and what felt like the onset of flu, or perhaps it was the fact that, despite renouncing arguably more fulfilling things to attain them, no one spoke about life's apparent luxuries with the passion Glen displayed when showcasing musical tennis. It didn't make their priorities wrong, though it did make me wonder why they pursued them with such ruthlessness.

Piroska came in carrying the baby, who looked cute and cuddly in a blue onesie with a teddy bear and the imperative HUG ME on the front. She had somehow managed to attend to every need of both adult and child the entire evening, though Glen had left the meal on occasion to help in the bathroom and kitchen.

'Jack to sleep,' she announced, waving one of his tiny hands.

'Goodnight, Jack,' said the party.

'Sweet dreams, little man,' added Sarah.

'Kiss for Mummy,' said Margaret, reminding us that she was the boy's mother.

Piroska wiped the resulting lipstick off Jack's cheek and took him from the room, breaking into a lullaby as she left.

'Still no plans on the family front, Sarah?' asked Margaret, retaking her seat.

POP!

'*Arrrgh!*'

'*Sorry, Alan. I wasn't aiming there.*'

'*Don't rub them, darling. Count them!*'

'Mixed doubles,' informed Glen. 'Mind if I go and watch?'

'Think I'll join you,' I said, grabbing the Château Laroque.

9

Direct questions

A chilly morning. Spring was thinking twice. Collar up on my incompetent coat, I took the shorter route to school via the children's playground on Chalcot Square. Expensive silence among the pastel facades of rainbow-coloured terraces – a pocket of Prague in Primrose Hill. Fair-haired young women pushing dark-haired children on the swings, a pendulum between carer and mother. What vain travail could mean more to a mother than spending the clumsy years with her young?

I often saw my students pushing other people's offspring around Primrose Hill. Pushing uphill, putting their backs into it, designer strollers laden with organic, fair-trade groceries. Were the exhausted, underpaid nannies ever tempted during one of their ward's tantrums to turn around, release the brake and say, 'Sod it, junior, you're not actually mine'?

Despite the cold I stepped slowly, reluctantly, as though towards a showdown. Suspicions aroused by conversations with

Walter, and urged to intervene by Sarah, I was hoping to find a way of learning more about Eva's potentially unsavoury situation in the monthly counselling session after class that afternoon. But when my horoscopic crossword unearthed the clue *Chin up, Len. Worried it's end of story? (5, 4)*, the answer to which was *punch line*, I had the uneasy feeling that Walter's vulgar joke about the little boy talking to his sister in their St John's Wood home might ring true. It wouldn't have been the first time that clues to Eva had appeared in my crossword.

A WELCOME BACK, FRANK banner adorned the staffroom, hung between the noticeboard and the clock. He'd been off for two weeks, convalescing and celebrating. We cheered him as he strode in, stood on a pile of textbooks and recited 'Peter Piper Picked a Peck of Pickled Peppers', a tongue-twister which, before plummeting from the hammock, would have been im-per-per-possible. Frank said he'd contemplated sending Margaret a thank-you card for ridding him of his speech impediment but then thought better of it.

Frank had recovered but Walter was ill. A finer, if not fitter example of a hypochondriac would be difficult to find; in fact, when I taught the word in class I wheeled Walter in as a real-life example. That morning he was clutching his side as he approached me in the staffroom. I was bickering with a photocopier that was also on death row.

'What side's your appendix on?' he gasped.

'Neither,' I replied.

'What do you mean, *neither*?'

'It's been removed.'

'Oh, very clever,' he snapped. Mornings were his nemesis. 'What side's it supposed to be on?'

I checked my scar.

'The right.'

'Well, it's not appendicitis.'

I assumed he was going alphabetically.

The bell rang. He limped off, going through the motions until he'd perk up in the pub. I performed my pre-class routine, splashing more water on my face than usual in the hope of waking up. Cold corridors helped – the boilers were on the blink again. Rather than greet my students I sneezed at them on entering the classroom.

'How to spell?' asked Doughnut.

I wrote it on the board.

'Pronunciation spelling,' demanded Jean-Paul.

I wrote /sneez/ on the board.

The cold snap had ruined my warm-up. Straight into the lesson today.

I called the roll and managed to pronounce my new Turkish student's name – Simge Ghanem – without her assistance. Years of practice give you a head start with hieroglyphics but they can still trip you up. I once had a French student called Arageme who I accidentally christened Aubergine. She forgave me, after I gave her some Aragemes from my allotment by way of apology. Other names can prove prickly even when you do pronounce them properly: Lee Bum Suk, for example. But some foreign names were such confused collections of letters that I often thought our admissions officer had let her cat stroll across her keyboard.

Only Eva was absent. Did she know it was counselling day? Had she deliberately stayed away? Frustrated, yet somewhat relieved, I was preparing to begin my lesson when I heard a faint knock on the door – the hail of a hesitant knuckle. Opening it revealed a child in a stroller steered by my Czech student, breathless and bashful.

'I sorry,' she begged, red-cheeked. 'No vont miss class but must look baby. Is okay?'

'How on earth did you get everything up the stairs?'

'I to carry.'

She was stronger than she appeared.

I looked down at Zeus in his Superman suit. Rhonda's twenty-five-page school code of practice didn't cover situations when au pair students bring their wards to class. I should have said no, cited some health and safety claptrap that neither I nor Eva would have understood for entirely different reasons. Instead, I moved a desk aside, allowing access for the stroller.

'Does everyone remember what a "secret" is?' I asked the class.

Only Doughnut needed reminding, but didn't ask for the spelling as she was busy moving chairs, bags and books to accommodate the latecomers.

I pointed at the stroller, which Eva parked next to her desk.

'Well this must be a *secret* between you and me. If my boss finds out, I'll get fired.'

'What means "fired"?' inquired Fernanda.

'It means I lose my job.'

The class agreed, though they were clearly wondering why I was willing to risk my neck for my least attentive student.

In an improvised show-and-tell, Zeus provided some novel vocabulary. The first half-hour of my class was spent with the students crowding around his stroller and me decorating the whiteboard on demand with /náppi/, /dúmmi/, /dríbb'l/, /téddibair/, /Īthingkheedídaypōō/. Eva handled him with tenderness, lightly brushing his cheek with her fingers to keep him reassured in a room full of strangers. Zeus was well behaved and the students seemed to enjoy his presence; apart from Lee, who was on the receiving end of a couple of raspberries.

On top of his help with vocabulary, Zeus proved a handy prop on a day when my lesson plan was modal verbs of obligation. As part of a role play, each student was told to pretend they were a parent disciplining their child and to write ten rules using the target grammar. When they had finished writing they stood in front of the class, looked at Zeus and laid down the ground rules.

'You *must not* talk wid full mouth,' said Giuseppe, recalling Italian dinner tables on which more than the food is heated.

'You *shouldn't* cry,' said Jean-Paul, confusing obligation with advice.

'You *have to* serve in army,' said Lee, who I hoped never had children.

'You *need to* eat your green,' said Sibylla, unaware that one little 's' could do such harm to her intended meaning.

I then conducted an hour-long analysis of modal verbs of obligation, which almost put everyone except Zeus to sleep; there are only so many ways to make English grammar fun. No one was more relieved than the teacher when the bell rang, until I remembered the counselling session after lunch and that further obligations lay ahead.

Every four weeks teachers sat down privately with students to ensure the present perfect was more than just a grammar point. It was a chance to help students with any difficulties they were experiencing beyond those that could be aired in the classroom, plus it gave them an opportunity to whinge about their host family's cooking, their classmates, how expensive London was, how hard it was to find part-time employment with inadequate English . . .

When counselling day came around we were teachers, psychologists, diplomats, tour guides, relationship counsellors, careers advisers and financial planners. When pay day came around we were teachers.

Ulrica was first to return to the classroom after the lunch bell emptied the canteen. The others began their homework – half a page on the pros and cons of English weather – in the classroom next door. I liked Ulrica, a husky German au pair. She reminded me of a Bavarian barmaid: thick-set, cheerful and direct. No affectation – humbled every day by a dozen dirty nappies.

'How are things?' I asked her.

'Yar, fine,' she replied. 'Oosual shit. No money. No free time. Same as prison but better toilet paper.'

Her verve was effortless.

'And are you happy with the progress of your English?'

'Is zere progress?'

'I think so.'

'Zen I am happy.'

She was easily pleased.

'And is there anything I can help you with, Ulrica? Anything you want to ask me?'

She hesitated. Crossed her legs. Tugged at the tassels on her cowperson boots (as a teacher I was an expert on political correctness).

'Vell, I think to get my tongue pierced. Do you think is good idea?'

'Umm . . . I'm afraid I'm rather conservative when it comes to such matters. I mean, aren't your ears, nose and bottom lip enough?'

'My best friend do it and say it improve pronunciation.'

'Really?'

'Yah.'

I thought of my colleague Clarissa, desperately searching for a topic for her master's in linguistics dissertation. Perhaps I had found it: *Can Piercing Aid Pronunciation?*

'Well, Ulrica, there's no definitive research on the subject, but why not give it a go and we'll monitor the results?'

Tassels swaying, the human pincushion smiled and left the room. Jean-Paul swaggered in next: aviator sunglasses, hair gelled back and mobile phone strapped to his belt. I'd had my fill of the French upstart, who often read (or pretended to read) an English newspaper in class when he'd completed an exercise. It was his way of showing fellow students he was superior, which he might have been if his answers were correct.

'How are you getting on?' I asked as he settled into his chair and made me aware it was uncomfortable by turning his nose up as it creaked.

'Zis class too easy for me,' he replied. 'I sink I ready for upper intermediately.'

'Upper what?'

'Intermediately.'

It wasn't in Rhonda's manual, but my own rules stipulated that if a student couldn't pronounce a level then they weren't ready for it. I told him I'd defer the decision until his next class test.

'If you get more than eighty per cent you can progress to upper *intermediate*.'

'But I am not good on ze paper.'

'So stop reading it in class.'

His eyes narrowed, though he didn't dare confess he hadn't understood as it would damage his cause.

'Any other problems?' I inquired half-heartedly.

'I sink Ludmila is in love wiz me.'

'Ludmila is in love with everyone. Don't take it personally. Next!'

She must have heard her name, because the Ukrainian then sashayed in as though the tired carpet in room nine was a catwalk in Milan. Nicotine and hysterical perfume were once again locked in battle. She sat on the chair and leant forward, demanding my eyes descend. Each time Ludmila broadcast that blubber I felt like a crash-test dummy.

'How are they getting on?' I inquired, chatting with her chest and throwing political correctness to the dogs.

'She dangerous,' replied Ludmila.

My brazen mood dissolved.

'Sorry, Ludmila, what did you say?'

'Eva – she dangerous. Don't tvust zis voman. You vill regret.'

Her cadence was staccato – like a robot with a Soviet accent.

'And what makes you say that?' I asked, doing my best to remain relaxed.

'You teacher but don't know everysing.'

She was more cryptic than my crossword.

'Do you know something about her, Ludmila?'

'I know film star actress ven I see. Eva is good performance.'

I looked out the window. Some tourists were photographing Yeats' former home. I hadn't had a holiday in years.

'Well, thank you for the advice, Ludmila. And is there anything else I can help you with?'

She flashed her jaundiced smile.

'I sink I need private lesson.'

'For Christ's sake, Ludmila, I'm a scarecrow next to Johnny Depp.'

'Vot means?'

'It means we just aren't meant to be.'

'To be?'

'Very good. Now conjugate: I am . . .'

She continued, confused, '. . . You are, he/she/it is, we are, they are.'

'Brilliant! See, you don't need private lessons. Now is there anything else?'

'I sink Jean-Paul is in love with me.'

'Jean-Paul is in love with himself. Please send the next person in.'

Ludmila cast me a glare that could have pierced Ulrica's tongue. Though Walter had somehow repaired the boilers, I felt a sudden chill. Her capricious pong lingered long after she'd left the room. I opened the window to clear the air. The tourists, like Yeats, had gone.

Doughnut was next – I prepared my indelible marker to spell every word I said. Giuseppe followed – happy with the course but disgusted that English bathrooms had no bidet. Fernanda after that – wondering if I could speak more slowly in class. Then Yoon Pong – could I write him a reference so he might open a bank account? Lee – looking for help with applying to City University. Sibylla – too polite to suggest she was better than the rest. Agnes – said she'd pray for me at church on Sunday. Kazuki – could she bring a Japanese-style cake for her birthday next week? Natalina – nothing to report other than her host family's poodle was a jealous beast who had piddled on her pillow. Simge – so far so good and well done for nailing her name.

I heard Zeus's stroller roll along the wooden corridor. Eva wheeled in her load apologetically, said sorry when she dropped her books, said sorry when the stroller scraped the door and woke the passenger. Zeus began to cry when he saw me. Eva apologised for that too and pacified him with a plastic bottle containing what looked to be orange juice. She was less shy with Zeus in her care because she had no time to consider her behaviour, responding dutifully to his needs without regard for her own. It stripped her of some of her mystery. Filled in some of the blanks. Gentleness replaced austerity. She was intriguing either way.

Only her clothes stayed the same – the genre, not the garments. Tracksuit bottoms and dirty trainers today; she had been walking somewhere muddy. The chair creaked as she sat down and tucked a strand of blonde hair behind her ear, then hovered a hand near Zeus as a safety net for his drink. Her clothes may not have been beautiful but her movements had a certain style; nervous yet sophisticated, like chewed fingernails on elegant hands.

I was surprised when she spoke first.

'I sorry for bring Zoos today. I not to choose.'

'Oh, that's okay. He helped me teach the grammar.'

Eva smiled generously, her eyes involved. Then, as though some burden stirred, she frowned and lowered her head.

'I'm just glad Lee isn't his father,' I continued, 'or he'd be playing with a tank rather than a teddy bear.' I had hoped to coax another smile. Perhaps she hadn't understood. 'Anyway,' I rambled on, 'he's a lovely little boy. You are very good with him. He's lucky to have you.'

'Oh, tank you,' she replied. 'He easy . . .' She searched the roof for the word. '. . . *Leaving*?'

'*Going*.'

'Okay.'

She tipped Zeus's bottle to ease the flow. Her wrist was slender. Veins aquamarine.

'Right, Eva, well, this is your first counselling session. Basically it's a chance for me to help you with anything that you are having problems with, either at school or . . . at home.'

The chair creaked again as Eva shifted slightly. She volunteered nothing. I would have to dig.

'Is everything okay at school?'

'Yes, everyting okay.' She hesitated. 'You good teacher.'

We both blushed.

'Are you happy in class?'

'Is difficult for me. I sink other student angry for slow.'

'Don't worry, you're doing fine. No one is angry.'

Her smile flickered like a flame fighting wind.

I paused, struggling with the weight of the lid to Pandora's box.

'And is everything okay at home?'

Eva's Adam's apple pulsed. She fussed over Zeus's blanket. Appeared flustered. Avoided my gaze.

'Home also okay,' she said plaintively.

'What about work?'

She sighed. Her eyes seemed to moisten. I followed them out the window. Were they holding back tears?

'Verk much stress. Very much stress.'

'Really? But Zeus seems so agreeable. I mean, as you say, easy-going. Not a difficult boy to look after.'

'Oh,' she said, straightening his fringe as though he were her own, 'yes, is true, he good. But Zeus mother no here and I more busy.'

I was as casual as I could manage.

'I see. I'm sorry to hear it. Where's his mum?'

It was of course none of my business, but when students have a linguistic disadvantage they are so busy trying to understand and respond to a question that they tend not to evaluate its relevance.

'She is verk. USA. Two veek.'

How long does a love bite last? Had Tim deemed the coast clear?

Zeus dropped his drink. Eva dutifully retrieved it and placed it on the desk between us. Then she passed him a Mr Men book that was fastened to his stroller with a velcro strap.

'Any other problems?' I asked, aware I was playing with fire but for some reason fanning the flames. 'You can tell me if things aren't okay, Eva.'

'Nussink to tell.'

'It is confidential – stays in this room. If I say anything to anyone, I will lose my job.'

'You say dis before but break rule.'

'That was to help you.'

'I no need help.'

I stood and stepped towards her, pointing at her neck.

'When I first saw you, Eva, you had a mark there.'

She stood her ground.

'Vot means "mark"?'

'It means a blemish.'

Her brow furrowed.

'A bruise?'

Her brow furrowed.

'A colour?'

Her brow relaxed.

Perhaps I wanted her to need me. Perhaps that's why I persisted. Perhaps, despite my reservations, I needed to be someone's father.

'I know I shouldn't ask, Eva, but why did you have that colour on your neck?'

She thought for some time. For too long. Her lie was telegraphed. I stepped back.

'From violin,' she said.

'From violin?' I echoed, too taken aback to say it correctly.

'Ven I play it sore my neck.'

'I didn't know you played the violin.'

'My farzer vont. I hate. Zen bad sing happen and I like. Memory.'

My mind was a cacophony of discordant thoughts. It wasn't credible. Cellists don't limp around with bruises on their thighs. Or do they? Perhaps Eva wasn't a damsel in distress. Perhaps Walter was wide of the mark. Or was Eva protecting her boss? Somebody famous perhaps. This was, after all, Primrose Hill.

I walked to the window. Leant on the sill. Eva and Zeus followed my movements like cats eyeing prey. No mystery man in the window across the street. No father figure to preach caution, to stop me walking headlong into mistakes . . .

'If I'm wrong, Eva, I hope you will forgive me for the mess I am about to make.'

'I no understand.'

I searched the window for the silver-haired man. His last chance to stop me . . .

'I have a friend who is very insightful. Do you understand *insightful*?'

'No.'

'He sees things other people don't see.'

'Like blind man.'

'If you like. Anyway, this friend, he told me a joke the other day. Do you understand *joke*?'

'Sometingk funny.'

'Yes – something funny. But not always.'

'Okay.'

'Because today is about obligation, I must ask you a question that my friend's joke has made me wonder about you.' I heard Eva's chair creak and assumed she was shifting uncomfortably but I couldn't face looking at her. Then I took a deep breath. Summoned strength. 'It's because you seem so sad,' I cushioned. 'It's really none of my business and please stop me if you don't want to answer, but I think that . . . colour on your neck . . .' Why wasn't the old man there?! Why wasn't my father there?! 'I'm worried that colour on your neck was . . . was put there by . . .'

I searched the street for the courage to continue. Two Japanese students were smoking on The Future Perfect's front steps. I wondered why they weren't in class. They were startled by the arrival of someone and looked up from their conversation as a blonde girl ran from the building below me. For a second I thought it was . . . She looked uncannily like . . . I spun on my heel to find Eva's chair empty and the classroom door ajar. She hadn't shifted in her chair earlier; she had abandoned it.

I darted from the room and down the stairs, taking four at a time, but by the time I reached the street Eva was nearing the end of the block, her ponytail swinging back and forth like a pendulum. I heard her trainers slap the pavement like applause for my stupidity. She dodged the postman, who turned his head. Then she turned the corner. Gone. I wanted to call her name, to beg her to stop, but Primrose Hill was quietly ticking over and I'd already created a scene. I wanted to follow her but found eleven reasons not to in my classroom upstairs.

The Japanese students nodded as I retraced my steps into the school. In shock I climbed the stairs less frantically than I had descended them, before stopping off at the bathroom to wash the anguish from my face, closing my eyes and grasping at a deep, shuddered breath. When I found the composure to return to class most of my students had finished penning their personal appraisals of English weather. We shared a couple, as is customary. No surprises – a general thumbs-down.

I was doing my best to explain the meaning of *miserable* when a child started wailing on the other side of the wall.

'Holy fuck!' I exclaimed.

'How to spell?' asked Doughnut.

10

The present

When Ludmila raised her hand to ask who was crying in the room next door, I panicked and said it was Walter, head of IT, attempting to tame the machinations of one machine too many. Despite their suspicions, my students agreed to add a paragraph to their critiques of English weather (a simple enough assignment) while I officially dashed off to thwart the suicide of the school's handyman, even though it was my own neck on the line. I had forced a smile before entering many a classroom; this one, however, was my cheesiest effort yet.

Little Zeus, mercifully, was still strapped in his stroller, though his toys had been cast far and wide around the room. The tear-stained two-year-old howled when he saw me, doing little to reassure me I was the right person for the task. These were uncharted waters. My experience of tiny-tots was itself tiny. I had once taken a friend's four-year-old to an Arsenal match, although he ended up comforting me when we lost three–nil.

Step one was to curb the crying. It wouldn't be long before colleagues came to investigate, or, worse still, the principal. Unable to recall the words to 'Postman Pat', I performed a less than glittering rendition of 'Twinkle, Twinkle, Little Star'. Zeus fell silent for a second, out of sheer horror at my singing no doubt, then began to howl even louder than before. 'Mary Had a Little Lamb' met with a similar tantrum, while 'Humpty Dumpty' wasn't even given a chance to be put back together again; Zeus preferred both him and me in pieces.

I grabbed my mobile and frantically phoned the mother of the aforementioned four-year-old, who said her preferred method of staunching infant outbursts was to act more childishly than the child. I went cross-eyed, stuck out my tongue, waved my hands about my ears like wacky antlers, but without a spinning bow tie or water-squirting flowers I would never forge a career in children's entertainment.

When Zeus began to shake his stroller with all the muscle of his namesake, I realised it was time to retire Coco the Clown. I noticed a bag hanging from the stroller handles and madly rummaged through it in search of a dummy, all the while saying 'shhhhhhhh' to no good effect. A squeaky duck, a food-stained sunhat, a bib, a bottle of juice, a packet of cigarettes (Eva's, I hoped!), a spare nappy and, hiding behind a packet of crayons, a dummy. I brushed it off and shoved it into Zeus's mouth as you might a frantic finger in a leaky pipe. The noise perished, like flicking a switch, but relief was short-lived and rudely interrupted by Zeus firing a twenty-one-gun salute into his Superman suit. Now I was in the shit in more ways than one.

Soiled but silent, Zeus could be left alone for a few minutes, so I raced down to the staffroom, where I surprised Walter perusing porn on one of the school computers.

'Still searching for an au pair?' I asked him.

'I was just, er . . .' he stammered, hastily exiting the spicy site.

'Never mind,' I interrupted. 'I've got good news for you. You know how you've been dying to get back into teaching? Well here's your chance. I need you to take over my afternoon class.'

Walter's face lit up like a child's, a comparison I found painful given my predicament. He jumped to his feet, after ensuring he'd left no cyber-footsteps to his site.

'Superlative!' he exclaimed. 'What will I be teaching? The future progressive? Delexicalised verbs? Don't tell me, don't tell me – the mixed conditional.'

I'd started back up the stairs, Walter snapping at my heels like a deranged dog.

'You'll be pressing play on the DVD player, I'm afraid. They'll be watching a film – *Bridget Jones's Diary*.'

The rom-com was always on standby, justifiable as an English class by selecting the English subtitles option. Combined with a worksheet asking whether Renée Zellweger looked good in knickers, it was the perfect plan B when a teacher had no time to prepare a lesson, was simply feeling lazy, or, less often, needed to buy time to smuggle a baby from the building.

Offended, Walter stopped on the stairs.

'Why can't *you* show them the film?' he asked.

'No time for questions. Just do it.'

'Sebastian Pink, I'm looking forward to an explanation in the pub this afternoon. Your attempts at procreation are doing you no good at all.'

'I've got a baby. That's the problem. Alive and well in the room next door.'

Walter looked more confused than usual.

'Does this concern the au pair?'

'Eva.'

'Does it?'

'Look, I haven't got time now. Just do me this favour. Oh, and I don't suppose you remember the words to "Postman Pat"?'

Walter closed his eyes and pinched the bridge of his nose.

'Postman Pat and his . . . black and white cat. All the birds are . . .' He opened his eyes only to narrow them. 'All the birds are . . . singing. The day is just beginning. Pat feels he's a really happy man.' His head bounced merrily as he recalled the simple rhyme.

'How the hell do you know that?'

'Only show on TV with any depth to it these days, although I'm pretty sure we'll soon be able to tele-vote which parcel Pat delivers first.'

In essence I was asking Walter to babysit my class, an irony he pointed out as I dragged him into my classroom and introduced him to its occupants. They played along by applauding half-heartedly when I told them I had talked Walter in off the window ledge, but were less enthused when I informed them he would be their teacher for the afternoon. I broke every rule in Rhonda's rulebook that day, although I decided to rationalise that later as I left Walter and my students nervously eyeing each other like blind dates.

Rushing next door, I couldn't decide what worried me more: leaving my class in Walter's hands or my predicament with Zeus. As Sarah always said, it was important to keep things in perspective. The situation was bad but it could have been worse had Eva decided to abandon Zeus at The Future Perfect the following day, when the annual British Council inspection of the school was scheduled. They'd probably knock off one of our five hard-earned stars for a soiled superhero in room nine.

The smell was foul: decomposed broccoli. This good little lad was eating his greens, probably at Eva's conscientious insistence. There was no escape – I would have to change him. But where? On the overhead projector? A rickety desk? Time to move him to the bathroom. After checking the coast was clear, I pushed Zeus's stroller across the hallway at high speed. Aptly, it was a Maclaren.

The CELTA course claims to prepare teachers for every classroom contingency. I must have been absent when they did nappy changing. I locked the toilet door and unzipped Zeus's Superman suit before placing him in the bathroom sink. His shit shield had done an admirable job, deflecting what appeared to be a devastating blast. I suppose it was appropriate that I sang 'Postman Pat' while bundling up a package that needed to be handled with care.

I wiped, washed and dried the boy's bottom, not such a tall order after all. I had cleaned up after Claude countless times, and the late Bullseye had been incontinent towards the end. But just when I thought I was doing a good job, my confidence – and shirt – was doused by the water pistol between Zeus's legs, a pert little squirt like a blast from an udder.

'You little . . .'

Anger was my first reaction. Then I looked at the boy, shy smile on his face, and realised what a good sport he was to have his nappy clumsily changed by his au pair's English teacher. Suddenly I was overcome with a sense of selfishness. The day's developments must have been far more traumatic for him than me, yet he had stopped crying and, judging by the temperature of the splash, was warming to me.

I had the duration of *Bridget Jones's Diary* to return Zeus to his rightful owner. How long did the film last? Ninety minutes? Perhaps a hundred with all that signature Hugh Grant awkwardness and bumbling dialogue (or was that *Notting Hill?*). All I knew was that Eva's host family lived in Humpstead, not exactly the precise coordinates you'd feed to a sat nav. And even if I had the address, what if Eva, in distress, hadn't gone home?

After applying the clean nappy (back to front initially) and resealing his suit, I strapped the boy into the stroller and crouched down to his level.

'Zeus, little fella, can you tell me where you live?'

'House.'

His charm had worn off. I parked him back in room nine, placed the dummy in his mouth, handed him the squeaky duck and raced downstairs to the office. Our admissions officer, Audrey, had the foreign and local addresses of every student at the school, but the greying spinster wasn't supposed to divulge them except in an emergency. This was an emergency, if not the kind that ticks boxes. When I appeared in front of her desk, looking as though I'd tried to outrun a storm, Audrey was serenely dunking a Hobnob into her tea. We had petitioned Rhonda to make office staff teach a lesson now and then so they might understand the rigours of our work. She said she'd consider it, two years ago.

'Can I help you, Sebastian?' snapped Audrey, visibly annoyed at my arrival. She wasn't unhelpful; she simply took her mid-life crisis out on the teachers and students who interrupted it.

'Um, well, yes you can, as a matter of fact.'

Audrey's soggy biscuit plopped into her mug, splashing hot tea onto her hand. She glared over half-glasses. I would need to be convincing.

'I, er, need the address of one of my students.'

'For what reason?'

'Er . . . because the student . . . yes, the student forgot some textbooks in class this morning.'

I wasn't a bad Hugh Grant myself.

'And why can't *said student* collect them when *said student* comes to school tomorrow?'

Audrey brushed a crumb from her desk. The Hobnob in her tea keeled over and sank.

'Because said student has a test tomorrow and needs the books to prepare.'

'Isn't that the student's problem rather than yours?'

'My students' problems are my problems.'

She raised her eyebrows – prickly parabolas.

'I never knew you were such a professional, Sebastian.'

Gling-glong as an email arrived in her inbox.

'Look, Audrey,' I said, tired of playing games, 'she's been studying so hard for this test. I'd hate to see her fail just because we couldn't bend the rules slightly.'

'She?' repeated Audrey, interested suddenly. She turned to her computer. 'What's her name?'

'Ah, Eva Kaliv . . . Kalivoda? Something like that.'

Audrey tapped at her keyboard.

'Eva Kalivkova?'

'That must be it.'

Audrey stood and pulled a folder from her bookcase, then produced a thinner folder from inside the first.

'That her?' she asked, holding up Eva's file.

My eyes widened. The photo was ravishing – from shrinking violet to sunflower. No frumpy clothes or ponytail but flowing hair riding suntanned shoulders and an engaging, confident smile. Her teeth seemed whiter, her eyes more alive, and her necklace – a crucifix, not the opal – nestled on a crest of cleavage: declivities leading to destinations I dared not contemplate. No trace of sadness. No hint of shyness. The photo had clearly been taken some time ago and appeared to prove that my Czech student was currently dressing down, though it also reminded me of what Ludmila had said about Eva putting on a performance.

Audrey sat in her swivel chair, spectacles on a string, ladder in her stockings.

'Emergencies,' she said robotically, 'include illness, fire, suspended classes, family bereavement . . .'

'She's left Superman in my class with a cape full of Kraptonite and if I don't get him home soon he will self-destruct from the bottom up. The future of humankind depends on it, so tick whichever box you like but give me that fucking address.'

Audrey dunked another Hobnob. 'My, my,' she said, 'that *is* an emergency.'

She scribbled on a scrap of paper and handed it to me, convinced she wasn't the only one in the grip of a mid-life crisis.

Exhausted, I retreated from her office.

'Sebastian,' she called.

'Yes, Lois Lane?'

'Why is your shirt wet?'

I pointed at her packet of biscuits. 'Same problem,' I replied. 'Think I'll switch to Rich Tea.'

Our admissions officer had seen enough surprises for one day.

■

I inhaled until the acrid anaesthetic of Eva's cigarettes reached the soles of my feet, smoke in my wake as I pushed Zeus along the pavement as fast as the tiny wheels on his stroller would allow. I must have cut an appalling father figure. As I streaked past the window of the Princess of Wales, no doubt the dusty daytime congregation commented that fathers didn't have enough time for their children these days. It struck me that I might push Zeus past his real father, turning this bad dream into a full-scale nightmare. I shortened the cigarette. Sucked for sanity.

I was heading for our apartment, where I planned to put Zeus in the car and drive to the scribbled address. I figured I should be able to make it before Bridget realised Hugh was a philandering twat and plumped for the other toff whose name I couldn't remember. Then I realised I had no car seat in the car (why would I?) and would have to take the bus. If I bumped into a friend I would simply say one of my au pair students had forgotten the boy in class: a stock-standard Tuesday.

'Do I need to pay twice?' I asked the driver.

'Say what?' he replied, half-interested.

'Do I need to pay for the boy as well as for myself?'

Passengers looked up from their smartphones and free newspapers. The driver ignored the query and waved me and Zeus onboard, glancing at his side mirror before assaulting the accelerator and careering us down the aisle like a bowling ball. I imagined these barnstormers back at their depots of an evening, tallying the number of pensioners they had crippled, collecting bets, claiming personal bests. It was the same each time we stopped – the driver hit the brake as a last resort and sent me and Zeus lurching. A large woman leant across and applied the brake on the stroller. 'First child?' she asked rhetorically. If only she knew.

Approaching Hampstead Village, computerised voice ramming route number and destination down passengers' throats, I unscrunched Audrey's note and saw that Eva lived, or Eva's boss lived, in Pilgrim Lane. I figured that it was an appropriate name, although my mind was too muddled to think why exactly. Was I the pilgrim, or was Eva?

I knew the area because a colleague of Sarah's lived in nearby Willow Road and held numerous soporific dinner parties, where they discussed things such as shared-equity transactions while I combed the bookshelves or tickled the cat. We got off the bus and raced downhill towards the Heath, the wheels on the stroller beginning to wobble. Streets with cobbled gutters were choked with four-wheel drives. A red phone booth added a village feel. It started to rain but I resisted the temptation to call in for courage at the Wells Tavern. The piddle on my shirt had dried and been replaced by sweat. I could only imagine how I looked and smelt.

'Will Mummy be home?' I asked Zeus as we turned into his street. Construction work and renovations on both sides of the road. The banks were blindly funding a property boom. Zeus's inheritance was gaining value before our eyes.

'Mummy hopital,' he replied.

I was alarmed before remembering Zeus's mother was a doctor, who was also, according to Eva, currently away in the States.

'What about Daddy?'

'Daddy work.'

'Do you like Eva?' I asked, feeling sorry for the child.

He smiled and raised both arms as though celebrating a goal. 'Love Eva!'

With each frantic step along Pilgrim Lane, counting the numbers aloud with Zeus – 'seven, nine, eleven' – I had the uneasy feeling that I was wading into waters where I'd be out of my depth. Arriving at the house, sole of one shoe separating, I resisted the temptation to park Zeus at the door, apply the brake (which I now knew how to do), ring the doorbell and run for the nearest pub. But if no one was home he could be sat there for hours, if no harm came to him before then. I couldn't abandon a defenceless boy. Like father, not like son.

Audrey had written one address but the house had two doorbells. The building had obviously been bisected into apartments. Real estate agencies such as Sarah's were turning stately homes into hotels. I unbuckled Zeus and held him up to the height of the buttons.

'Which doorbell is yours?' I asked him.

Rather than reply, he pressed.

I had a lot to learn.

When no one arrived I peered through the front window like a cat burglar checking for dogs. The living room became a dining room which became a kitchen which became a garden. Furniture was pricey and posh, though the designer chair by a magazine rack appeared more conceited than comfortable. Shellacked wood floors, original artwork above the fire, charcoal nude on the opposite wall, a tinsel HAPPY BIRTHDAY banner strung between upright lamps.

'Is it your birthday?' I asked Zeus.

'Hip hip hooray!' he replied.

I rang the bottom bell. A dog growled hazily, more dozer than deterrent.

'Is that your dog?'

'Hercols.'

'Is that the dog's name?'

'Big dog.'

Zeus had a habit of anticipating the next question. Conversation with him was like a *Two Ronnies* sketch.

Still nobody. I rang the top bell. Footsteps. My heart pounding. Surely Eva didn't have her own apartment. What if it wasn't her and the neighbour recognised Zeus and began asking questions? I felt as though I was standing in quicksand and was livid with Eva for dragging me into it. Stairs creaked. A silhouette increased in size as it approached the frosted glass.

The latch clicked. No turning back.

Her face was as pure as snow. I often thought of snow when I saw Eva – freshly fallen, milk white, sun playing in the prism of each flake, a temporary novelty for a tired landscape. My anger melted as Zeus ran from behind me and jumped into his carer's arms. Hercols (strange name for a dog) flapped his tail but didn't rise. Reunification met with relief all round.

'Congratulation,' said Eva.

To my surprise she carried Zeus off down the corridor, leaving me on the doorstep unsure what to do. The dog's head found my hand, wet nose on dry fingers; dogs have a knack of knowing who will pause to pat them. He sniffed my trousers as I crouched beside him and reached for the silver disc on his collar. *Hercules*. I smiled – Zeus's infant effort to pronounce his name was admirable. I wondered if all his parents' 'possessions' were named after Greek mythology? Why couldn't the hound have a normal name such as Flop or Biggles or Beethoven? Not only was it snooty, it was wildly inappropriate. Hercules was supposed to be strong and courageous. This dog was an ageing wuss. The worst guard dog since . . . er, Claude.

I stood and craned my neck in an attempt to see along the corridor. Was I supposed to follow Eva or take my leave? Was I as WELCOME as the doormat suggested? I realise now that she was giving me a chance to end this story early and return to the comfort of my crossword. In that moment, however, I had a real riddle to solve. For the first time in a long time I had no idea where my day was headed. If I followed her down the hall perhaps I wouldn't while away the afternoon with Walter or wind up with a bottle on my lonely bench. Fear of the known – that's why I didn't turn. Was I helping her, or helping myself?

I closed the door quietly and boldly stepped inside (so nervously that I split the infinitive). The polished wooden floor made it impossible to walk silently, so Eva was less than surprised when I clunked into the kitchen.

She looked my way, expressionless, and sniffed the air like Hercules.

'You have smoke?' she asked.

'I smoked your cigarettes. I was stressed. You know why.'

The rain had stopped, or weakened, and Zeus was climbing on a cubby house in the garden, a high-quality plastic contraption, a palace for a two-year-old prince. The garden was a mix of grass and mud. Laces tied, Eva's soiled trainers lay on their sides by the open French doors. It explained her dirty clothes.

It was the first time I had seen Eva anywhere other than at school and I was confused by her confidence. She appeared at home, in control, as though it were her child playing outside, as though it were her silver fridge she opened and from which she took an uncorked bottle of wine and poured two glasses. If, as Walter suggested, she was an unwilling participant, was an illicit relationship with her boss possibly worth a swanky address? Or perhaps, like a teenager when parents are away, she was simply playing queen of the castle while Zeus's mother was in America.

I eyed my watch. Renée Zellweger was beginning to see the real Hugh Grant. No time for chitchat. I would need to get right to the point.

I cleared my throat to avoid the possibility of a false start.

'Eva, I know I'm only your English teacher, but if you want to tell me what's going on here I'm all ears.' She hesitated. Appeared confused. Looked at my lobes. I was living proof of the idiom, but that didn't mean Eva had understood it. 'I will gladly listen,' I explained.

She closed the fridge with the nudge of a hip and handed me a glass of chardonnay.

'Zoos play,' she replied factually, 'you, me and ears drink.'

I accepted the wine and followed her to the leather sofa, lumpy in parts yet plush. It farted as we sat down, mocking the gravity of the moment.

'I don't mean that. I mean what's happening to you in this house?'

She rolled her eyes and barked louder than Hercules: '*Typický učitel, pořad se jen ptá.*'

I almost spilt my wine.

'I hope you're going to translate that.'

'Oh,' she said, flustered, 'alvays teacher, alvays question.'

I turned towards her. The sofa farted again.

'Why did you run away from school? You could have got me in a great deal of trouble.'

'Vot means?'

'You put me in a difficult situation. I could have lost my job.'

She gulped her wine. Her feet were bare. Toenails undecorated.

'Ha – same me! I could lose job too.'

'So why did you do it? Was it because of what I said about my friend's joke and the mark on your neck?'

She frowned. 'I no hear joke. I am already leave.'

I cast my mind back to the counselling session. Her chair had indeed creaked before I'd summoned the courage to spill my theory, and even then I hadn't managed the final blow. I was frustrated and relieved in the same deep breath.

I leant towards her, palms open, importuning the truth. 'So why then?'

'Because I vont help you.'

'To help *me*?!'

'Yes.'

'So why did you run away? Why did you leave me with Zeus?'

She finished her wine. Contemplated the empty glass. 'If I say, you no believe.'

'Try me.'

'Vot?'

'I promise I'll believe you.'

She looked into my eyes for the first time since the counselling session. 'I vont see you good farzer.'

Silence was uncomfortable as I returned her timid gaze, which she immediately shifted out the window, half to escape mine, half to check on the child in question.

'Oh, my stupid English,' she lamented. 'You no understand.'

'No, no . . . I understood. I just . . . I just don't quite know what to think.'

The phone rang. We held our breaths till it stopped, as though the caller might hear our conversation.

'Is that why you said "congratulations" when I arrived?'

A slight but perceptible nod.

'But why would you want to show me that I'm a good father?'

'Because must to know.' She smiled. 'Obligation.'

'You took such a risk, Eva.'

Her eyes were still out the window. 'You say me vont practise farzer. I help you practise farzer.'

I studied her face, shaking my head slightly, flattered yet alarmed that she would entrust Zeus to me. Then I sat back and sipped, thinking the surprises were over. But Eva was full of surprises.

'I buy for you prissent,' she declared, standing and leaving the room.

I stood too, though by the time I was on my feet I was alone. The stairs squeaked as Eva climbed them. I went to the window and watched Zeus – gentle boy with a powerful name. I checked my watch again and realised I was due back at school. I felt irritable, nervous. I was used to being in control around students but Eva seemed to know how to manipulate me. I had spent my life solving puzzles. Now I felt as though I was living one. Eva's life was cryptic. Perhaps that's why it intrigued me.

The stairs squeaked again. When she walked back in both our cheeks were flushed: hers with effort, mine with embarrassment. She held out a bag bearing the message *This is not a plastic bag*. Nothing was as it seemed or should have been.

'*Otevři to*,' she said

Even language had mutinied. I held up my hands, tried to refuse the bag. Eva shook it.

'*Otevři to!*' she insisted.

'You don't have to give me a present, Eva.'

'You frighted?'

'No, I'm—'

'So to open!'

I put down my wine and accepted the bag. When I opened the top and tipped it up, the toes of a pair of men's slippers slid onto my hand.

'What are these for?'

'For cold feet.'

'What?'

'You say can't have chiltren because cold feet. Now no problem zis.'

I searched Eva's face for a clue as to whether she had genuinely misunderstood or was playing with me. I never knew if she was behind or one step ahead. I retrieved my glass and drank, holding it to my lips long after it was empty.

'More vine?' inquired my unlikely host.

I ignored the offer and studied her neck. The opal lay in the hollow of her throat as though in a gift box.

'Speaking of presents, Eva . . .'

Her turn to be embarrassed, for her cheeks to fill with blood.

'I need vine.'

I followed her to the fridge, allowing her no escape.

'Admit it – that opal wasn't a present from your brother.'

Each utterance was akin to a chess move.

'So who from, this *opal*?'

She opened the fridge. I stepped in and shut it.

'From your boss.'

Checkmate.

I retreated, allowing Eva to pour a drink. There was only a quarter of a glass left in the bottle.

'I know what's happening to you, Eva. It's not unheard of and it's not your fault. I can get you out of here without making a big thing of it. Without anyone knowing the details. I can find you a new job. I can find you a new family.'

'No,' replied Eva. 'Is no easy and you no understand.'

'It is easy and I do understand. You won't have to do anything. Leave it all to—'

'No,' she repeated. 'I no leave zis house.'

'But why not? You're unhappy here.'

Eva turned and looked to the garden. Zeus climbed through the window of his cubby house, knocked on his own front door, then climbed back inside to answer the knock. 'Who's there?' he shouted, peering left and right.

'I here,' shouted Eva, running barefoot into the garden.

■

I was almost as anxious outside the door to my classroom as I had been outside the door to Eva's house. I had been gone for two hours and had expected to hear Van Morrison's whisky voice singing *Bridget Jones's Diary* to a close. Instead, I heard raucous laughter.

I inched the door open to find Walter standing on a chair, holding one arm in the air and sniffing his own armpit.

'Phew,' he exclaimed, coaxing a response from his audience, 'I don't arf . . .'

The students eyed their notebooks. Doughnut and Fernanda conferred.

'Pen and ink!' shouted Giuseppe.

'*Bravo!*' hollered Walter.

Then they noticed me, open-mouthed in the doorway, wondering where in the intermediate textbook was the lesson on rhyming slang.

'Look, everyone!' continued Walter. 'It's Grandpa Grammar. I think he's a little bit surprised to see us. Have a butcher's at his . . .'

The students eyed their notepads again. Kazuki's eyes lit up. 'Boat lace!' he declared.

'Give that man a cigar,' yelled Walter.

Amid applause for Kazuki I put down my bag, sat at Eva's empty desk and examined the whiteboard. Walter's handwriting was steadier than I remembered it. *Adam and Eve, China Plate, Brown Bread, Dog and Bone, Frog and Toad, Pork Pies . . .* His list almost filled the board.

'What happened to *Bridget Jones's Diary*?' I asked Walter.

'Far too dull for these fertile minds,' he replied, 'as were most of the grammar points we discussed. They're tired of traditional teaching methods, dear boy. I've promised them you'll spice up the syllabus, bin the nuts and bolts and teach them something whole.' He turned to Jean-Paul. 'What's tomorrow's lesson, *mon ami?*'

The Frenchman read carefully from his pad. 'Ze lurve poetry of Jean Donne.'

Elbows on Eva's desk, I rested my chin in my hands. It had been a turbulent day. This was surely the final bump.

'You are tired,' stated Jean-Paul, putting his books away and checking for messages on his mobile.

I nodded.

'Vot happened to you?' asked Ludmila.

'Trouble and strife,' I replied.

The students laughed in chorus, thinking it rhyming slang.

11

Determiners

Three middle-aged women in sensible underwear wandered the school like rising damp. Our orders were to ignore them, to pretend they weren't there, to teach our classes oblivious to the clipboard brigade, ticking boxes here, tut-tutting there. British Council inspections can make or break a language school. The Future Perfect had performed well in the past. Rhonda was adamant it would continue.

The principal had outlined her five-star plan at a recent staff meeting, the kind of meeting where you counted the minutes while taking them:

- Walter to hide in the broom cupboard.
- Caretaker to pick up all the cigarette butts between the bricks in the courtyard. (Clarissa ended up getting her students to do it so she could elicit the word 'backache'.)
- The Polish students have finally completed renovations in the

foyer and the school's entrance looks smashing.
- The fish tank in the foyer has been cleaned and the Bubble Eye goldfish with fin rot has been flushed down the toilet.
- Only the most recent textbooks to be used in class. No home-made supplementary materials and no films to be shown in lieu of lessons.
- If posing a question to students in a class under inspection, be sure to choose a student who knows the answer.
- Teachers to be in class on the dot of 9 am rather than five past.
- No jeans, and shoes polished please. (Rhonda had looked at my well-trodden size-tens when making this point.)
- Use interactive whiteboards where possible. (A big thankyou to Walter for yesterday's demonstration and an even bigger thankyou to Frank for stepping in and demonstrating it to Walter.)

Our Ts were crossed and our Is dotted. We had been preparing for months. It was the ELT equivalent of the Olympic Games – interminable chaos to be shipshape for a fortnight.

The assessors had access all areas, barring broom cupboards. As well as passing judgement on existing practices, they would recommend ways of improving the school and its facilities. We were confident we would pass, that our five stars were safe, but resting on our laurels would be wrong, insisted Rhonda, who, to thank us for our efforts and commemorate the day, had organised a lunchtime barbecue in the courtyard to which students were invited. 'It will showcase The Future Perfect's emphasis on teacher–student rapport,' explained Rhonda at the staff meeting, 'as well as providing an opportunity to get the assessors cheerfully pissed.'

The night before D-day I was as jumpy as a flea on my mattress. London was sultry and my quilt made me sweat. Events with Eva and the school inspection were making me anxious.

Rhonda usually steered assessors towards the classrooms of full-time teachers, so there was a good chance my lesson would be scrutinised. I had prepared a personal favourite on the first conditional, which I could teach in my sleep and, without caffeine, might have to. Walter's promised masterclass on the poetry of John Donne would need to be postponed.

Amid a strange mist, both in my head and on the hill, my morning walk with Claude was more slog than stroll. My crossword turned up ominous solutions such as *bind*, *pickle* and *scrape*, all of which had different meanings in the puzzle but which could easily have been synonyms if applied to Eva's situation and my quest to do something about it. As I dropped Claude home I passed Sarah on the stairs, heading off to work, and greeted her like a neighbour before realising she was my wife. We kissed at high speed. Like married jousters.

'You home for dinner?' I called over the sound of her high-flying heels.

Claude and I cocked our ears in the hope of an answer.

'I promise I'll try,' came her response.

I hated closing the front door on Claude – it's only a dog's life twice a day. The brutish ritual reminded me of third-class passengers on the *Titanic*: he'd shove his snout into a narrowing gap before I pushed him back and shut the door in his face. He whimpered when I turned the key in the lock and only settled when I reassured him I'd be home as soon as possible. Then, as my linen testifies, he skulked off and slept on our bed all day.

The staffroom was particularly manic that morning, with skirmishes breaking out in the queue for the photocopiers. Most teachers were well dressed for the first time since the Christmas party, making everyone ill at ease, like wearing a tie when unaccustomed. Inexperienced teachers were the most nervous, putting finishing touches to vital lessons and seeking suggestions from senior colleagues.

As per Rhonda's request, I was in class before the bell had finished ringing. Only Doughnut had arrived and was surprised to see me so early. Some teachers got angry with students who were late for class but I put myself in the students' shoes and figured that if my parents were paying for me to learn a second language then I'd roll out of bed rather casually too. I had once heard Clarissa yell at a Spanish latecomer: 'Classes start at nine. If this were a job you'd be fired!' To which the Spaniard replied: 'But I no pay a thousand pound a month to go to work.' He obviously didn't commute on Network Rail.

Doughnut capitalised on the fact we were alone by posing a tangential teaser we wouldn't have had time for in class. (The words 'Teacher, can I ask question?' cause me nightmares.) Excitedly, she took a spiral-bound notepad from her bag, turned it in her hands and read from the back cover.

'What means "shampitka"?'

I crossed my arms and contemplated the question. Avoiding such interrogations was precisely the reason I turned up later than the latecomers.

'"Shampitka"?'

She eyed the scribbled word again.

'Yes – "shampitka".'

'I'm not sure what you mean, Doughnut.'

'"Shampitka" – I hear it tomorrow . . . sorry, yesterday.'

'It doesn't mean anything – on any day.'

'But I hear it.'

'No – not "shampitka". Shampoo? Champion? Paprika?'

'Oh . . . I not know,' she said, deflated.

Statistics suggest a new English word is created every ninety-eight minutes, but at The Future Perfect it was more like every ninety-eight seconds.

Only while Doughnut was searching her electronic dictionary for the mystery word did I notice that she was dressed somewhat differently from her usual black jeans and Mind the Gap T-shirt. I had to look twice. I may even have rubbed my eyes. Was my otherwise unremarkable Thai student actually wearing an Elizabethan ruff around her neck? While she tapped at her keypad I examined the bizarre frill. It appeared to have been fashioned from the paper in her notebook, and closer inspection (to which she displayed no protest) revealed ruled blue lines and the words *Homework for Tuesday*.

'Er, Doughnut,' I asked, 'what is that around your neck?'

She was confused for a second, then she twigged, sat straight and modelled the accessory.

'Luff,' she replied, like a dog with a speech impediment.

'Right. Okay. And why are you wearing it?'

'Is oligami. Kazuki make for everyone. Today is John Donne lesson, no?'

I was fumbling for a reply when through the open door came Fernanda, Jean-Paul and Giuseppe, looking like the court of Elizabeth the First. Crude concertinas adorned their necks, Jean-Paul was clad in cloak and codpiece, Giuseppe was sporting a strap-on goatee and from their pencil cases they pulled quills rather than biros. On any other day I would have admired their enthusiasm. Today it needed to be nipped in the bud.

'I'm so sorry to disappoint . . .'

A harmonious flourish of notes as Yoon Pong strolled in playing a lute. I snatched it from his hands and closed the door.

'Where the hell did you find that?' I asked, hiding the instrument in the cupboard.

'Host family,' he replied. 'I look on Google. Was most popular instrument in time of John Donne.'

'Well, that's wonderful, but I'm afraid we're not . . .'

The door squeaked again. Through it filed Agnes, Sibylla, Kazuki, Ulrica, Ludmila, Lee, Natalina and Simge, looking like a lounge, a cluster, or whatever the collective noun is for frill-necked lizards. (A lethargy of lizards? If that's not it, it should be.)

As usual Eva was last to arrive, sneaking in breathless, rose in each cheek. She had missed Walter's class – for reasons known only to her and me – and arrived at school expecting to find Sebastian the First rather than Henry the Eighth. She was as surprised as I was by the fancy-dress party, and in her soft-spoken way apologised for being the odd one out. Kazuki wasted no time in tearing a page from his notebook and folding another ruff. Never again would I ask Walter to cover a class.

'Don't bother, Kazuki. I'm afraid we're not having the lesson on John Donne today.' A chorus of disappointment – the word 'boo' is universal. 'We'll be doing the exhilarating first conditional instead.' Disappointment turned to protest – the word 'nooo' is also widespread. 'So kindly remove your ruffs, lay down your lutes, and turn to page seventy-two of your textbooks.'

Yoon Pong and Lee conferred in Korean. Ludmila made sure that her chest was on show. As far as her cleavage was concerned, the Ukrainian didn't need a fancy-dress costume to belong to Tudor times.

'But we already do first conditional,' objected Lee. 'We study before in pre-intermediate.'

'Is tlue!' seconded Kazuki, who had ignored my request and continued to work on Eva's ruff.

'Alright then, give me an example,' I challenged, wondering if they realised how mutiny was dealt with in Donne's day.

The lizards looked eagerly at Sibylla – the strongest student, whose cheeks went crimson when she realised she had the stage. Clever Clogs took a deep breath. Time to live up to her nickname.

'We'll . . . always . . . do our homework,' she said cautiously, 'if you teach us a lesson on John Donne.'

An eruption of applause from her classmates, though most weren't sure whether she'd nailed it or not and hoped the volume of their praise might disguise any errors.

'Okay,' I said, 'well done, Sibylla. We'll do the second conditional instead.'

'Done it,' declared Lee.

'Example,' I demanded.

All eyes on Clever Clogs. Another deep breath.

'If . . . you . . . taught us a lesson on John Donne,' she said deliberately, 'we . . . would . . . always do our homework.'

Riotous applause. The stomping of feet. I hoped the assessors weren't outside the door.

'Very well,' I continued, 'we'll turn our attention to the third conditional.'

Was that sweat on Sibylla's brow? She closed her eyes. Rehearsed the sentence in her head. Served it up methodically when she thought it was cooked.

'If . . . you'd . . . taught us the lesson on John Donne, we . . . would . . . have . . . done our homework.'

A standing ovation. I was tempted to join in. Sibylla really should have been in a more advanced class. Students such as her were often graded incorrectly because of shyness at the placement interview.

Queen Elizabeth's courtiers returned to their seats.

'So?' said Jean-Paul.

'So what?' I replied.

'Can we 'ave ze lesson on lurve poetry?'

I surveyed my students in their homemade costumes. Kazuki had finished Eva's ruff and presented it to her on bended knee like a crown to a queen. I felt a strange fondness for them, delight at their eagerness, jealousy for their youth. An oddball lot — diamonds in their ruffs.

'Okay,' I said, 'we'll do it, but on one condition.'

'Argh,' objected Lee, 'we already do this.'

'No.' I laughed. 'Not that kind of condition. I mean we'll do it if you agree to do one thing.'

'What?'

I tossed him a piece of paper.

'Make me a ruff.'

As Rhonda always said – if something is worth doing, it is worth doing well.

■

While the class made my costume I went in search of Walter, but all I found in the broom cupboard were mice droppings, broken furniture and a few ping-pong bats hanging, appropriately, upside down. I eventually found him in the staffroom looking busy near a photocopier. I had never heard the school so quiet. The assessors, according to Audrey, were in Frank's class. Good job his stutter had gone.

'You fixing that?' I asked Walter.

'Officially, yes,' he whispered, 'though for once it's not broken. Just looking busy till the coast is clear. How are you getting on?'

'Thanks to you, terribly. My students have all turned up in Elizabethan dress and are demanding that lesson you promised them on Donne.'

Walter smiled and tweaked his moustache.

'Pleased to hear it. Good group you've got there.'

'You couldn't have promised them "Incy Wincy Spider" or "Baa Baa, Black Sheep", could you?'

'Too easy, dear boy. Donne will challenge their curious minds.'

'They're not a bunch of randy sixth-formers, Walter; they're foreign language students yet to nail their ABC.'

'You underestimate them, Seb. They'll understand more than you think. The language of love defies linguistic boundaries.'

'Is there any Donne in the school library?'

'*The Complete Works and Selected Prose.* Donated it myself. Poetry section. Top shelf.'

'Any particular poem you'd recommend?'

Walter was something of an expert on Donne and often quoted him. He could encapsulate modern incident with ancient verse, which was usually lost on me after several pints in the Princess.

'Hmm, let me think,' said Walter, separating his fingers across his whiskers. 'Given our conversation in the Princess last week, I'd suggest perhaps his best and arguably most famous elegy.'

'Which is?'

He raised his eyebrows and grinned mischievously.

'"To His Mistress Going to Bed".'

I saw immediately where he was going.

'You know, I think we might be wrong about Eva.'

His sly grin became something more curious.

'What makes you say that?'

I surveyed our surrounds to ensure no one was in earshot.

'I spoke with her and she said the mark on her neck was from playing the violin.'

Walter laughed. Threw his head back.

'Is that what she said?'

'That's what she said. I asked her about it and that's what she said.'

He laughed again. Less of a reflex this time.

'That's a symphony in itself. Sounds as though she's playing you rather than the violin.'

'And she gave me a present.'

'A present?'

'A pair of slippers.'

'Why the chicken's cluck would she give you a pair of slippers?!'

'For my cold feet.'

151

When Walter squinted his moustache rose at the tips.

'Your cold feet?'

'A misinterpreted idiom.'

I turned to leave for the library. The bell rang.

'Sebastian,' called Walter, raising his voice over the bell, which sounded more suited to a fire station than a school.

'What?'

'I'd suggest you be careful. As Donne himself said, "Send not to know for whom the bell tolls. It tolls for thee."'

Walter raised his head when quoting poetry, lending the phrase thespian gravitas.

I stood at the door and raised my own head.

'Bastard you are, Walter. Bard you are not.'

■

I made twelve photocopies of Walter's suggested poem, reading it briefly as I did so. Though risqué in parts, it was actually quite appropriate for an English class thanks to a rhyming couplet towards the middle of the verse:

Licence my roving hands, and let them go
Behind, before, above, between, below.

If the assessors walked in I could easily justify it as a lesson on prepositions. *Behind, before, above* . . . such words in language textbooks refer to banks, cinemas, supermarkets . . . Boy, were my charges in for a surprise.

I raced back to class to find that Yoon Pong had retrieved his lute from the cupboard and was plucking it with aplomb in front of the class. I confiscated the instrument once again and sent its strummer to his seat.

'No problem,' he said. 'Prefer electric guitar. That too quiet for me.'

Donne's subtlety would no doubt be equally wasted on a young man who could squeeze an expletive into a sneeze.

'Take one and pass it along,' I said, peddling the bygone porn. When I saw Agnes, beginner in English but advanced religious fanatic, take her copy and squint at the title, I suddenly thought I had made an error of judgement. I hesitated, gazed at the fast-thinning pile of copies, last chance of censorship slipping away.

'What means "mistress"?' asked Fernanda.

I hadn't realised what a minefield of vocabulary lay waiting in the poem. It would be akin to explaining the birds and the bees to a child.

'Extra wife,' suggested Giuseppe, with clumsy precision.

Well, perhaps not to a child.

'Ah, well,' I hastened to clarify, 'shall we just say a "lover"?'

'How to spell?' asked Doughnut.

I wrote it on the interactive whiteboard.

'Pronunciation spelling,' demanded Jean-Paul.

I wrote /lúvvər/ on the board.

'Okay,' I instructed, 'I'd like you to get into groups of four. Read the poem first and then discuss what you think is happening. Then I'd like you to underline ten new words and we'll discuss them as a class.'

Never had they been so obedient. Sex can sell everything, even prepositions. I enjoyed the contortions of my students' faces as they silently studied the verse. I often reassured them that to understand the gist of a text it wasn't necessary to grasp every word. It was something teachers drilled into students so they wouldn't get discouraged and give up. I didn't need to worry about them giving up today. They tried desperately to understand. I think they were flattered Walter deemed them capable of comprehending the material. Whatever their motivation, they pored over the forty-eight-line rhyme as though it were the fine print of a crucial contract.

After their group discussions, the class admitted to understanding only the first three words – *Come, madam, come* – which was sufficient for them to agree that Donne was trying to convince a woman to sleep with him, although Giuseppe suggested she couldn't have been keen on the idea given the length of the poem.

'Not good if you must to beg,' he informed the class. 'Look desperate. Woman no like.'

Ulrica nodded but Ludmila's eyes expressed doubt.

'Is he begging?' I wondered aloud. 'Or is he seducing her with words?'

Silence as they digested the concept.

'Like chat-up line?' asked Ulrica.

'If you like.'

'Very long chat-up line,' said Natalina. 'Voman say yes so he shut up.'

Half the class laughed. The rest hadn't understood and Agnes had started to pray.

'At least he ask,' said Eva. 'Some man no ask, just take.'

The class was shocked, first that she had spoken, second by what she had said. She hadn't looked up from her handout to drop the bombshell; she merely stared at the poem on her desk. Perhaps Walter was right after all. Perhaps she was playing me rather than the violin. Or was I to interpret the remark as an official cry for help? If so, Sarah was right – it was my duty as a human being to help, to get her out of there, regardless of her protests and her attachment to Zeus.

'Did chat-up line work?' asked Ludmila.

My mind was elsewhere, out the window, pondering Eva's salvation.

'Did ze chat-up line work?' repeated Ludmila.

I returned to the room. 'Er, I assume so,' I replied, scanning the poem for proof.

'Not for me,' declared Ulrica, pointing at Donne's portrait on the interactive whiteboard. 'He too thin for good lover. No muskle.'

'And zis beard!' declared Natalina. 'Horrible!'

It seemed a good time to move on.

The prickly part of the lesson was explaining lascivious language such as *hairy diadems, unlace yourself, happy busks* and *heaven's zones glistening*. I explained the terms as best I could without devout Agnes organising a lightning strike, and did the funny spelling to only a smattering of sniggers. But in truth I was thankful for the knock at the door, until I remembered that Rhonda and the assessors were on the prowl. I ripped off my ruff and signalled for the class to do likewise.

My students stared at me, confused.

Another knock. More insistent this time.

I looked at the poem's last two lines.

'*To teach thee I am naked first*,' I begged, throwing my ruff in the bin. '*Why then: what needst thou have more covering than a man?*'

My students continued to stare.

'Take off your fucking costumes!'

Finally they did as instructed, apart from Giuseppe, whose codpiece – thankfully – was out of view under his desk.

'Okay,' I whispered, 'the first conditional. Page seventy-two of your textbooks.'

Rhonda and the assessors observed a lesson I could have taught in my sleep rather than one which almost caused me nightmares. Two hours later we filed out of the classroom and headed for the courtyard, where the barbecue was starting to sizzle. Like the captain of a plane I was the last to leave, switching off the lights and, as is customary, cleaning the whiteboard. I froze despite the heat. In the corner of the board were the words /lúvvər/, /pyōōbic hair/ and /párrədīss/. So that's why my boss had observed my lesson open-mouthed. And I had deemed it awe at the quality of my lesson.

I trudged downstairs towards the courtyard, wondering if the school would survive with only four stars.

■

For every cobblestone in the courtyard there was a different language spoken. Despite constant reminders from teachers that students should speak English rather than mother tongues, most couldn't help letting off the handbrake, so to speak, with new friends from old countries. I loved listening to the patchwork of languages: a linguistic washing machine. Walking towards the punchbowl to fill my plastic cup, I detected Spanish, French, German, Italian, Swedish, Japanese, Korean . . . Yet I couldn't help thinking that, by the time the bowl was dry, it would be Walter who'd be the most indecipherable.

Having graded every student, I was their familiar face at the school and popular beyond merit. Most teachers only knew the students in their class but I knew everyone: their pasts, their presents and their futures. It was crowded in the courtyard but I wandered as best I could and chatted here and there. The first student I bumped into – quite literally – was a young Spaniard by the name of Fernando. I had taught him as a beginner and he was the worst student I had ever suffered. The verb 'to be' was beyond him and he'd repeated the textbook twice. So I was amazed when he confidently apologised for our collision before saying, 'Hiya, Seb. Alright?'

'Fernando? Is that you?'

'The one and only, my man.'

'What the hell happened to your English?'

'Got myself a girlfriend, innit?'

Kiwa and Keiko were timid girls from Tokyo who I'd taught in a class a few months back. They were sweet, smiley and inseparable, so I was happy to stop and converse when they waved and nodded subserviently.

'How are you both?' I asked.

'Vely well,' they said, nodding.

'Enjoying the barbecue?'

'Vely good.' They nodded again.

The slightly awkward silence was punctuated by metronomic nods. I saw Rhonda guiding the assessors towards the punchbowl. It would be weeks before they delivered their verdict, but clouding their short-term memories couldn't hurt.

'Can I ask question?' said Kiwa.

I nodded lukewarm consent. Nodding is like yawning – remarkably contagious.

'Have you decide if to move to Amelica?'

'Er . . . sorry, Kiwa, I'm not sure what you mean.'

'In last lesson you say can't decide if to move to Amelica or stay in England.'

I scoured my mind. The afternoon sunshine was bright but that wasn't why I was squinting.

'Was that the lesson we did on dilemmas and decisions?'

'Yes.' Keiko nodded.

I smiled. 'That was a hypothetical example so I could use the target language of the lesson – *Should I? Shouldn't I?*'

'A hyper . . . ?'

'It wasn't true. I just needed to have a dilemma. I thought you realised I was making it up.'

'Ohhh,' exclaimed Kiwa, disappointed.

'So you not want kill mother-in-law?' figured Keiko.

I tipped my punch.

'Well, it wasn't *all* hypothetical.'

I left them to their nodding and headed for the safe insanity of Walter. He was smoking by the barbecue (frightfully close to the gas bottle) under the pretence of helping Robert – our resident chef – by handing him a utensil now and then. We sipped our punch. Walter tossed a cigarette butt behind the barbecue. If he ever got the sack as head of IT, he would be a shoo-in for health and safety officer.

'Did you fix the photocopier?' I asked him.

'Think I broke it, actually. You must show me how to do double-sided copying sometime. How did your lesson on Donne go? Were they suitably seduced?'

'I chickened out when the assessors came in. Things were getting dangerous. You were wrong about them understanding it, though. They only got the first three words.'

'Don't be so sure, dear boy. Like Donne the lover, his words seduce slowly.'

We watched my knot of students, huddled around a table partaking of Robert's wares. They had put their costumes back on and were laughing and joking together. Yoon Pong strummed his lute and Ulrica sang along, a speck of silver in her tongue flashing every time she sustained a note, although I hadn't noticed any perceptible difference in the quality of her pronunciation.

Eva sat quietly with her classmates, her long blue skirt tucked demurely under her legs, blonde hair like spaghetti in a tortoise-shell claw. She wore a simple blouse which neither revealed nor concealed. The opal had been replaced by a crucifix – the one from her student photo, I presumed. Her slender fingers plucked apart a bread roll. She speared the olives in her salad with a plastic fork. I had to talk to Rhonda about how best to approach her rescue, though I would need to be discreet.

Natalina sat on Giuseppe's lap, rested her elbow on his codpiece and tried on his Prada shades, which were big even by Primrose Hill standards. It was all too blasphemous for Agnes, who crossed herself three times and lashed out in her native tongue before disappearing into the canteen.

'My word,' quipped Walter, observing the outburst. 'I think she's having a Tudor period.'

I sniggered and wandered over to the group. 'Everything okay?' I inquired.

'Everysing fine,' replied Natalina, before Giuseppe tickled her and she exploded with laughter. I only had myself to blame for their friskiness: Donne's poetry isn't frigid and the first conditional has a charm of its own.

'What was Agnes upset about?' I asked Ludmila.

She looked Giuseppe's way and put her fingers to her temples in an attempt to recall language from our lesson.

'Roving hands,' she replied.

As usual, Walter was right; they had understood more than I thought.

12

Predicate

Ten to nine and business as usual, or unusual business as usual. Rhonda hovering in the staffroom to ensure it was aptly named, tea and textbooks, caffeine and chat. Apart from the fact it was Rhonda's last day (she always took a week off to de-stress after the school inspection, though this year she might need a fortnight), activity in the staff room was reassuringly routine, with photocopiers jammed and CD players on the blink. The grammar bullies were at it again, dunking Hobnobs into milk and two sugars while lamenting the whoring of their mother tongue. They gravitated into groups, often generational, having long ago identified who sympathised and who couldn't care less.

'It's *on* the weekend, not *at* the weekend,' complained Cynthia, marking a test aloud. 'I won't accept *at*, mainly because of the types of people you hear using it.'

And she wondered why she was a spinster.

'I won't accept *backpack*,' drawled Toby, a recent arrival from California. 'It's a *rucksack*!'

'Well, I've been teaching *backpack* for twenty years,' countered Peter from Dollis Hill. 'You don't go *rucksacking*, you go *backpacking*.'

Not in Nevada, you don't.

'Prefer *camping* myself,' joked Walter, putting his arm around me and making most of his colleagues laugh. 'Have you recovered from last night?' he inquired. 'You drank me out of Laphroaig.'

Despite my strengthening flu I had drowned my sorrows over the school inspection by going back to Walter's after a few in the Princess and drinking a few more to forget.

'Still a bit rough around the edges, actually. Don't suppose you fancy covering my class?'

'Twice in one week! Enjoyed their lesson on rhyming slang, did they?'

'Thought it was Robin Hood.'

Walter nodded applause.

'I'm sorry to say I can't. Rhonda's computer is playing up and she can't do the pay round till I fix it.'

'God help us!' I announced, startling my colleagues. 'Ladies and gentlemen, we are going to starve!'

The bell rang. Walter jumped to his feet, unusually keen to get started. He seemed livelier than usual, though I couldn't think why.

'See you in the Princess,' I said, settling back into my chair in denial of the day ahead.

'With half the school in tow?' he asked, indicating the noticeboard. 'Your turn for social calendar, dear boy. A pub crawl by the looks of it.'

My groan drowned out the bell.

Sure enough, I discovered by walking to the wall, I was rostered that evening to chaperone hordes of thirsty students on a tour of the capital's watering holes. Had I known I would have called in sick, closed my eyes and slumbered with Claude. Now I had no escape. My only hope was that those hordes, while my responsibility, didn't drink as much as Walter and I had the night before. It was the kind of hypocrisy, I supposed, that parenting is all about, though it was beginning to look as though social calendar duty was as close to fatherhood as I would come.

My students arrived with their customary casualness, as though punctuality was a foreign term I was yet to teach rather than a universal concept. I marked the attendance log as they trickled in like drips from a tap: Sibylla (first again), Doughnut, Natalina, Ulrica, Yoon Pong, Jean-Paul, Ludmila, Eva, Agnes, Fernanda, Kazuki, Giuseppe and Simge. Lee had left the previous Friday to fly home to Seoul, to the relief of his host family's dalmatian, who had reportedly developed a nervous condition during the South Korean's stay. (No, not the spots.)

Lee's replacement was Mercedes – a Spanish girl, not a German car – who Rhonda had mentioned at the last staff meeting in an appeal for sympathy and special consideration because the *senorita* suffered from narcolepsy. When a couple of colleagues expressed shock and disgust, the principal informed them they had confused the condition with something more sinister. 'She has pills to keep her awake,' Rhonda added, 'but they don't always work.'

'Next month you have a test,' I informed the class when it had finally arrived. 'I want you all to do well, so start revising from today.'

Ludmila raised her hand. I nodded her way.

'Ukrainia people say don't vash hair night before exam because vash out knowledge.'

The class eyed Giuseppe, who according to Ukrainian proverb was losing his knowledge, though it didn't seem to be harming his self-confidence any.

Prefixes and suffixes was our topic for the day and, as usual, I kicked things off with a game. Playing with a partner, students had to form as many compound words as possible by joining word dominoes. Most combinations were straightforward: *under-cooked, over-confident*; others more complex: *tact-less, post-modern*; some slippery to explain: *anti-abortion, ex-Communist*; several downright wrong: *relax-ment, shock-centered*; one had a euphemistic feel: *self-use*; while my favourite was the politically correct: *post-married*, which seemed softer than the stark proper term.

I was explaining to Yoon Pong that *Tate-Modern* didn't score him a point when Kazuki touched my arm and whispered in my ear: 'I solly but partner has to fallen asleep.' Mercedes crashed for the entire morning class and half that of the afternoon. I have since managed to convince Rhonda to give her a refund. As a teacher of ten years I thought I had seen and counselled every impediment to foreigners learning English. Narcolepsy, I have to say, trumps them all. Even if you talk in your sleep.

■

The best thing about *We Will Rock You* running for 'seven smash-hit years' at the Dominion Theatre was that it gave English language teachers on social calendar duty a London landmark that never changed. The other Queen changed her guard, Prince Charles changed his wife, Big Ben changed its time, Downing Street changed prime minister, but it seemed Freddie Mercury would never leave the building on Tottenham Court Road.

Six o'clock was the designated meeting time, when every car in the capital was a cab. It wasn't just my students who were invited. Anyone was welcome as long as they put their name on the sheet of paper outside the staffroom and paid the requisite pounds. Swiss students arrived first, followed by Spanish, Italian, Mexican, Brazilian . . . It seems punctuality and longitude are related, at least until you reach the equator.

I watched the evening news in the electronics shop adjoining the theatre, until the number of revellers outside on the street resembled the number of names on my sheet. Then I emerged, performed a quick head count and politely reminded those gathered that if they weren't eighteen it was best they were tucked up in bed, which was where I longed to be. My flu had taken a turn for the worse. I suppose it was fitting that I was on duty that evening, given a crawl was all I was capable of.

I wasn't pleased to see Eva emerging from the tube since I was yet to devise a plan to solve her problem. Step by step she bobbed to London's surface, blonde hair defying the drizzle. Cars and buses hissed along the streets, leaving gossamer mists in their wakes. Pesky and persistent, it was rain that soaks you slowly because it doesn't deserve an umbrella. As an Englishman I was waterproof but my students only bowed their heads and put up with it because they deemed it part of the cultural experience for which they'd signed up. I hoped the heavens would open fully so we could have more pub and less crawl.

Soho beckoned like the orange lantern on a black cab. I knew my way around the labyrinth from my days at the school on Oxford Circus. The Three Greyhounds was the first dry knot in our wet rope. A bygone boozer, the pub's exposed Elizabethan beams prompted the Asian students in our party to fire up their cameras and snap a thousand shots, or ask their teacher to snap a thousand shots. Do Japanese cameras work if the people in the photo aren't holding up two fingers like a bunny rabbit's ears? I would ask Kazuki over a pint, if we ever got inside.

Rhonda insisted such outings be educational, so despite the drizzle I kept them waiting on the doorstep while I rattled off the pub's history. The rule when speaking to students of varied levels is to pitch to the middle ground. Unlike most things in my life, however, I aim high.

'This area of Soho, would you believe, used to be parkland,

and this pub is named after the dogs that were used to hunt hares here!' Two tourists and a gay couple stopped to listen. The Asian students took photos of both. 'Greek Street, on which you are standing,' I continued, 'is so named after a Greek church that stood here in the 1600s.' The students looked confused. 'A long time ago!' I clarified. 'There has been a pub here since the middle of the nineteenth century and Casanova reportedly stayed in this street on a visit to London.' The rain grew heavier so I decided to wrap it up. 'If you haven't understood something, I suggest you steal a coaster!' I held the door open. 'Ladies and gentlemen – cheers!'

What I didn't mention in my spiel was that the Three Greyhounds is also aptly named because that's about all you can squeeze into the poky pub. At six-thirty on a Thursday it was already packed with drinkers; by the time twenty-five of our party had burrowed in, the place was bursting at its beer-stained seams. We were shoulder to shoulder, or in my case boobs to beer given that Ludmila had snuggled up close. To sip the ruby-red pint of Hobgoblin she'd bought me I almost had to dislocate my elbow. Loud music made her lean even closer to talk. Her breath was pure nicotine.

'Good lesson last week,' said the Ukrainian.

'You mean when we did Donne?'

'Vot?'

'Or when we Donne did?'

She was rightly confused.

'I sink you drink.'

'Very good – you're something of a poet yourself, Ludmila.'

I was wrong to amuse myself at her expense but the Hobgoblin was living up to its guest bitter blurb: *What's the matter, Lagerboy, afraid you might taste something?* After four days of heavy drinking it was something of a hair of the dog, an idiom I decided not to share with Ludmila in case she wrongly attributed it to one of the greyhounds. Sleep-deprivation mixed with alcohol and cold and flu medicine. I felt unusually self-assured and blasé.

'Lots of single men sitting at the bar, Ludmila. Why don't you go and find Johnny Depp?'

'I no need Johnny Depp,' she replied. 'I haf fall in love viz English gentleman of dreams. Look.'

She fished a digital camera from her brand new Louis Vuitton handbag and treated me to a dozen or so sexy shots of her draped across the bonnet of a beaten-up Rover. She was fully clothed in all of them, though racier than the car.

'They're lovely, Ludmila. Very classy. But where is the English gentleman?'

'He take photo.'

'Did you suggest climbing on the bonnet or did he?'

'He suggest,' she replied, lacking a past tense, though now equipped with a future.

'I wish you every happiness,' I said mechanically.

She put the camera back in her bag and took a sip of her drink – spirits of some sort with Coke.

'You no jealous?'

'No, I've never liked Rovers – too difficult to find spare parts.' I dislocated my elbow and downed my pint. 'Drink up, folks!' I yelled, pushing my way towards the exit. 'The ale trail continues!'

We were outside in seconds. They were more obedient than Claude. Each pub we visited was a mixture of history and histrionics. At the Marquis of Granby, named after the military leader of the Seven Years' War, Agnes started another conflict without even being there by phoning Natalina to tell her she would go to hell for her public display of affection with Giuseppe. Natalina burst into tears and went home. Giuseppe didn't seem too concerned by her departure and set about finding another companion.

More tears were spilt at the Argyll Arms, again thanks to untimely phone calls. The etched partitions that once divided drinkers into 'snug' social castes weren't enough to stop news spreading of a Swiss student's cat with a tumour in its mouth that would need to be put down. The girl was devastated, sobbing, '*Einschläfern! Einschläfern!*' Walter was right about pointless inventions; without her phone the girl might have enjoyed her evening.

Ulrica cornered me in the Clachan to seek my opinion once again on adding shrapnel to her body. This time it was her belly button that she wanted to pierce.

'Aren't you worried you might rust?' I protested. She didn't understand but my tone was sufficient to convey disapproval.

At the Pontefract Castle I reminded the students that their classroom wasn't the only place to learn English and they should keep their ears peeled if they wanted to speak like a local. During the following few minutes I fielded the following few questions: What means *bovvered*? What means *innit*? What means *we was finkin' of grabbin' a curry*? I reluctantly vowed to drop that activity from future school excursions.

Our last stop was the Crown, on Brewer Street of all places. Generally speaking, unlike the English, foreign students don't drink until their stomachs rebel and decide to dabble in abstract art. I can't think why, but Continental types find vomit on the morning pavement less decorative than we Brits. It was only eight o'clock but most of my followers had already wandered off either to restaurants, nightclubs or each other's bedrooms. Fortunately I only had to count their heads at the beginning of the evening; they weren't children and were free to get hit by the bus of their choice.

A man of medicine couldn't have prescribed anything that would have picked me up as well as four pints of bitter. Students love shouting teachers drinks. Perhaps they think we will remember them fondly when marking their next test, though, more likely, their folks are footing their bill. My stomach was a long way from discovering its inner artist, but I had fluffed my spiel on the Crown by suggesting it was Beethoven rather than Mozart who had given a recital there when it was a concert hall. Not that my audience was capable of contradiction, or so I thought.

All the students from my class had left, other than Eva. Ulrica had stayed at the Clachan after bumping into some friends from another language school; Giuseppe had stayed at the Argyll Arms in the hope of convincing an English lass to come home and spread her Argyll legs; Kazuki and Doughnut had tickets to *Mamma Mia*, and Ludmila had disappeared, perhaps to do a night shoot on the bonnet of a Rover P6.

Eva, who had been sitting at a table of Japanese students, wandered over to join me at the bar. Crucifix at her neck and lightly made-up, she wore an elegant white blouse with a pullover tied around her waist and designer jeans that led to black leather shoes. I smiled at the vibrant young woman of her student photo rather than the recoiling girl who'd hidden in my class for the past month.

'Hello,' she said.

'Do I know you?' I replied.

She looked over her shoulder, wondering if I was talking to someone else.

'I Eva.'

'No, no – I mean your clothes are different.' She was still confused. 'I didn't *recognise* you,' I said didactically. 'We studied this word . . .'

'Please,' said Eva with raised hands. 'School close. Pub open.'

'Quite right,' I said, remembering my manners and tipping an imaginary glass. 'Drink?'

She reached for her bag, the same bag she brought to school. 'I buy.'

'No, let me. I haven't bought a drink all night. What would you like?'

'Vodka,' she replied in that deep dramatic way only Eastern Europeans can, lending the drink a dark persona.

'With anything?' I asked, thrusting hands in pockets on the hunt for penny and pound.

'Red Bull.'

She made London Pride look like tap water.

'Think I'll join you – my stomach's bored with beer.'

The barman looked at Eva while leaning towards me to take my order, which I screamed over some musical haemorrhage.

'Ah,' exclaimed Eva, 'now understand vy is "shout".'

'No . . .' I began, before realising I didn't have a better explanation.

We watched the barman make a show of things but a lemon is a lemon is a lemon . . .

'Your story for all pub interesting,' said Eva, 'but you do mistake about here – is Mozart not Beethoven which come.'

'How did you know that?'

'Mozart favourite composer. Know everysing him. Farzer take me Vienna ven I young.'

'Mine took me to the Coventry Toy Museum.'

'Vot means?'

'It means I'm jealous.'

Eva sat bolt upright. *'Jealous?!'*

'It means I wish—'

'I know vot means,' she interrupted, 'but *jealous* to my life no possible.'

The love bite on her neck may have faded but other memories were clearly more than skin deep. I would need to be tactful when convincing her to leave Zeus. From what Glen had said, she would be attached to the boy as though he were her own.

Our drinks arrived. I removed my straw. 'Cheers,' I said, passing Eva hers and holding up my own.

'*Na zdraví*,' she said, clinking her glass against mine.

We sipped. I grimaced. I wasn't used to adolescent alchemy and must have looked alarmed because Eva began to laugh.

'You are well?' she inquired politely.

'Fine,' I replied, coughing slightly.

'Is no good?'

'No, it's fine. It's fine. It's just, well . . . potent.'

'Potent?'

'Strong.'

Different adjective. Same hangover.

The remaining Japanese students stood and nodded my way. I waved back. Social calendar duty was over.

'Shouldn't you go back to Zeus?' I asked, finding an excuse to bring up the subject.

'Is free night. Muzzer home. First free night six week.'

'That doesn't sound fair.'

'*Fair?*'

'Right.'

'Hah – I au pair. Ulrica right say "servant".'

My second sip went down easier than my first. 'What's she like?'

'Ulrica?'

'Zeus's mother.'

'Oh, Angelique.'

I nodded. The music was making an already clumsy conversation more cumbersome.

'She like clothes, restaurant . . .'

'No, I mean what kind of person is she?'

Eva's teeth were whiter for the embarrassment in her cheeks. She pursed her lips. Looked beyond me. 'She busy.'

'Is she nice?'

She shrugged her shoulders. Pulled an indifferent face. 'Yes, she nice, but sometime too busy for nice.'

I sighed at the curious concept – too busy to be nice.

'Is she a good mother?'

Eva thought for a moment. Rested her elbow on the bar and her chin on her closed fist. 'Vot is goot muzzer?'

I wasn't expecting the question and looked beyond her for the answer. 'I don't know. I wish I knew. It sounds old-fashioned, but for some reason I've always thought that being a mother involved staying home and seeing the children at least through their early years. Otherwise . . . well . . .'

Eva saw me struggling and stepped in to assist.

'And ven Zeus no need Angelique more, vot Angelique do? Job go. Money go.' Her face fell. 'Perhaps farzer go.'

'Yes, but that takes instinct out of the equation.'

Eva shook her head.

I tried to rephrase a complex opinion with rudimentary words. Vodka and grading your language do not mix. 'If you think of human beings as animals,' I continued, 'it is natural for the mother to care for the children, while the father . . .'

Eva laughed – dimples in her cheeks. 'But no live forest. Live London.'

'So the problem is the society we have created in which people bring up children. A society where money is more valuable than love.'

Eva frowned. Stirred her drink with her straw. 'I no understand.'

I sipped my own. 'It doesn't matter.'

But she was deep in thought.

'Angelique modern muzzer. Much difficult. Big problem her. If to no verk for Zeus, she can later haf problem ven Zeus old and no need her.'

Deep down I knew I was prehistoric. Deeper down I knew my stance on raising children was grossly patriarchal. And even deeper down I knew I was being too hard on Sarah, and perhaps on Margaret, who were simply doing their best in a world that

171

made contradictory demands on them. Eva's spelling it out in simple terms helped me realise how simplistic I was being. There was still some bitterness left over from my childhood, however, and no doubt always would be.

'Yes, but why have Zeus in the first place if you'd rather work?'

'Rather?'

'Prefer.'

She regarded me as if through fog. 'No *prefer* work. Who *prefer* work? But, no live forest. Live London. Must to verk. Obligation.'

I studied her face. For the first time I noticed a tiny scar on her right temple, a pink apostrophe between eyebrow and ear. She took a long sip through her straw this time, which made her look like a child.

'What about the father, Eva?'

She closed her eyes for a moment. Clenched her jaw. Reached for her handbag.

'He important for different sing.'

'What kinds of things is a father important for?'

Again she closed her eyes momentarily, before turning her head, opening them and looking deep into mine.

'Farzer for love, Sebastian.'

It was the first time she had called me anything other than Teacher, perhaps because she had herself assumed the role.

'Just love?'

She smiled sorrowfully.

'Just love.'

I took a rapid sip, holding it in my mouth like a tablet before swallowing it. I was starting to acquire the taste, starting to enjoy the sweet slap of pleasure as the drink did its damage. Beer tends to loosen my tongue but otherwise leaves me unscathed. Spirits grab me by the ear and drag me out the back for a caning.

'What about Tim?' I continued. 'Is he a good father?'

She seemed irritated. Took a Marlboro Light from her bag and persecuted a piece of fluff in the filter – she couldn't smoke it so she decided to torture it.

'He busy too. Both busy.'

'I suppose that's good and bad.'

'Vot?'

'Well, if Tim and Angelique weren't busy and stayed home with Zeus then you'd be out of a job.'

'Vot means?'

'You would not have a job.'

Eva flicked her hand as though shooing a fly. 'Oh, I find anuzzer.'

She contemplated her tumbler before emptying it, then sucked on the first of three ice cubes.

'Speaking of finding other jobs,' I continued, 'have you thought about what we discussed the other day?'

Eva's brow knitted. She clearly didn't remember, or didn't want to remember.

'About finding you a job with a different family,' I persisted.

She ignored the question, eyed the crowd and moved her head and shoulders gently to the music – 'stool dancing' it would be called if it had a name.

'I vont go out!' she declared.

I surveyed the bar. Shrugged my shoulders. 'We *are* out.'

She smiled – first pityingly, then playfully. 'You vont gamble?'

I looked at my drink. 'I thought I was.'

'How much money you haf?'

The question should have alarmed me. 'Not much – I was supposed to get paid today but . . . well . . . not much.'

'Come casino wiz me.'

'A casino?!' I held up my hands. 'Not really my scene, I'm afraid.'

Eva's grin was cheeky. 'I sink you fright . . . er . . .'

She searched for the word. I helped her look.

'Frightened?'

'I sink yes.'

Was I frightened? Normally at eight-fifteen I would be slouched on the sofa on a slow hunt for 6 across, correcting some BBC presenter's grammar while tickling Claude with my toes and hoping to hear Sarah unlatch the front door. Eva was jamming a stick in the tedious turning of my spokes. Maybe I wasn't destined for a TV dinner tonight. Maybe *Question Time* would have one viewer less. I might even forget to put my painstakingly separated rubbish out. Was I frightened? Yes. Not of Eva, not of casinos and crazy cocktails, but of the fact I couldn't remember the last time I'd been frightened. *What's the matter, Lagerboy, afraid you might taste something?*

'I'll come to the casino if you promise me one thing.'

'*Promise?*'

'If you agree to do one thing.'

She rolled her eyes. Tapped the cigarette she was itching to light. 'Vot?' she said impatiently.

'If and when we lose, you agree to let me help you change your host family.'

Eva thought for a moment. 'And if vin?'

I downed my drink. 'I've never won anything in my life.'

13

Countable nouns

'Sorry, sir,' said the man on the door, raising his hand to stop me, 'you need a tie to get in here.'

The night was breezy but the plastic palm tree at his back didn't budge, and neither did he.

'What if I do my top button up?' I improvised.

'I'm afraid the casino makes the rules, sir, not me.'

'Couldn't you make an exception?'

'I'm afraid the casino makes the rules, sir, not me.'

His vocabulary appeared more limited than Eva's.

'Fine,' I said, giving up. 'It's probably your loss.'

I turned and stepped into the street. Eva followed, confused, having not understood a word of my altercation with the talking bicep. The rain had stopped and despite nearby neon from Piccadilly Circus I could see a few stars in the sky, though that may have been the Red Bull browsing the china shop in my head.

'Is problem?' inquired Eva.

'I don't have a tie and you need one to get in.'

'Vot is *tie*?'

I imitated the tying of an imaginary knot at my throat and then ran my hand down my torso. I charged more for private lessons but decided to waive the fee in this case. We resumed walking before Eva stopped abruptly and rummaged through her bag. I expected her to produce the cigarette she was eager to smoke earlier. Instead she produced the ruff Kazuki had made her for the John Donne lesson.

'What are you doing with that?'

'Is tie.'

'What?'

'Is tie for Donne. Is tie for you.'

I laughed – head back, hands in pockets. 'Don't be ridiculous.'

'Is no ridicolos. Is tie!'

'Eva, that's the Elizabethan equivalent of a tie, but times and fashion have moved on. If you examine the dress code of the Palm Palace Casino I'm confident you won't find a ruff.'

But it was already around my neck, bestowed upon me as though I'd won a medal at the 1596 Olympic Games.

Eva stepped back and sized me up. '*Bezvadný*,' she exclaimed, adjusting my collar.

'I'm not going in there dressed like this.'

'Vy?'

'Because I look silly.'

Eva removed the ruff. Took a step back. Sized me up once again. The holes at the elbows of my faithful blue pullover were wider than a week ago, my checked shirt was half untucked and the corrugations on my corduroy trousers were flattened in certain sections.

'Hmm,' mocked Eva, 'much better.'

For some reason I didn't mind. We English make fun of the people we care about. It's strangers who scare us polite. I wondered if Eva used to rib her father in the same way. I was always jealous of Walter when he spoke of the affectionate mocking of his late father. Apparently he pulled his trousers up to the shadows of his armpits and Walter called him Captain Mainwaring. I would have loved such banter with my father – with either of my fathers. Oh, the irony, the savage and twisted irony: two fucking fathers and neither of them deserving the title.

'Okay, Eva,' I said, 'you win.'

We returned to the door of the casino. The bouncer flexed his muscles once again. Indeed his arms were so overinflated that he couldn't put them by his side. He looked like a human corkscrew.

'I'm sorry, sir. I thought I said you needed a tie?'

I lifted my head to model my frill.

'I have a tie.'

'That's not a tie.'

'I can assure you this is a necktie; primitive, but a necktie nonetheless.'

'Looks like someone hit you over the head with a concertina.' He laughed at his own joke.

'You are mistaken. In Elizabethan times this was a tie. Now are you going to let me in or are you being ageist?'

His bald brow creased. 'Whatist?'

'*Ageist*. It's a form of discrimination. Wouldn't look good on the cover letter for your next job.'

As I said – self-assured and blasé. It didn't happen often.

The doorman smiled at Eva as though apologising for the impasse. 'Can I see the . . . *tie*, please, sir?' I removed the ruff and handed it to him. He held it up to the light. 'What's this?' he said, examining it closely. '*Subject + have/has + verb in the past participle*?'

'That's the brand – The Present Perfect. Similar to Armani only more exclusive.'

He returned Kazuki's handiwork and took a reluctant step back. 'Good luck, sir, madam.'

We were high rollers after all.

I had never been to a casino and was unnerved by the artificial atmosphere. Brass fittings, fake flora, patterned carpets, chandeliers . . . At least in the Three Greyhounds there was history on the walls and personality in the wooden furnishings. At Palm Palace the only wood belonged to a Turkish man drooling over one of the waitresses. His forearms were forested with black hair and gold bracelets. Her skirt would have been dwarfed by a teabag. They saw my ruff and smirked. I must have appeared as alien as I felt.

How many mortgages had gone into the tacky décor? How many children's trust funds had paid for the flashing lights? I wanted to leave but Eva had me by the elbow. I had never seen her so confident. She ordered two drinks with umbrellas in them. They turned our tongues blue. We faced each other at the bar, her legs twisted like tentacles through her stool.

'So,' she said, brushing her fringe from her eyes, 'vot game to play?'

I raised my hands as though under arrest.

'You choose. I haven't a clue how to play any of them.'

'Twenty-one?'

'Yes, I'm old enough, I just don't know the rules.'

Eva laughed. 'You are stupid man. Come.'

She stood and walked towards several felt tables that were sliced in half like the lime in our cocktails. I abandoned my sickly-sweet drink and followed.

'Twenty-one,' she repeated. 'Blackjack. Now to give me every money you haf.'

Being robbed is less traumatic when you're starting to like your assailant.

'There's sixty,' I said, handing it over. 'The rest is shrapnel.'

'Good,' she said, rummaging through her bottomless bag. 'And I to put fifty – all I haf.'

As we took our places at the table alongside a hunched man with a moustache, I remembered less than fondly our game of Find the Liar, when Eva had been flippant about losing a car. 'Is okay,' she had said. 'I prefer valk.' I was convinced I wouldn't see my sixty again.

Eva swapped our hard-earned for tokens; it was a silent exchange and felt like the death of something. After expressing polite confusion at my unconventional tie, the man with the moustache stared my playing partner up and down. I felt like clubbing him. Being father to a beautiful daughter would be a daunting task.

Our stack of tokens looked less than imposing: as far as skyscrapers went it wouldn't have cut the mustard in Manhattan. I shifted my stool back from the table a little to show Eva that she was captain of our team. Slot machines cackled in the corner, musak spewed from the speakers, low lamps begged for contemplative smoke that was banned except in Hollywood.

'Bets please,' said a bow tie.

My watch, while I still had one, told me it was seven minutes past nine.

Eva placed a white token in a red circle and a blue one near a yellow square. The man with the moustache staked a pink token and put a black one near his yellow square. It appeared a rather colourful pastime – except when you were in the red, I supposed. Our card slid silently on the felt. Eight of hearts. The dealer flipped the seven. Eva tapped the table as though picking up a crumb. The nine of clubs arrived. She waved her hand across her cards as though casting a spell on them. The dealer turned a three and an eight. Our tokens vanished so quickly I hadn't time to see how much we'd lost.

Another player arrived at our table, which I supposed would at least slow the game down and buy us our money's worth. The man looked Indian and was plump like the wad of notes he placed emphatically on the felt. The only safe bet in the house was that his money could have been better spent elsewhere, though he could have said the same about ours. While the dealer counted his donation, making a bit of a show of things, I leant towards Eva to talk tactics. Here was my chance to discover how she had found herself in such a mess, and perhaps how to get her out of it.

'Every time we lose,' I said softly, 'you must tell me something about your life. That way at least my money buys me something.'

Eva sat back abruptly and looked at me as though I'd whispered something obscene. 'You sink to lose?'

'I think you'll find it's the rule.'

She grinned knowingly. 'Okay, I am agree. But if vin you say me about you life. Deal?'

We were buying each other's biographies.

'Deal.'

Deal. Our card arrived. Another eight. (I thought there were only four in a pack?) Then a three and a seven. He turned the seven of spades. We won our token back.

'I grew up in Rugby,' I said, keeping my side of the bargain.

We won another token, red this time.

'My mother and father were obsessed with work so I was raised by a woman called Elaine who stole money and kicked the dog.'

We lost the red one.

'I born in suburb Břevnov in Prague.'

And another white one.

'Parents better if no marry. Muzzer chiltren and farzer...' She turned a token skilfully through her fingers. 'Farzer music... music...?'

She looked at me hopefully.

'*Musician?*'

'Yes.'

We won two pink ones. Eva's unpainted fingernails looked plain among the spectrum of colour.

'I moved to London when I was twenty-seven and got a job in a real estate agency.'

We won again. Our stack looked stronger.

'I met my wife at the agency.'

Two blue ones gone.

'Parents to fight for money.'

Two blue ones back.

'Mine too, but only because they had too much of the stuff.'

Two blue ones gone.

'I vont study architek in Prague, but . . .'

I must have been the only player in the casino hoping the dealer won.

'I haf bruzzer, but . . .'

'But?'

She scratched her cheek. 'No more.'

'How?'

A black token vanished. Our stack was fragile again.

'He die himself.'

'Jesus.'

She was silent.

'Eva, I'm so sorry.'

I forgot the cards but Eva kept playing. We won three pink tokens. Our agreement seemed silly all of a sudden.

'I left the agency and became a teacher.'

We lost four white ones. Our heaviest blow yet.

'Farzer crazy for bruzzer dead.' She looked at me for a split second. Her face had lost its youth. 'Horrible, horrible, horrible.' She sighed. Closed her eyes. Shook her head.

I wanted to hug her. To offer sympathy in some way.

We won the tokens back.

'I'm afraid that's my life story, Eva.' I looked at our stack. 'Worth about eighteen pounds fifty.'

We lost them again.

'Is better my story finish too.'

Our game had gone far enough.

I pushed our entire stack into the circle, my hands leaving a trail on the felt. Having regained her composure, Eva smiled gently and crossed her fingers. The other players at our table decided to sit out the round. Our first card was the queen of hearts, our second the ace of clubs. The man with the moustache sat up straight. The Indian man wobbled as he clapped. Had they played the round our cards would have been different, but that thought was as close as I came to thanking them. I clapped but Eva didn't celebrate. Perhaps it was the memory of her brother.

We cashed in our chips, tipped the dealer (on Eva's instruction) and went to the bar to order drinks. She chose some kitsch concoction but the best I could do to join her was plonk an umbrella in my pint. I had been drinking for four days and was drowning in alcohol and adrenaline.

'How much have we got?'

'Perhaps fife hundret.'

'You keep it – I'm sure Walter will fix the computer someday.'

'Keep? No keep. Blackjack only start. Now to play roulette.'

I smiled and sipped. Eva clearly wasn't familiar with the term 'quit while you're ahead', neither in my language nor hers.

'Okay, but remember our bet – when you lose, I win.'

Eva rolled her eyes again and stood, eager to return to the tables. 'Ready?'

I took off my ruff and put it on the bar, hoping they might kick me out. 'Mind if I stay here? If I watched that spinning wheel I'd fall over.'

'I can to bet everysing?'

'Just leave yourself enough to get home.'

Eva turned to go before remembering something and stopping. 'Vot number is lucky you?'

I thought for a second. 'Two.'

'Vy?'

'I'll tell you later.'

'Bye,' she said, waving.

It felt unusual, as though she didn't intend to return. Her eyes seemed moist again, though this time not with tears.

While she was gone I perused the menu, which reinforced the fact I was out of place. Why do chefs overcook the adjectives in fancy restaurants? *Box-baked camembert.* Wouldn't an oven be simpler? *Maple shallots.* Surely a snack for squirrels. *Red onion tarte tatin.* Sounded like Ludmila in a kilt. I had no idea what tzatziki or Belgian endive were, but figured prawn wanton to either be a typo or a reckless amount of shellfish.

Categories were as cryptic as individual dishes. I hoped 'Sharing Plates' didn't mean their dishwasher was on the blink, and surmised that 'Leaves' was trendy for salad. Most diners only need the menu explained to them in foreign restaurants. These days I need it done in SW1. Nouvelle cuisine and I are like chalk and boxed-baked cheese. I just hoped Eva wasn't hungry, as explaining the menu to her would have been the blind leading the blind.

I was wondering if 'rarebit' was a threatened species of rabbit (I should ditch crosswords and take to solving modern menus) when the bartender asked if I wanted another pint. Half an hour later she asked again, and half an hour later once more. I was on my third and seventh for the evening when a vague voice reached me. I thought I was hearing things until its first grammatical lapse.

'Now Sebastian life worth more eighteen pound fifty.'

'What's that?' I replied, pulling myself out of my pint and spinning round on my stool, almost to my peril.

Eva sat beside me and ordered a bottle of French champagne, which she pronounced better than I would have, and not because I was drunk.

'Must to celebrate,' she said. 'Obligation.'

'How much did you win?'

She moved her mouth to my ear.

The volume of my laughter surprised me, and those near me.

'I see you've finally learnt how to play Find the Lie.'

She leant towards me and opened her bag. Bundles of cash like a Hollywood briefcase.

'Fucking Aida! How did you do it?'

'You do it. Number two.'

I lowered my voice and looked over my shoulder as though the winnings were ill-gotten gains.

'Congratulations. I'm dead impressed. What are you going to spend it on?'

'Is no mine. Is yours.'

I held up my hands. 'Nonsense. I don't want it.'

'But is yours.'

'No, Eva, it's yours. It takes me six months to make ten thousand pounds and that's the way it's supposed to be. You keep it. You won it.'

'I no haf place to put. No even haf account.'

'What do you do with your pay?'

She scratched her neck. Appeared reluctant. 'Tim give money ven I need.'

His shadow was never far away.

'So put it under your mattress.'

'I can't take money home. Boss come to my room. No vont they know I haf money. Come casino bad for person who care baby.'

She was sweet and selfless. Utterly sweet and selfless. The Tim man had no heart.

'Well I can't take it home either. Sarah wouldn't understand me gambling, and she certainly wouldn't believe I'd won. I'm not the kind of person who wins.'

Our champagne arrived. The bartender poured two flutes and put the bottle back in the fridge. Had she known we'd just won ten thousand pounds she would no doubt have placed it in a cooler.

'Cheers,' said Eva, raising her glass.

'*Na zdravi*,' I toasted, raising mine.

'*Na zdraví*,' she corrected.

'You're a good teacher.'

'You goot student.'

We smiled and tipped our glasses.

'You are hungry?' she inquired. 'I get menu?'

I sprayed my champagne across the bar. The waitress jumped back fast.

'I'm terribly sorry,' I said, blotting up the bubbly with my ruff.

Eva giggled hysterically, though her mood darkened when she opened the same menu I had been deciphering earlier. She read in silence for a few minutes, head in hand, shoulders slumped. Suddenly she was the old Eva – shy, sullen, distant. I had also found the menu unappetising, though this seemed an extreme reaction.

'What is it, Eva?'

She chewed her fingernail. I pulled her hand from her mouth.

'What is it, Eva?'

She snapped the folder shut and tossed it back on the bar.

'My English shit. Horrible, horrible shit.'

I laughed when she expected it least. Eva pushed me away, almost off my stool. 'No funny. Vy to laugh?' she said, so offended she'd forgotten her gloom.

'I'm laughing because I don't understand the menu either.' She couldn't have looked more confused. 'Don't worry, it's not in English. Well, it's in English but it's full of culinary . . . er . . . cooking words that I've never heard before.' Eva still looked uncertain. 'Did you bring your English–Czech dictionary?' She nodded at her bag. 'So get it out and look up "pretentious".'

She reached for the bag.

'Repeat,' she instructed, having found the bonsai book.

'*Pretentious.* P-R-E-T-E-N-T-I-O-U-S.'

She scanned the columns. Placed her finger on the target.

'*Nóbl,*' she announced. 'So?'

'So "*nóbl*" people use words you don't need.'

Eva smiled shyly, reluctant to look at me. I had never met anyone who went from bold to bashful with such speed and frequency. She reached for the menu and opened it cautiously, like patting a dog that had once bitten her.

'Vot means "leaves"?' she asked.

'As a noun, probably salad. As a verb, what I'd like to do now.'

Eva thought for a moment before smiling and closing her dictionary. 'But still haf problem for money.'

I pushed away my half-finished flute. 'Grab your bag, Eva. I think I know where we can put the money.'

14

Intensifiers

'Vot means "allotment"?' asked Eva as our cab raced past Regent's Park.

Her bag was on the seat between us, strapped into its own seatbelt.

'An allotment is a small piece of land used for growing fruit and vegetables.' I ensured the driver's listening latch was shut. 'And for burying casino winnings.'

The lights of a passing car illuminated Eva's bemused face.

'And you haf?'

'I have.'

'Where?'

'Near Hampstead Heath.'

Eva looked out the window at Camden Town: at graffitied shop awnings, at a crimson mohawk, at a skirmish at a bus stop, at a jogger, at a woman walking her dog . . . at the 'boiling mug' that is the London I love and hate. Several silent minutes later the driver shouted over his shoulder.

'Here we are, boss!'

Eva seemed surprised by residential surroundings.

'Vy to stop here?'

'I need to get a spade.'

'A *vot*?'

'*Spade*. Look it up in your dictionary while I'm gone.'

Eva plunged her arm into her bag.

'Won't be a moment!' I yelled to the driver.

When I returned a few minutes later, followed by a labrador madly wagging its tail, both driver and passenger were wide-eyed.

'Is dog!' exclaimed Eva.

'Dog *and* spade,' I clarified. 'You should see him dig.'

We climbed aboard. Claude sniffed Eva's cautious hand before allowing it to rest on his head.

'I can't take the dog!' said the driver.

'Why not?'

'Against the rules.'

'Can't you make an exception?'

'Sorry, boss.'

The London I love and hate.

'Look, I've consumed almost ten pints of beer. He's practically my guide dog. Now are you going to let him ride or do you wish to discriminate against the physically impaired?'

He thought for a moment. The old engine chugged. 'Where to?' he said finally.

'Fitzroy Park allotments.'

He put his foot to the floor and followed the street map in his head.

Eva moved the loot and Claude jumped up on the seat between us. She scratched his ear. He fell her way, tongue lolling, eyes glazing over. A learned hand behind the lobe is the canine equivalent of class A drugs.

As Chalk Farm became Gospel Oak a wretched smell filled the cabin. We opened our windows slightly. Claude appeared to be grinning.

'I'm sorry,' I said. 'He's been inside all day.'

Eva pinched her nose as we stopped at traffic lights.

'Dog haf name?' she asked in an altered voice.

'Claude.'

The stench had softened. She removed her fingers.

'He is name Claude?'

'Claude Pink.'

'Is name for person, no?'

I made a mental note that we needed a lesson on question tags.

'He is like a person to me.'

'Much hair person.'

Her 'h' was rough, like summoned spit.

'Are you angry that I brought much hair person?'

Every so often a mistake was too memorable to correct.

'No – I luff dog. In Czech Republic ven young haf dog.'

'What kind of dog did you have?'

'Oh,' she said, flustered. 'How to say – bits of everysing?'

'Very good – "bit of everything". A *mongrel*,' I said deliberately. Teaching was all I knew.

The Heath was on our left, the lungs of London, canopies of giant oaks silhouetted against the sky.

'This is perfect!' I yelled to the driver.

His eyes in the rear-view mirror before he pulled over obediently, brakes screeching as we slowed to a stop. I opened the door and Claude bolted as though we had fouled the air rather than he. Eva followed more sedately. I leant in the passenger-side window.

'That's forty-four pounds sixty, please, guv.'

Normally I would have baulked, perhaps accused him of taking the scenic route. Instead I looked at Eva, who reached into her bag and handed me a fifty-pound note. I'd never realised they were the colour of blood.

'Keep the change.'

'Very good of you, guv. Mind how you go.'

He switched on the cab's lantern and turned back towards the city. On his boot an advertisement for the airline Sarah had flown with to Dubai. I wondered how the prawn-shaped hotel was coming along.

Eleven o'clock and the midsummer sky was reluctantly dark. The rain was a memory, the breeze had dropped and the shirt-sleeve evening was warm and still. England is a paradise on earth when those minor miracles merge. Walter likens his homeland to a surly sovereign who manages a smile once or twice a year. King Tightarse, he calls him.

'Beautiful night. Perhaps to here first,' said Eva, pointing in the direction of Parliament Hill. I looked over at Claude, backed against the trunk of an oak, snubbing the nearby sign demanding NO DOG WASTE.

'Vot means?' asked Eva, indicating the sign.

'Means he can't do what he's doing.'

'*Tak jdeme!*' commanded Eva, clapping her hands in the dog's direction. Claude turned his head, pinched his load and kicked his legs, then ran towards us with liberated glee. 'Hah,' exclaimed Eva. 'He speak Czech.'

NO DOG WASTE wasn't the only rule. English parks seem to prefer statutes to statues. 5MPH OVER HUMPS. SHARED-USE PATH. NO KEEP NETS OR SACKS PERMITTED. DO NOT FEED PIGEONS: FOOD DEBRIS ATTRACTS VERMIN . . . Eva better understood the menu at the Palm Palace than the ubiquitous signage on Hampstead Heath. She could comprehend neither the amount of rules nor their elusive meaning. Only when viewed through the eyes of a foreigner can the linguistic complexity of *shared-use path* be truly seen.

'*Use* is verb!' she protested. 'Ve are *use* path!'

'Yes, but it can also be a noun and, in this case, a compound adjective,' I explained.

'Vy?!'

'To explain the *function* of the path, the *purpose* of the path, the *use* of the path.'

'Shit stupid language,' she declared.

'Shit stupid language,' I agreed.

The wind gusted. Flapped my flimsy collar.

'I never learn English. You must to correct me more. You never correct.'

'"School closed. Pub open," you said.'

'I change. Now you must to correct everysing I say. And to tell me all meaning of word – noun, verb, adjec . . . adjec . . .'

'*Adjective*.'

'Yes. If no I never learn.'

'Okay,' I lied. 'No problem.'

Eva stopped walking and rummaged through her bag once again, producing a slender bottle of transparent liquid. She unscrewed the lid and took a swig before handing it to me as though it were a given I would accept. *Cannabis Vodka* announced the label, which was slightly amateur and featured a marijuana leaf.

'From Czech Republic,' said Eva patriotically. 'Smood, sweet, no headhurt.'

'Is it legal?' I asked, scanning the label for the alcohol content and finding forty per cent.

'Everysing legal in internet.'

I shook the Bohemian bomb. Seeds billowed through the liquid like snow in a child's snowglobe.

'Good wid tonic water, orange juice, Coke or nosink,' said Eva, whose vocabulary seemed boundless all of a sudden.

'What else have you got in that bag of tricks?'

'*Tricks?*'

'Noun in this case, meaning when something's not real.'

Eva thought for a moment.

'Ah – like rabbit in hat. I watch TV Zeus.'

I tipped the bottle. Swallowed flame. Coughed till my stomach convulsed. 'Good example, Eva,' I spluttered. 'Though a better one might have been when you said Cannabis Vodka is smooth and sweet.'

The breeze was at our backs and, though still warm, grew stronger with each step towards the crown of the hill. We continued our climb in silence until London lay at our feet, flickering with nocturnal industry. I squinted into the darkened distance but, unlike from my bench atop Primrose Hill, couldn't make out Sarah's building. I had watched it many times, hoping to see the light in her office extinguished.

A portable radio, voices here and there, scattered bottles of beer and cigarettes glowing in long grass. The heat had brought people onto the Heath. London's best lookout turned bar and café.

'Is fantastic,' commented Eva.

'What's fantastic?'

'Freedom. People freedom. In England can do all. Nobody say me must do different.'

'Except doormen. And taxi drivers. And all the signs . . .'

'Vot means?'

'It means English people are starting to feel that their freedom is disappearing; their freedom of speech, freedom of expression. There will probably be CCTV on this hill in a few years, to stop people daring to enjoy themselves as they're daring to enjoy themselves this evening.'

'Perhaps revolution in England one day.'

'That would be nice. Hopefully on a Monday.'

Eva laughed. Her teeth were brighter than the city's neon.

'Vot is vord to say person like you?'

'Cynical?'

'I sink yes.'

'I'm old enough to be your father, Eva. Let's see if the next twenty years don't make you cynical.'

'My farzer say time fix but muzzer no listen.'

'What did your father want time to fix?'

Eva looked at me. Shook her head slightly. Some things she left unsaid for more than linguistic reasons.

I didn't push. Eyed the city.

'*Time is a very bankrupt, and owes more than he's worth to season.*' I was speaking to London rather than to Eva. '*Nay, he's a thief too: have you not heard men say that Time comes stealing on by night and day?*'

The wind gusted again.

'I no understand.'

'Forgive me. It's Shakespeare – *A Comedy of Errors*.'

'Vot means?'

'When dramatic things happen based on misunderstanding rather than reality. A bit like my classroom from Monday to Friday.'

Eva smiled.

'You like Shakespeare?'

'Very much.'

'But he say old people. Old life. No modern sings.'

'I don't think people have changed all that much; people and their predicaments.'

'*Predicaments?*'

'Problems.'

I had drunk too much to watch every word.

'Anyway,' I continued, 'you're right – it's not much of an interest to have these days.'

'Vy?'

'I don't know really. The world seems to have dispensed with subtlety. This is the era of the exclamation mark. You can't bring up *A Comedy of Errors* when everyone's talking about *The X Factor*. People think you're strange, except for Walter.'

'Valter?'

'My friend. My best friend. The closest I ever got to a real father.'

Eva saw my eyes moisten and knew it wasn't the wind in my face. She touched my arm. I knew she was only understanding the stepping stones in my river of words, yet I could talk to her better than I could talk to anyone. She understood me least, and made me understand myself most.

'Vy no haf real farzer?' she asked.

I looked at Eva, then at the city, wondering if he was out there somewhere. Wondering if *they* were out there somewhere. When I'd become an adult in the eyes of the law I had refused the chance to look for them. Maybe that was a bad decision. Just another bad decision in a long line of bad decisions. Yet I was grateful for the breath in my lungs, even if I regretted never having the courage to use it to share my secret with Sarah. My secret that had started out small and snowballed in size and strength, to my mind at least. Perhaps the time had come to free the flightless bird, to face my fears about Sarah's reaction. I wasn't to blame for what happened. Surely she would only be angry about my keeping the secret from her, rather than the secret itself. And my position on motherhood and parental responsibility would perhaps be more palatable, or at least comprehensible, if she knew.

Eva touched my arm again. 'No matter if no vont tell,' she said. 'And I no sink you strange.'

I smiled, but she was no judge of 'strange', considering she was about to help me bury ten thousand pounds at my allotment.

■

Flanking Hampstead Heath, Fitzroy Park laneway is lined with grand houses and even grander gardens. When King Tightarse smiles and Londoners venture outdoors, most must rely on public parks for their picnics, their kick-abouts, their sunbathing spots, while the fortunate few who reside in Fitzroy Park simply open double doors and step into their own private playgrounds.

Adorned with ivy and with its wood turning green, the gate to one such garden had been left ajar. Through it crept Claude, snout to the ground, hunting down the source of a scent. I wasn't concerned at first; he usually returned as swiftly as he strayed, after briefly tormenting a cat or a squirrel. But after five minutes, and nearing the allotment entrance, there was still no sign of him so we were forced to retrace our steps.

Enthused voices from the garden suggested a contest of sorts. We edged through the ivy gate and stretched our necks around the side of the house to find two men playing cricket, a golden retriever taking his breed literally at short leg, and Claude in the outfield humping another golden retriever who had taken signing autographs for adoring fans to a new level. Every light in the house was on to provide sufficient illumination. Kerry Packer would have been proud. Environmental activists less so.

The batsmen skied a catch and the bowler rather unnecessarily yelled 'mine' in case the dog was about to get under it. He didn't take his eyes from the plummeting cherry, skilfully sidestepping a compost heap to snare the wicket of a batsman who, by the time the catch had been taken, had poured himself a glass of wine, which wasn't that significant a feat given the bottle comprised his stumps.

'Vot they do?' asked Eva.

'Cricket – our summer sport.'

'Is noun?'

'Yes.'

'Only one meaning?'

'Er . . . 'fraid not, it's also a kind of insect – but don't complicate things. For the moment it's a game played on a grass oval by two teams, usually of eleven players but, as you can see, people cut corners.'

'*Cut corners?*'

'Improvise.'

'*Improvise?*'

'Change the rules.'

Not wishing to interrupt Claude, and amused by the eccentric scene, we waited at the edge of the garden and watched. Between the house and a weeping willow our vantage point would have been classed as 'restricted viewing', although that was soon to change.

'My turn to bat,' declared the exuberant man who'd taken the catch. Though in his sixties and learnedly stooped, he seemed to have more puff than his friend, who looked younger and more fashion-conscious. His son perhaps.

'To *bat?*' asked Eva.

'Verb – to hit the ball,' I explained. 'Cricket has its own vocabulary. It's part of the fun.'

'Vot he haf in hand?'

'Er, that's a bat too, but a noun.'

I felt sorry for her: first the menu, then the signs and now cricket.

After pausing for a drinks break comprising beverages usually confined to the pavilion, the two men swapped equipment, while Claude closed his eyes and continued to exploit the gap in the outfield. The first few deliveries of the older man's innings were, rather sensibly, met with forward defensives, fielded by the drooling dog and returned to the bowler, who didn't need to add his own spit to the leather. The fourth delivery, however, with back foot flair, was sent scuttling in our direction at a speed which defied the untrimmed outfield and caused Eva to screech and run from its path.

'Who's there?' yelled the batsmen, not disagreeably.

'Just us,' I announced, walking through the weeping willow. 'Sorry to trespass, but I'm the owner of the dog who appears to have taken a liking to your deep fine leg.'

The two men turned to watch the dogs, who had finished humping and were rolling on their backs in the grass, not unlike modern cricketers celebrating a dismissal.

'Bloody pitch invader,' complained the younger man, collar up and shirt unbuttoned. 'I was down a fielder for that over. We'll have to replay it.'

'Why don't you join us?' said the older man, carefully picking the ball out of a rosebush. 'We could do with tightening up the field. The dogs are fine fielders but rather fond of their canines when it comes to the crunch.'

'Why don't you indeed?' said the younger man, shamelessly eyeing Eva.

'What'll it be?' asked the old man as he offered me the ball. 'Spin or pace? If you've got a long run-up I'll move the mower.'

'Er,' I stammered, 'thanks, but we can't. We're—'

'Oh, come on,' urged the younger one, pouring Eva a glass of wine. 'It's only day one of a five-day Test.'

'We really can't,' I continued, wondering what on earth Eva was making of all this. 'We have to—'

'Nonsense,' interrupted the young man, handing Eva the glass. 'Come on!' he said to me. 'You keep wicket and your daughter can bat.'

Eva appeared uncomfortable, though it was impossible to say on account of what exactly: the invitation, the ogling, the suggestion she was my daughter. She accepted the bat and was led to the crease. I crouched behind her as wicketkeeper and turned the bat in her hands so it was facing the right way.

'Vot to do?' she asked anxiously.

'When the ball arrives hit it with the bat.'

'Hit where?'

'Wherever you like, but try to avoid those empty bottles.'

The older man went to cover and ordered his dogs to square leg and mid-on. The young man stood tall, puffed his chest, tested the wind direction and rubbed the ball on his groin.

'Vot he do?' asked Eva.

'Um, he's *shining* the ball.'

'Vich ball?'

'Good question.'

'I'm Tristan, by the way,' yelled the young man as he came in to bowl.

Eva missed the first three deliveries, or the first three deliveries missed Eva. They were sent down far too quickly. I wasn't sure why he thought he could bowl her over by bowling her out.

'You need to watch the ball,' I coached. 'Keep your eye on the ball.'

Like that of the young man's previous over, the fourth delivery was loose. Eva swung wildly, more agriculture than cricket, fluking the target and dispatching it towards the boundary, though not along the ground this time. If the sweet slap of willow on leather wasn't heard from the Heath, I've no doubt the shattered window was. Assorted screams ensued, followed by a clang of cutlery. I presumed it was a dinner party but deemed it impolite to ask. The young man stared at Eva, collar still peaked, before running towards the house, his pride in as many pieces as the window.

'I sorry,' shouted Eva, dropping the bat as though it were a bloodied dagger and putting her hands over her mouth.

'Six and out,' said the older man. 'Sorry to nip your innings in the bud but I think that's probably stumps. Better go and see if the other guests are okay. Do help yourselves to more wine.'

His dogs followed him inside. Claude didn't even receive so much as a farewell kiss from his catch in the outfield.

As invited, Eva and I took some wine and skulked through the ivy gate. The moon was yellow as butter and trees cast ghostly shadows along the laneway to the allotments. The hoot of an owl as I pushed my key into the padlock. Eva shuddered. I indicated the bag containing our winnings, gestured that we should keep quiet and pushed the rusty gate. Claude led the way along crossword paths dissecting rhubarbs, turnips, vines, potatoes . . . Pitchforks and shovels stood to attention. No matter how well maintained, allotments are ragged places. All plots are similar yet no two are alike. Fertile junkyards of tin sheds and turned earth. Two fingers up to pesticides and Tesco.

We followed the path towards the top of the slope, zigzagging now and then up the hobby farm grid.

'Crazy garden,' whispered Eva. 'In Czech Republic yes, but for olt people.'

A veiled insult from anyone else.

'In London people get old waiting for these,' I explained. We could talk now that we were inside the gate. 'Would you believe there's a thirty-year waiting list for these plots?'

'Thirty-year . . . ?'

'Before you can have one. They're very popular and a great way to save money by growing your own food.'

'You grow food?' asked Eva, surprised.

'Strawberries, artichokes, the occasional carrot. I'm not much of a green thumb.'

'*A green* . . . ?'

'Thumb.' I held one up. 'Idiomatic expression. Means "good in the garden".'

'So vy you haf?'

I presumed she meant the allotment rather than the thumb.

'Because I sit, do a crossword and watch other people grow food. It's my escape – noun and verb. I watch the Heath change colour with the seasons and pretend I'm in the country all year round.'

My plot was at the very top of the slope, tucked under trees at the end of the path. Given the reasons I visited the allotments, my shed was better cultivated than my crops. I opened it on darkness but had done so before and knew the way blind to candle and match.

A faint glow revealed the room, and lack of.

'Welcome to Villa Sebastian,' I announced.

Eva looked around, which didn't take long.

'I'll give you the grand tour.' I pointed to each furnishing as it was listed. 'We've got a fold-up chair, some bottles of beer, a packet of . . .' I picked up the sachet and read the label. '. . . Bolivar Beetroot seeds, newspapers, gardening gloves, a shovel, a trowel, Wellies, a blanket, a tin of dog food and some sacks of fertiliser.' I crossed my arms. 'What more could you need?'

'Litte bit vodka,' added Eva, pulling the bottle from her bag.

Claude roamed outside and lifted his leg on the usual spots – shed, tap, my neighbour's coriander. I lit the remaining candles on the rickety shelf. Eva noticed a small frame on the wall and went to inspect the shed's only decoration. She delicately lifted the frame from its nail, which indelicately fell to the ground, though we were too drunk to look for it. She clunked through the first line but then gave up, looking to me for an explanation.

'It's a poem,' I said, 'by Lord Byron. A eulogy for his favourite dog.'

'Vot means *eulogy*?'

'It means a goodbye.'

I sat down on the cold cement. Eva held out the frame.

'Read,' she commanded.

'No,' I complained. 'I've drunk too much to do it justice.'

She thrust it under my nose. 'Read,' she repeated.

I took the frame and turned it in my hands, though I knew the poem by heart.

'"Inscription on the Monument of a—"'
'Stand,' ordered Eva.

We had studied the imperative the previous week in class. Eva had clearly been paying attention.

I stood as best I could. The evening had taken its toll.

'"Inscription on the Monument of a Newfoundland Dog".'

Eva sat on a bag of fertiliser and closed her eyes. I took a swig for stage fright.

When some proud son of man returns to earth,
Unknown to glory, but upheld by birth,
The sculptor's art exhausts the pomp of woe
And storied urns record who rest below:
When all is done, upon the tomb is seen,
Not what he was, but what he should have been:
But the poor dog, in life the firmest friend,
The first to welcome, foremost to defend,
Whose honest heart is still his master's own,
Who labours, fights, lives, breathes for him alone,
Unhonour'd falls, unnoticed all his worth –
Denied in heaven the soul he held on earth:
While Man, vain insect! hopes to be forgiven,
And claims himself a sole exclusive Heaven.
Ye! who perchance behold this simple urn,
Pass on – it honours none you wish to mourn:
To mark a Friend's remains these stones arise;
I never knew but one – and here he lies.

Eva opened her eyes. Tears had pooled in mine.
'Vy haf poem here?'
'My dog Bullseye is buried outside.'
'*Buried?*'
'In the ground, keeping the carrots company.'

Candlelight was sufficient for me to see Eva's surprise. 'Can to put dog here in ground?'

'No, it's against the rules, but he's been there for years and no one's objected.'

'*Dobrý nápad,*' said Eva to herself.

'What does that mean?' I asked, reversing our roles.

She returned from private thoughts. 'Er, means perfect place for to put money,' she translated, opening her bag and taking out the stash of cash.

I grabbed the Tesco bag that had housed the beetroot seeds, put the money inside, folded the bag into the smallest possible size and tied the handles closed.

'Right,' I said, 'time to put this in the bank.'

We returned to the night and surveyed my plot, holding the torch to the stretch of earth. Towards the middle was a patch of vacant soil, flanked by rhubarb leaves and a tomato vine. I stood back and allowed access to a fascinated Claude.

'Dig!' I ordered.

My labrador planted all my crops – or cash crops in this case. His paws moved frantically, spray of soil through his legs, nose sinking slowly into the ground. He'd have struck the Northern line if I hadn't stepped in, his snout poking through somewhere between Archway and East Finchley. 'Severe delays in both directions,' the announcement would go, 'due to a labrador-induced signal failure.'

When Claude was up to his elbows I stepped in and took over, digging a further inch with a standard spade before deeming the hole deep enough. Eva handed me the bag, which I placed into the ground and covered over, flattening the soil with my shoe and marking the spot with a cracked flowerpot. Claude lifted his leg on the burial site, perhaps watering it in the hope it would grow.

'There,' I said, standing my spade in the ground. 'Quicker than queuing at Barclays.'

Eva sat on the step of the shed – sipping, smoking and gazing at the trees in the direction of the Heath. The owl hooted at regular intervals, its eyes brighter than the glow from my candles.

'You say England people not free,' she said. 'If people haf allotment and play cricket zey free.'

I wiped my hands on my trousers and sat beside her.

'You think those people were free? That young man playing cricket made me uncomfortable. He was too prickly to be free.'

'*Prickly?*'

'Adjective – like the sharp thing on the rosebush.'

'Young man strange – before he look me then he leave garden no say goodbye.'

'Because he liked you. You broke more than his window.'

'He sink I am your daughter.'

'No he didn't – he was trying to point out my unsuitability. You see, Eva: jealousy, insecurity, vanity, lust . . . People's predicaments haven't changed since Shakespeare put down his pen.'

She lit a cigarette. Spoke with smoke.

'Vot means?'

'It doesn't matter. Pass me that bottle.'

I took a sip of vodka. Held it in my mouth to savour the taste or perhaps burn my tongue. That bull in my china shop had done with browsing and was ready to make a purchase. He found the specials section, eyed a triangular stack, lowered his head and charged.

'What about Tim? Is he like the man at cricket?'

Eva sighed as though exhausted, leant against the door and took a deep drag of her cigarette. She was silent, so silent I looked across to see if she had fallen asleep. Tears glistened in her eyes. This time I was sure they were tears. Perhaps they had been tears all along.

'I'm sorry, Eva. I shouldn't have—'

'Alvays zis problem!' she interrupted. 'It no go away. Tim wrong man. Much wrong man. You must stop. Please stop.'

I turned towards her. The concrete step felt cool.

'I will stop it, Eva. I promise I'll stop it. But the person who can help me is away for a few weeks. Just kill time and everything will be fine.'

'You no understand,' she said, suppressing tears. 'You no understand. He buy me flower. He touch me. I say him sad story and he touch me. I can't to haf zis problem no more. Alvays you speak. Vy you no stop?'

'I do understand and I will stop it. As soon as my boss returns from holiday I promise your problem will be over. Just kill time till then, Eva.'

Her head in her hands. Her chest heaving. I grabbed her bag and helped her stand.

'Come on – I'll walk you home.'

'No,' she said, pushing me away. 'I can do. Leave me myself.'

'It's almost midnight. I can't let you walk home by yourself.'

She wiped her eyes and tossed away her cigarette. 'You must,' she said. 'Obligation.'

Then she ran down the path, down the slope . . . The dark consumed her, though for a second I could still hear her crying. When the glow of her discarded cigarette vanished I could have sworn I'd spent the evening by myself. Then I heard her voice in the night.

'Sebastian no understand language he teach.'

15

Modifiers

One advantage of working at a language school is that you can turn up without shaving and if your boss objects you simply claim to be eliciting new vocabulary: *beard, unshaven, stubble, five-day shadow, blunt razor, couldn't be arsed* . . . After sleeping in my allotment shed clutching an empty bottle of Cannabis Vodka, I could also have elicited a lesson on prefixes by having the students simply describe my appearance: *unkempt, unchanged, unwashed, unwell* . . . I may not have spent the evening preparing lessons as dedicated teachers should, but when I reported for duty at The Future Perfect that Friday I was a walking, if slightly swaying, dictionary.

All this talk of teaching . . . I felt more like a student: hungover, with my homework not done. Twenty years younger last night. Twenty years older this morning. When Eva had said 'no head-hurt', she'd lied. How I longed, just once, to be behind the desks rather than in front of them, to swap sarky notes with fellow students and biro out the teeth on the faces in my textbook. But as we filed into school, London drizzle our shared crown, I abruptly exited that dream by being the only arrival to wipe his feet on the mat. Students continued straight on to the classrooms while I veered left to the staffroom.

Shiny shoes from Monday week when I return, read a note on the staffroom door, attached with sticky tape and signed by the principal.

'She's cracking down,' commented Clarissa.

'She's cracking up,' corrected Walter.

We wouldn't have dared gossip were she not on holiday.

Other than that, the morning staffroom was routine: queues for the photocopiers, colleagues calling in sick, replacements being found, teachers consulting colleagues over how best to begin their lessons.

'I'm doing extreme adjectives,' said Clarissa. 'Any ideas for a lead-in?'

'Slap them about a bit,' advised Samuel. 'You'll soon elicit the target language.'

I was splayed across my chair, eyes closed, head back. It wouldn't have been a lie had I called in sick. Sleeping in parks and sheds is no cure for the flu. Some chirpy sod was daring to whistle. The tune grew louder and found the seat next to mine. I opened my eyes on the last person I'd expected to see saluting the morning in the manner of birds. Two days in a row. What had made him so happy?

Despite my condition, I spoke first.

'How's the IT charlatan this morning?'

'Better than you by the looks of it, dear boy. Forgive me for prying but are you trying to elicit the word "forage"?'

I sat up straight. Slapped my cheeks in the hope of waking up.

'What makes you say that?'

'It's just that between your knees and your fingernails there's enough soil to plant cucumbers. Indeed you look, if you'll forgive me, like a cross between Gerald Durrell and a squirrel.'

'I won ten thousand pounds at a casino before burying it at my allotment,' I replied robotically, as though such goings-on were akin to a night in.

Walter laughed, assuming I was joking but entertaining my explanation.

'So you're filthy rich, as it were.'

'Ten thousand is nothing these days.'

'Well at least you can afford some shiny shoes for Monday week.'

The bell rang. The room groaned.

'See you in the Princess,' said Walter.

'Not a chance,' I replied, 'unless they've turned it into a hotel and made me up a king-size bed.'

■

Not for the first time in my career, as I opened the door to my classroom I had no idea what I would teach come the other side of it. As a teacher you never stop learning. That morning, for example, I discovered there is even a seminar in a sneeze.

'Good morning!' said the students in clumsy unison as I entered.

'*Atchooooo!*' I replied.

'Bless you,' declared Ulrica.

'You are look terrible,' added Natalina.

'I have flu,' I informed them.

'No,' contested Sibylla, thumbing her textbook for the relevant page, 'you have flown.'

And there was our topic – the present perfect, which I recruited Clever Clogs to teach since she knew it so well. I gave her a marker pen and slumped into her seat, at long last on the fun side of the desk.

Shoved into the spotlight, though slightly nervous, my Dutch disciple did a competent job of introducing the grammar and was only thrown when Yoon Pong traipsed in late without knocking.

'Solly,' he stammered. 'Happen bad, bad ting: yesterday night host family buggered.'

My brain may have drowned in vodka but my teacher's ear was still dry. I stood, took the pen from Sibylla and wrote *burgled* on the board. Jean-Paul's hand shot up so I wrote /búrg'ld/ alongside.

'What does a *burglar* do?' I asked the class, to check the concept.

'Take my lute,' replied Yoon Pong.

'Yes, but do *burglars* only take lutes?'

'No,' he replied, 'cunt take TV as well.'

I suspected the experience would do little to purify Yoon Pong's polluted opinion of 'teenager with hood and twenties with white van', regardless of who had *buggered* his host family's house.

Again I gave Sibylla both the pen and the floor, which she took without hesitation this time. She seemed to enjoy the role and her board-writing was neater than mine. 'Come in!' she hollered when the next latecomer knocked. The door squeaked, revealing Ulrica dressed in a half-length top to brandish her pierced belly button. Had I asked why she was late she might have said she had a puncture. Agnes pretended not to notice the show of skin. Giuseppe and Jean-Paul appeared hypnotised.

The only name missing on my attendance log was Eva's. She might simply have overslept after our late night, although I knew her cry for help had traumatised her. But at least she had finally appealed for help directly. Now I could talk to Rhonda and, come Monday week, Eva could be on the path to a new job.

'Work in pairs for next exercise,' ordered Sibylla. 'Think of five things you do now which you also did in past, like play piano.'

Hands behind her back, Sibylla wandered the room, monitoring students preparing their material. It was spooky how well she had watched me. Her lesson on the present perfect got off to an excellent start, but I'm afraid I can't vouch for its end. I had always despised students who fell asleep in class, until joining their ranks.

■

Other than my snoring in class it was a standard Friday, though that was to change when I went home to collect Claude for a stroll on Primrose Hill. There was, strangely, no mail in our slot. It seemed unlikely we hadn't received any mail that day because I couldn't remember the last time I hadn't been offered easy credit on the threshold to my house, a catalogue of credit cards we could punish now and pay off later.

The mystery was solved when I opened our front door and saw Sarah's suitcase propped against the hall wall. The only thing I found more difficult to remember than the last time I hadn't received junk mail was the last time I'd come home during daylight hours to find Sarah on the sofa doing Sudoku in her socks. Claude was curled beside her. Hobnobs by her tea. For a moment I was happy. Then I saw her tears.

'What's the matter, sweetheart? I thought you were in Dubai.'

'I came back early. Haven't you seen the news?'

'I only look at the crossword page.'

Sarah pointed at the newspaper beside her on the sofa. 'They're calling it the Credit Crunch. I've lost my job!'

My mouth fell open. It was difficult to digest. Had I needed to elicit the expression 'out of the blue' from my class, my wife's announcement would have been ideal.

'I'm . . . I'm . . . I'm sorry, sweetheart.'

'No you're not. You've been wanting me to stop work for years.'

'Not like this. And only if we had a baby.'

'Well now we have neither.'

Claude sprawled on the floor like a polar bear carpet. I picked up Sarah's airport copy of the *Evening Standard* and studied the front page. For the record, what I said next was an attempt to cheer her up. Humour had always been the way to cheer her up.

'The Credit Crunch, huh? Nice to see the corporate world is capable of alliteration, even if it does sound a bit like a breakfast cereal for bankers.'

Sarah looked at me wide-eyed. 'Did you hear what I said, Sebastian? I've lost my job! Why are you trying to be funny?'

Her tears had muddied her mascara. With the best intentions, I proceeded to make things worse. 'Because you'll find another job. You're the best. And you're certainly hard-working. If they want someone to vouch for that, put me down as a referee.'

She dropped her puzzle and pen on the coffee table, which in our house was more of a tea table. 'I don't think you understand. I'm not the only one. Hundreds of people have lost their jobs and it looks like thousands more will too.' She searched for a dry patch on her Kleenex. 'I could tell you the reason but you wouldn't understand.'

'I promise I'll try.'

I fell into the old leather armchair and cuddled a cushion. In hindsight I should have cuddled her.

'Well,' said Sarah, turning towards me, 'basically, Fannie Mae and Freddie Mac . . .' I bit my lip. Sarah noticed and simplified. 'Basically, two giant US mortgage lenders offered money to people to buy houses that were way beyond their reach.'

It sounded as negligent as me putting a beginner in an advanced class, though – in my first correct decision of the conversation – I opted not to share that with Sarah. I kicked off my shoes, which according to Rhonda's note were treading death row.

'So, to cut a long story short,' she continued, 'the value of those assets fell and people had over-borrowed. Those people then faced negative equity.'

'*Negative equity?*'

'They had borrowed more than their assets were now worth.'

For the second time that day I felt like a student. Sarah uncrossed her legs and sat forward. Just talking about her industry energised her, regardless of how rotten it was. 'So those borrowers then defaulted on their mortgages and Fannie . . . the mortgage lenders have exposed themselves to massive losses.'

'So why have *you* lost your job?'

Sarah slumped back on the sofa and took a deep breath. 'Because it's not just Fannie Mae and Freddie Mac who have done the wrong thing.'

'I see.'

'You see what?'

'I see what you're saying.'

She turned her head in my direction without it leaving the sofa.

'What am I saying?'

'That greed is not merely an American concept and the UK's upstanding financial institutions, mortgage lenders and real estate agencies have been drinking from the same dirty trough.'

Anger in her eyes, her bloodshot eyes. 'Why does everything you say have to sound like a lesson?'

'I didn't mean it to sound like a lesson.'

'This is serious, Seb. We're talking about the livelihoods of millions of people.'

'No we're not, Sarah. We're talking about human nature. Walter – a man the corporate world would view as an underachiever – was spot on. He said it would end in expensive tears and he was right.'

Why was I more ready to praise Walter than I was to comfort Sarah? Her own tears had started to flow again. I moved to her side and embraced her.

'I'm sorry I was insensitive and I'm sorry you lost your job. But it sounds as though rules were broken, warning signs were ignored and some people might get what they deserve, though I'm sure it will all blow over and you'll soon be back at the top of the skyscraper.'

She was sobbing. Her head found my shoulder. 'There's something else,' she said.

I waited patiently before realising I would have to prompt. 'Something else?'

Tears stained my unironed shirt.

'I think . . .' Her voice was meeker than I had hitherto heard it. 'I think I might have lost all our savings.'

I moved away from her, if only to see her face.

'You've done *what*?'

She closed her eyes as though the mess she was about to describe was physically in front of her in our ground-floor living room rather than just numbers that had vanished from a computer screen. Then she opened them again as though realising she needed to face up to what she had done.

'I invested heavily in hedge funds linked to those sub-prime mortgages and it looks like those will be the hardest hit.'

Life can go from predictable to perilous in the time it takes your heart to miss a beat. Yet for some reason I felt no anger. My parents' love of money nurtured my hatred of it, and I had never seen the money Sarah spoke of so I struggled to feel its loss. All I knew is that it would have been safer alongside the rhubarb at my allotment.

'Why didn't you consult me?'

'Because you don't know about these things.'

Her voice was its usual sure self. I embraced her again. Kissed her forehead.

'In the light of what's happened, will you forgive me for saying that it appears you don't either?'

Claude sighed deeply, nostrils flaring on the floorboards. I extended my leg and tickled his ribs with my toes.

'What the hell happened to the knees of your trousers?' asked Sarah.

'I won ten thousand pounds at a casino last night and buried it at the allotment.'

Sarah sat straight and looked at me, frown dissolving, face lighting up. Tears turned to laughter, raucous laughter. When it subsided she returned her head to my shoulder.

'Thank you for cheering me up, sweetheart. In your own unusual way you always know how to cheer me up.' My wife blew her nose. 'What really happened to your trousers, Seb?'

'How about . . . I dived to save a boundary playing cricket?'

Her lips met mine.

'That's more like it.'

Sarah wiped off the lippy she had left on my lips, stood and walked to the window. She had been working such long hours lately that she hadn't had time to dye her hair. It was darker than usual; a strand had stuck to her tear-stained cheek. I watched her squinting at the afternoon as though a stranger to daylight hours. Her ears were adorned with pearls. The outline of her underwear corrugated her skirt. Her hands seemed swollen, rings suffocating that delightful dough I had fallen in love with all those years ago.

Then she turned abruptly from the window, a sense of purpose on her face. 'I think this has happened for a reason,' she declared. 'I want to adopt a baby, Seb, and I want to stay home and bring it up.' She strode over and sat beside me on the sofa. 'We'll play happy families. I'll . . . er . . . change nappies and, um, I don't know, whatever – bake cakes.' She was more fluent when talking about negative equity. 'And you can beat your chest like Tarzan and bring home the bacon.'

'I've never said you shouldn't work, Sarah. I just thought you should slow down and allow other things into your life. I'm proud of what you've achieved, but you had no time for me, for us.'

'Well I've got plenty of time now.'

I brushed aside a strand of her hair that had stuck to a tear.

'It sounds wonderful, really it does, but why don't we wait a little before planning the rest of our lives? You can't see the future through tears.'

'Okay,' agreed Sarah, wiping her eyes. 'But in the meantime let's spend some quality time together. Why don't we have a holiday to make up for lost time?'

I handed her a dry tissue.

'With whose money?'

'We'll find the money.'

I knew where to look.

'Work's full-on at the moment. My students have a test coming up.'

'Take some time off. Frank will cover you.'

'You're planning again, Sarah. One step at a time.'

She snuggled up, head on my shoulder, arm around my soft stomach. 'I'm sorry,' she said. 'For everything.'

I put my arm around her. Held her close.

'Everything's not your fault.'

Claude skulked over and sat at our feet as though guarding the conciliatory moment. Sarah sank her fingers into his fur. I couldn't remember the last time she'd touched him.

'Did you stop it?' she asked softly.

'Stop what?'

'The cricket ball you dived for.'

I thought for a moment. In her traumatised state Sarah needed the sanctuary of the status quo.

'Who me? Butterfingers? No, I just helped it on its way to the rope.'

■

We ate dinner together for the first time in months: bangers and mash washed down with a mid-priced red from M&S. Then we nested on the sofa and watched a property show that had been recorded while banks and mortgage lenders were tying the knot in their noose; it was like listening to plucky pilots discussing dinner reservations on the black box.

16

Qualifiers

As usual, my wife wasted no time. She simply didn't do depression. Early the following week, sunshine and showers the backdrop, Wendy from the adoption agency dropped by the flat to talk us through the process. Sarah's research had revealed she couldn't do IVF and apply for adoption at the same time because the adoption agency preferred couples who were over the emotional hurdle of not being able to conceive naturally. This made me realise that my wife may have been right about the clock ticking. With an average two-year wait for adoption, and a maximum age gap between adoptive parent and child of forty years, if the gamble of IVF didn't work Sarah might never mother a baby. To leave it late is to limit your options.

For the first of Wendy's dozen inspections, which she preferred to call 'visits', Sarah sat dotingly close to me on the sofa from which she had cleaned every trace of Claude's coat. The rest of the potential nest was also spotless; indeed, I wondered for a moment if she was trying to fill the flat or sell it. Playing the role of diligent housewife, Sarah served tea in cups and saucers rather than discoloured mugs. Biscuits were arranged on a plate rather than plucked from a packet. Windows had been cleaned for the first time in years and were as transparent as our London lives.

In her new wardrobe of casual clothes, blouse rather than business shirt, Sarah hoped to convince Wendy that, although her hand was forced, she intended to shelve her career to stay home and raise a child. The lost savings were not mentioned but, in Sarah's defence, were yet to be fully ascertained; it depended how much the hedge had been trimmed. Sarah rammed home 'the security of my husband's job' – a formal way of saying that, if the euro went the same way as the pound and students stopped arriving from the Continent, Rhonda would sack the newcomers first.

A heavily overweight, middle-aged black woman in sensible shoes, Wendy was no slouch when it came to peering under the carpet of our lives. Trying to put one over her, beyond the fancy biscuits, seemed a bad idea. Originally from Antigua, she had three children of her own plus one adopted nipper; I suppose some people are born to bear others. She oozed roly-poly affection. I wanted to adopt her as my mother.

When asked about our experience of children we spoke of our fondness for Sarah's niece, whose photo was on our fridge, and for my friend's four-year-old, who we'd *often* taken to Arsenal matches. Okay, the adverb of frequency was an exaggeration. We said we enjoyed home life, which for me wasn't a lie. To back this up, Sarah had found some wedding photos and displayed them on the mantelpiece in frames bought from Cancer Research so they wouldn't look new. She had bought some board games – Scrabble, Monopoly, Yahtzee – which lent a familial feel to our otherwise Spartan living room. She had also brought some books through from the bedroom and stacked them on the shelves, plus she'd tossed out morally questionable videos such as *Twin Peaks* and *Blue Velvet,* replacing them, somewhat saliently, with the *Planet Earth* box set.

'The house must look like a place where a child would be exposed to education,' Sarah had said, while crossing the 't' in deception.

'Don't worry,' I'd replied. 'If they dispute that, I'll point out all the grammatical errors in their brochure.'

The scrutiny, we were told, wouldn't stop when Wendy left the house. We would have to attend medical checks to confirm we were in good health and might still hope to be when our toddler turned teenager. I imagined a half-hour with a man thinner than his hatstand who would inform me I had flat feet and the occasional haemorrhoid, which I would happily have told him myself. Then he would test my lung capacity, presumably to check my ability to inflate balloons at birthday parties.

Police checks would also be run. We had no record of offences, apart from me appearing in the same CCTV shot as a hooligan at an Arsenal match who threw a coin at Didier Drogba. But I hadn't thrown it, so we would be okay.

Our referees would be interviewed. For a second I considered asking Eva to recount my smooth handling of Zeus that tricky afternoon, then thought better of it. I supposed I would recruit Rhonda, who would tell Wendy that I would make an excellent father and that my teaching experience clearly demonstrated an ability to deal with the needs of others patiently. (She wasn't privy to the time I'd locked Yoon Pong in the cupboard.)

Sarah had already decided that her referee would be Jane, a friend and colleague who had also lost her job. Jane would testify that Sarah always saw projects through to completion, which was true, and attest that my wife often babysat her five-year-old daughter Gemma, which wasn't. 'She's a delightful little girl,' Sarah told Wendy. 'The daughter I never had.'

When my conscience pricked at Sarah's subterfuge I pondered the plethora of ill-equipped parents siring unplanned offspring across the UK. What William Blake failed to mention in 'Jerusalem' after 'green and pleasant land' was 'the highest rate of teenage pregnancy in western Europe', though in his defence that strains to rhyme. What we were doing seemed blameless by comparison. I couldn't help thinking that if the rigorous checks applied to prospective adoptive parents were also applied to prospective natural parents then there wouldn't be so many disadvantaged children needing homes. However, I kept that to myself in case Wendy misconstrued it as a suggestion she sterilise every teenager in Hull.

Of course, the irony of it all was that our lies described a life I would have preferred, and that when Sarah was least herself I desired her most. I would have loved to stay at home playing Scrabble with my wife, or to cuddle up in our socks and follow Sir David Attenborough around the world. So even when Wendy informed us that, like over ninety per cent of applications, ours would probably be approved, deep down I felt uneasy. In buying Scrabble we were playing charades.

We were asked what our child preferences were and Sarah said she would love the newborn that nature had denied her. There were very few newborns available, Wendy explained, and we would have more chance of finding a match if we adopted a toddler. We were shown photos of beautiful but challenging young children: solitary souls, brothers, sisters, even siblings of three, smiling despite their attached profiles, which all too often contained terms such as 'developmental delay', 'attention deficit disorder', 'becomes angry when recalling incidents from his past'. We were saddened by their stories, their tender, total innocence, and felt guilty for wanting a healthy newborn. We simply didn't possess the necessary attributes to meet the challenges of these desperate darlings. Despite their hardships and handicaps, it was we who were deficient.

After Wendy's visit, Sarah and I worked on making up for lost time. Despite our new financial restraints (which rather than see us squabble were actually bringing us closer together), we went out to dinner and tried to recreate a first date. Smelling of eight-year-old aftershave, I left the flat and did a once-round the block, before calling on my sweetheart armed with Tesco flowers complete with barcode on the wrap. No chocolates. We were penny pinching.

'I can't seem to open the door,' shouted the woman I had supposedly just met on the other side of the door. 'Have you seen my keys?'

'Try your handbag.'

'I have.'

'Coffee table?'

'No.'

'Jacket pocket?'

'No.'

'Oh fuck it, I'll use mine.'

I had planned on saying 'Nice place you've got here', though it would have seemed stilted after letting myself in. Sarah finished her make-up in the bathroom while I patted her dog in the living room.

'What's his name?'

'Claude.'

Now we were rolling.

'What's *Planet Earth* like?' I asked, browsing her bookshelves.

'Amazing,' she replied, 'apart from that sad bit with the bears.'

I saw the wedding photos on the mantelpiece. Picked one up. Studied the happy couple. 'I didn't know you were married.'

'What?' said Sarah, sticking her head around the door, armed with a lipstick crayon that reminded me of Claude in the company of poodles.

I held up the photo.

'Oh,' she twigged, 'that's my first husband. He died several years ago.'

'My condolences.'

'Not necessary. I killed him.'

'Goodness! Really? Why?'

'Because when I lost my job and asked him to take me on holiday he refused.'

'I told you, Sarah, I'm busy at . . .' Then I remembered myself, or my invented self. 'And, er, what was your husband like?'

She closed one eye as though peering through a microscope, which in a way she was. 'Set in his ways. Frustratingly old-school. Diverted a dull life through the clues of a crossword.'

I had tried to tell her about Sebastian the high-roller and successful gambler but she had derided the idea. I would always be an underachiever in her mind – and no doubt in mine.

I dusted the photo and returned it to the shelf. Sarah turned the tap in the bathroom, water-hammer reverberating through the bygone building. Now wasn't the time to remind her to bring that up at the next freeholders' meeting.

'Glass of wine before we go?' she asked, appearing from the bathroom in a skirt above the knee. A low-cut top revealed freckled cleavage. A redcurrant gem echoed scarlet lipstick.

'You look nice.'

'*Nice?* Not ravishing? Not sexy? Not finger-lickin' good? Come on, Seb, this is make-believe. Tell me I look like something your tongue might trip over.'

'This isn't going to work, is it, Sarah?'

'Yes it is,' she insisted, pouring me a glass of red from last night's half-finished bottle. 'Tell me about you,' she coaxed, handing me the glass. 'Let your imagination run as wild as your hair.'

I combed it with my hands, to no good effect.

'Okay,' I said, retrieving the wedding photo. 'As you can see I've also been married.'

'Really?' said Sarah, feigning surprise. 'What was she like?'
'She was a polygamist.'
'No!'
'Yes, married to me but also to her job.'
'The tart. Whatever did you do?'
'I, er, well, I finished my crossword and took the dog for a walk.'
I never could do make-believe.

■

Dinner was the same fumbling role-play; I'd seen my students do better jobs in pretend cafés and travel agencies. Perched like bookends at a grubby table-for-two in our local Indian restaurant, I ruined our ruse when it started to rain and I interrupted Sarah outlining her taste in music to ask if she'd shut the bedroom window. Do that on a first date and you'll not be granted a second, unless your sweetheart has a soft spot for stalkers. It was a question I asked automatically as her highly strung husband of ten years but which I wasn't supposed to ask as her well-hung toy-boy of ten minutes.

I gave the farce one last fling when we left the restaurant and stepped into the rain. Ignoring the downpour, I closed my eyes and kissed her mouth. She retrieved her curried tongue, pushed me away and said, 'Couldn't we at least find an awning?' We were home in the time it took to hail a cab, ripping off our clothes only to replace them with dry ones for fear of catching our death.

■

The following morning, at a loss with the concept of spare time, Sarah joined me on my walk with Claude. My labrador sat between us as I solved the crossword and she browsed the career section – distinctly thinner in light of recent events. She was just keeping an eye out, she assured me, though I knew she wanted to see if she was as 'irreplaceable' as her boss had said.

Low cloud beheaded St Paul's.

'Anything naming racehorses or tropical cyclones?' I asked her.

'Um . . . no,' she replied, playfully pretending to check.

'Hmm, looks as though I'm stuck with teaching then.'

Sarah cleared her throat. 'I've been thinking I might join you,' she said. 'Just part time while I'm waiting for Wendy to find us a match.'

I turned my head. 'You want to teach?'

Sarah shrugged her shoulders. 'Why not?'

'Because your heart's not in it.'

'Is yours?'

'It has to be now.'

Sarah peered at me over Claude, who ducked his head when she raised her voice. 'Why do most people become language teachers?' she asked rhetorically.

I looked at London. A Heathrow-bound plane appeared to be hovering rather than hurtling.

'For some it's a profession. For others it's a passport.'

'And for me it would be a stop-gap. Why does that offend you?'

'Because I'd like to think you weren't doing it out of desperation.'

'You have a short memory, Sebastian Pink.'

The city hadn't changed despite the cull of workers; skyscrapers cannot bow, cranes can't hang their heads in shame. The sci-fi skyline defied the Downturn, the Recession or the Global Financial Meltdown . . . The name of the menace depended on which newspaper you used to wipe the sleep from your eyes, if you could afford to sleep. The media certainly weren't sleeping. Analysis was endless, as were predictions, tossed about by 'experts' who hadn't seen the hiccup coming, making their opinion of how to stifle it utterly redundant. Finger pointing became a sport worthy of the London Olympics, which suddenly seemed a most expensive booby prize.

Done with the career section, Sarah read the front-page denunciation of 'the Bonus Culture' in which bankers were depicted as Satan's spawn. Public hangings seemed imminent. Only the location was yet to be decided. My money was on Covent Garden; the lions were lazy in Trafalgar Square. London's hacks were on a ruthless, repetitive witch hunt. In London you're never more than four feet from a rat, the saying goes, but in The City, yelled the tabloids, that distance is drastically reduced. It wasn't only bankers whose blood they were after. Real estate agents and mortgage lenders had also had their greedy fingers in the till.

I watched my wife read the bilious rant, jaw clenched, expression pained, reluctantly glimpsing her own reflection like a pimply teenager in front of the bathroom mirror. If the biting wind had brought tears to her eyes, *The Times* tipped them over the edge.

'You okay?'

Sarah folded the paper and placed it neatly on her knee, stone hands across it so it wouldn't blow away. 'Blaming money-minded people makes the masses feel better,' she said, 'but we're not all greedy and immoral.'

'Don't take it personally,' I said. 'People simply hate professions that give nothing back. Politicians. Bankers . . . You're seen as self-serving. That's one thing we teachers will always have over you.'

'What people fail to realise,' said Sarah, 'is that capitalism can only function if people spend money they haven't got. Banks and mortgage lenders simply make that money available.'

'It's the teeny-weeny bit you take for yourselves that peeves them.'

'Why should that concern them if we make their plans possible?'

'Because they feel enslaved.'

'Well then the world's in a right pickle.'

I smiled at the thought the entire newspaper on her knee could be so well summarised by one who rarely read it.

'If I had a penny for every time I'd sat on this bench watching your world and wishing you'd come home,' I confessed to Sarah, 'I could single-handedly stave off this recession.'

'I'm sorry,' said Sarah, eyes on the city, hand on my shoulder.

'You were too busy lending to others to give to me. What did you like so much about that concrete cage?'

Claude darted off to chase a squirrel. Sarah shifted closer, risking splinters.

'When you're in it, Seb, you don't see it as a cage. Quite the opposite – it's a gateway to wealth and happiness.'

'Are you wealthy?'

'We've got the flat.'

'Are you happy?'

Sarah contemplated the view. Spoke to a world no longer at her feet.

'I'm not like you, Seb. I'm not a thinker. If I'm busy then I'm happy. I'm only unhappy if I'm sitting around wondering whether I'm happy or not.'

'I wonder what Descartes would make of that.'

'Who?'

'Descartes. *Cogito ergo sum*. I think therefore I am.'

My wife's hand retreated.

'Stop it,' she said. 'You sound like my dead husband.'

'The role-play's over, Sarah. It's reality from now on.'

'We'll be okay, provided you forgive me.'

Claude returned to the bench, panting, slobbering. We made it clear there was no room.

'I forgive you, Sarah, but can you forgive me?'

'What for?'

My chance to tell all, to wipe the slate clean. I took her hand, squeezed it slightly and gazed at her face, her eyes, her lips – the only lips that had ever said 'I love you', to me at least.

My courage evaporated.

'For "set in his ways. Frustratingly old-school. Diverted a dull life through the clues of a crossword".'

Sarah smiled gently as she recalled her description of me from the previous evening.

Claude bowed his head, disappointed.

17

Imperative

Fewer morning joggers, more steam off Claude's stool – the first chills of autumn were showing themselves. My collar higher, my dog's head lower: typical signs that the planet was turning. *Pumice, snooker, centurion, wasp* . . . I finished the crossword and flipped to the front page. I rarely read the paper beyond filling its grid, which Sarah once compared to ordering an entire pizza just to scoff an olive.

I find the news damning, particularly when age-old evils repeat and humankind fails to stop them doing so. I am not immune to the global perils of war, famine, terrorism and reality television, yet what troubles me most about modern times is when snowfall is measured in pounds sterling rather than centimetres. I would hate to be a child growing up in a world which strives for perfection while becoming imperfect. Could I raise a child in such a dystopia? I would try, if Wendy approved our application.

That morning, however, I needed the news. I planned on teaching the passive, of which a newspaper provides more topical examples than a textbook. In the passive, the subject is not the 'doer' of the verb, although that doesn't get humankind off the hook. The news is just as dire, though what's happened is more salient than who made it happen. It's a grammatical structure (to be + past participle) used in formal fields such as academic writing or news reports. The difficulty for students is that, in newspapers, the auxiliary verb 'be' is often dropped from the headline for reasons of space and sensation, making the news cryptic, if no less criminal. My paper that day contained an excellent example: BANKS BAILED OUT BY DARLING. The UK economy may have been finished but my lesson on the passive had the perfect start.

This thorough approach to lesson preparation was a result of the new importance of my job. With Sarah sidelined and our savings up in smoke, my constipated stipend was our bread and butter. I had bought those new shoes of Rhonda's staffroom-door decree, and hoped to show my boss an ounce of overdue effort. I was even considering doing a DELTA (Diploma in English Language Teaching to Adults) and turning the lark into a career.

I was scanning the front page and underlining examples of the passive when a small tract of text in the bottom corner caught my eye – the lead to a story continued elsewhere to allow space for the Longines advertisement. ALLOTMENT THEFT SOARS hollered the title, not an example of the passive but enough to make me active. I raced to page eight and read, heart in mouth:

> A spate of thefts at inner-city allotments is being blamed on the Credit Crunch. Police and local officials in the London Borough of Lambeth say they have seen a tenfold rise in allotment crime as more and more people struggle with household bills in times of recession. Once a target for petty vandals, allotments now represent a source of free vegetables for more sophisticated thieves . . .

And on it went. The scrimpers weren't spending less on wine or whisky; it was veggies they were leaving off their shortened shopping lists, then helping themselves to the healthy spoils of my hobby. I wasn't concerned about the masses stealing my marrows; it was the ten-thousand-pound Tesco bag that had me worried. Despite my anxiety I couldn't help but laugh at the thought that, if Yoon Pong had written the article, Britain would be waking up to learn that vegetable buggery was on the rise. Now that would be an unexpected consequence of the Credit Crunch.

Since burying the money and my suggestion she kill time, Eva hadn't been seen at school. I supposed she was taking me literally as usual and had decided to ride out the week Rhonda was on holiday, spending as much quality time with Zeus as possible to make up for the ensuing detachment. I'd been hoping she'd come to school, if not to prepare her for the upcoming test, to discuss the subterranean stash and arrange for her to have it. In light of the morning news I vowed to visit my allotment after work that very day and take Eva the money at her host family's house. Perhaps it was enough to enable her to study architecture.

As part of my bid to become unsackable I was in class before the bell rang. I may have become punctual but my students still dallied, wandering in late as every other morning. 'Anyone who comes late from now on will find the door shut and locked,' I warned. No more Mr Nice Guy.

After a warm-up game, which with the drop in temperature was living up to its billing in more ways than one, I cut out the headline and stuck it on the board. BANKS BAILED OUT BY DARLING. Students had five minutes to guess its meaning. At the starter's pistol they reached for their dictionaries, which in this case only made things worse. Breaking English into bite-sized pieces often makes it more difficult to swallow. Like a mosaic, focusing on constituent parts renders the whole indecipherable. *Banks* was easy enough. *Bailed* had them squinting until I told them to think of it as a phrasal verb to be joined with *out*. *By* posed few problems, except for Natalina who was looking for *good* before it and *e* after. The biggest stir, however, was caused by *Darling*, which seemed somewhat appropriate.

'I got it!' declared Ulrica, as though playing bingo. 'Banks are not going to prison anymore because of love.'

Hmm . . . not far off, though her cumbersome headline would leave little room for the Longines ad.

'Nice try, Ulrica. Keep going.'

I pointed out the capital 'D' in *Darling*.

'Is name!' twigged Sibylla.

When I held up the chancellor's photo they were shocked.

'How is possible to have white hair and black eyebrow?' inquired Natalina.

'Can we stick to the point?'

'Vot means 'eyebrow'?' asked Ulrica.

The only part of your body you haven't pierced, I thought, while indicating my own undisciplined examples.

'How to spell?' asked Doughnut.

I wrote it on the board, followed by /ībrow/ for Jean-Paul.

'I haf friend like zis,' said Ulrica. 'But he change colour himself.'

'*D*yed.'

'No, he alive but he change with, er, like shampoo but colour.'

Never mind.

Giuseppe's face looked typically mischievous. 'I wonder what colour is this man's . . . how to say?'

Ludmila sniggered.

'Now what does the headline mean?' I persisted.

'Means,' said Yoon Pong, 'that maybe not so difficult for me open bank account anymore.'

After its somewhat tangential beginning, my lesson on the passive was painstakingly direct. By its arduous end the class knew the construction inside out and had hours of homework just to make sure. The fact they cheered the bell like high-school students showed they clearly weren't enamoured with the new me.

'You change,' said Yoon Pong.

'You've changed!' I corrected.

They filed out like emperor penguins on the march.

After school I dashed home and collected Claude before driving like a Hollywood cop to Fitzroy Park. There wasn't time to wait until dark; the article made it sound as though my carrots were the Crown Jewels. Though peaceful, the allotments were as crowded as I had seen them; either everyone read *The Times* or they didn't have jobs to go to. I remember thinking that if the Credit Crunch turned more people to simple pastimes and pleasures then it wouldn't be all bad. I could see tomorrow's headline – FROM YUPPIE TO YOKEL. How would my charges go deciphering that?

I zigzagged up the slope to my overgrown patch and ordered my dog dig where X (well, the plastic pot) marked the spot. 'Don't suppose you'd rent him out!' hollered an old man resting on his shovel three plots down. I smiled tepidly and waved but thought better of engaging in idle chat; didn't want him wandering over. When the sound of Claude's digging changed from damp earth to dry plastic I tugged on his collar and pulled him away, kneeling down and using my own paws to finish the job. I scratched at the ground as though it were an instant lottery ticket. Soon the prize appeared, white smile in dark earth, then vertical blue stripes and the phrase *Every Little Helps*. I am a believer in the green revolution but confess, on that occasion, to relief that the Tesco bag wasn't biodegradable.

I withdrew the plump parcel and dusted off the dirt. Our underground investment may have lacked the returns of those stashed in John's hedge, though they did seem more secure. I put the prize in the bottom of another plastic bag before plucking some carrots and putting them on top to disguise the haul. Then

I locked the shed, nodded at the old man and zigzagged my way back down towards the gate.

'Lightning visit,' commented the fogey.

I held up the bag, carrot tops overflowing.

'Wife's making soup,' I said. 'Pot's on the boil.'

For the second time I travelled anxiously to Eva's London lodgings, and for the second time it was to return precious goods. I drove less hysterically than I had driven to the allotment; the money was safe and I didn't want to attract attention. I wondered if anyone had ever paid a speeding ticket with carrots. The way Sterling was going it wouldn't be long. I couldn't remember the precise address so I drove to the bus stop near West Hampstead tube and retraced the route I had taken with Zeus. When I eventually stood outside Eva's door I was so nervous I didn't think I had it in me to press the bell, although the bloodhound unblocked that impasse by barking at my silhouette in the frosted glass.

Ding-dong!

No turning back.

The sounds of a chair pushed back on a wooden floor and footsteps coming towards the door. The approaching shadow was too large to be Eva. I considered running. The latch clicked. She was tall and attractive, snappily dressed: designer half-glasses, pleated trousers, soft pink blouse and lilac pullover tied over her shoulders. With my scruffy hair and clothes I looked more like her dog, who recognised me and wagged his tail; pat them once and they never forget.

'Well, it appears Hercules knows you,' said the woman, 'but I don't believe I've had the pleasure.'

She eyed my bag while waiting for a response. Carrots covered the cash. I must have looked homeless.

'I'm, er, Eva's English teacher,' I said. 'I'm sorry to disturb you. Is Eva at home?'

'I'm Angelique,' she said, ignoring my question and offering the manicured fingertips of a limp hand. 'Have you been teaching the names of vegetables?'

I overdid the laughter in an attempt to make friends.

'I'm on my way home,' I said. 'I, er, would have left them in the car but I didn't want my dog to eat them.'

Awkward silence as Angelique pondered what kind of car didn't have a boot. Hercules pruned his front paw. The pads were not worn. Cushy life for some. No wonder he was plump.

'Why don't you come in?' said Angelique, stepping aside. 'Go on through to the kitchen. I presume you know your way around?'

A loaded invitation to explain Hercules's familiarity.

'Not really,' I defended. 'I just dropped some textbooks off for Eva once when she was ill.'

'Home delivery,' she mocked. 'That's quite a service your school offers. I'm pleased to hear my money has been going to good use.'

Zeus ran in from the garden and hugged his mother's left leg. Then he pointed at me from safety. 'Teacher,' he said.

My game was up. I would have confessed to everything but Angelique's mind was elsewhere suddenly. She seemed irritable. Looked at her gold watch and grimaced as though it had stopped.

'I need a drink,' she declared. 'Care to join me?'

I looked at my own watch, if only in search of an excuse not to accept her surprise invitation.

'I . . . er . . . I shouldn't. My dog's in the car and I just need to see Eva quickly.'

She eyed the carrots again.

'We feed her, you know.'

Again I overdid the laughter.

'I'm sure you do. I'm sure you do. It's just she hasn't been at school for the past few days and I need to tell her about an upcoming test that I don't want her to miss.'

'Couldn't have sent her a message?'

'I was passing and thought I'd drop in.'

As justifications go it was as lame as her old dog.

With her son clinging to her thigh as though in a three-legged race, Angelique hobbled with Zeus to the kitchen bench. An LCD screen had been built into the wall by the fridge. She turned it on and found Zeus a cartoon. Then she walked to a free-standing wine rack by the lounge and pulled out a bottle of pricey-looking red.

'Is Eva a good student?' she asked, twisting the corkscrew.

'Ah, yes, yes . . . she tries very hard and she's making good progress.' It seemed a rather twisted take on a parent–teacher meeting. 'She worries about holding up the other students. She's such a sweet girl.'

'No argument from me on that score,' agreed Angelique. 'She's a sweetie alright.' Did I detect a tone of jealous sarcasm, or was her boss being sincere? 'And very attractive,' she added, catching my eye deliberately as she handed me a crystal wineglass and indicated for me to have a seat.

I followed orders, keeping the carrots close. Silence was uncomfortable. I sipped my wine but didn't taste it.

'Right then,' I said. 'So . . . is Eva about?'

Angelique took a swift sip and looked at her watch again.

'I'm afraid not,' she replied, 'and may not be for some time.'

I tried not to sound surprised, but my acting ability was limited to the slapstick performance of new vocabulary in class.

'Oh, really? And why's that?'

She took another swift sip as though her ability to talk was powered by alcohol.

'Because she's gone back to Prague.'

My eyes darted. Again I tried and failed to sound unsurprised.

'Oh . . . right, well, no need to bother you further then.'

'At first I was angry,' she continued, picking at the wine label with a medium-length fingernail. 'She left me in the lurch with Zeus and I've had to organise time off work at short notice. It's not a good time to be taking . . .' Zeus turned the television up too loud. Angelique shot a stern look at her son. 'But then I realised Eva had actually done me a favour by making me spend more time with Zeus.'

Why was she telling me all this? It was as though she'd had some deep-rooted realisation and was talking to a shrink rather than to a stranger. I gulped the wine, half listening, half wondering why Eva had shot through.

Or perhaps she was lonely.

'He's a lovely boy,' I said. 'You're very lucky.'

'We're lucky because of Eva. This family would fall apart without her. She's a miracle worker. Do you know, I wouldn't be surprised if she invented her excuse just to bring me closer to my son?'

I didn't doubt her theory.

'What was her excuse, may I ask?'

'There's the English teacher in you,' observed Angelique. 'Most people would have said "can I ask?"'

I wasn't sure if she was flattering or poking fun. And I was drinking too quickly to care – a combination of nerves and the desire to flee.

'Well, may I?'

She stared into her glass, swirling the wine as though searching for sediment.

'Something about needing to see her brother.'

My mouth fell open. Angelique filled hers.

'But her brother's . . .' I stopped dead. Perhaps Angelique didn't know the truth. Perhaps *I* didn't know the truth. But if Eva had been honest at the casino and her brother had taken his own life, then what did her need to see him imply? Angelique spoke of Eva's concern for the lives of others. Why then would she waste her own? Had the affair with Tim caused her to contemplate suicide? Perhaps he hadn't known when to stop. I quaffed a mouthful. My heart was pounding so hard I felt sure that Angelique could hear it.

'When did she leave?'

'This morning. Told us at seven and was gone by eight.'

'Did she say anything else?'

'No, but she'd been behaving strangely before she left.'

'Strangely?'

'She was distant, distracted . . . Though if truth be told I often saw her like that. I think it was because of her father.'

'Her father? What happened to her father?'

Angelique sat up straight as though exiting a trance. Her silver belt buckle caught the light for a second before her natural slouch saw her blouse conceal it once again.

'Oh, it's probably not for me to say, but he died shortly before she came to London.'

Perhaps it was because Angelique was a doctor that she was capable of delivering such dramatic news without raising an eyebrow. My own eyebrows, however, were surely scraping the ceiling.

'Do you know how her father died?'

Zeus's mother looked squarely at me as she sipped her blood-red wine.

'Car accident apparently.'

I stared out the window in quiet contemplation. Why had Eva only told me about the death of her brother? She had mentioned her anger with her father and that he was, in her words, 'horrible'. But it was strange that she had skipped the detail of his death. Perhaps it was too traumatic for her to tell.

'So she didn't give you any indication when she'd be back?' I asked, before remembering I was merely her English teacher. 'I mean, should I expect her for the class test next week?'

'I'm afraid I don't know. I was too busy on the phone to work, organising patients and whatnot. Tim – my husband – took her to the airport.' She looked at her watch. 'But he should have been back ages ago.'

I looked at my own watch, drained my glass and stood up.

'Right, well, I'd better—'

'If you don't mind me saying so,' interrupted Angelique, 'you seem more like a detective than a teacher.'

I swallowed nervously.

'What makes you say that?'

She swirled her wine again. Looked out the window. Brushed her black fringe off her eyes.

'Oh, I don't know, the way you've turned up, the questions you've asked. You seem like a man on a mission of some sort.'

'I'm sorry for the invasion. I didn't mean to disturb. When Eva gets back from Prague please just tell her to try not to miss the test.' I picked up my bag and moved to the kitchen. 'Thanks for the wine,' I said, placing my glass on the table.

Angelique looked at her watch again and reached for her BlackBerry.

'Bye, Zeus,' I said, gently touching his head. When the boy looked up I noticed a bruise on his temple, a plum-coloured circle, faint yet distinct. And his eyes, trained upwards towards me, like those of a dog, seemed sad.

I wanted to embrace him but thought better of it. Angelique dialled and put the phone to her diamond-studded ear. I walked towards the corridor.

'I'll see myself out.'

My host didn't reply. As I pulled open the front door I heard Angelique say to her son, 'Where on earth has your father got to?'

'Father got to,' repeated Zeus.

18

Tense

*In memory of Peter Stevens,
musician and dreamer,
whose favourite place was Primrose Hill.
1 February 1981 – 9 June 2007*

There was pigeon poo on the plaque: a freshly fallen stain which only missed my shoulder because – as Sarah points out – I am far too hunched for a man of my age. I was relieved that it missed, until I remembered it is said to bring luck and brushed my sleeve against it.

It didn't.

For the second time in as many mornings the front page made me frantic and I resolved to halt my newfound habit of actually reading my morning paper rather than heading straight for the comfort of the crossword. BANKER FOUND DEAD shouted the headline to the story, which went on to sketch the suspected suicide of a young investment banker, an unnamed father of one, though foul play was yet to be completely ruled out given his black Range Rover and body had been discovered at . . . my jaw dropped . . . an inner-city allotment.

Mouth dry. Mind racing.

'*Where on earth has your father got to?*'

Angelique had been concerned for her husband's whereabouts, but surely he had since turned up safe and sound. I chose to ignore the uncomfortable coincidence and put the sad death down to the Credit Crunch, to the anonymous actions of a man who had lost everything and forgotten that everything was in fact the people who loved him. Distressed – and somewhat disrespectfully – I didn't finish his story, scampering instead for the safety of 6 across.

Committed by crude Mr Rude (6).

It was *murder*.

Not often am I aware of the blood in my veins. Rarely is my heartbeat louder than London. Never is my hand too shaky to fill the grid.

I tried to calm down, to reason things out, to ignore the coincidence of today's clues to yesterday's questions. There was no way. It was simply too far-fetched. Even if Eva did have a pressing problem with Tim, I had assured her it wouldn't be for much longer. So why had she suddenly shot through? She'd said nothing about returning to Prague during our night out. She'd seemed happy, before taking to the darkness . . .

'*Just kill time, Eva.*'

Sunny, but I was shivering. Must have been the fear – they say it can trigger ill health. Ten years I'd been teaching. Ten years I'd been checking that students understood my instructions. The one time I forgot could cost me everything. Had my mysterious Czech student, hitherto clumsy in comprehension, killed Tim rather than time? Surely, no matter how wronged or mistreated, that sweet girl wasn't capable of such a desperate scenario.

Each time I told myself there was an innocent explanation, my mind joined the hazy dots of happenstance. Work would be the best distraction. I stood up slowly and looked at my dog – the only witness to the conversation that night at the allotment. '*Tak jdeme!*' I said softly. Claude obeyed my clumsy command. His Czech was coming along, as was he, faithfully down the hill at my heels.

■

I taught a lesson on the past continuous that I had already taught a few weeks earlier, though only Sibylla seemed to realise. After picking up Claude, I rushed to the Princess for medicinal purposes. There was only one man capable of giving me sound advice, and, like most father figures, he would dispense it whether I asked for it or not.

Walter raised his glass. A clink as it met mine. 'To dogs' ears and the will o' the wisp; to keenness, and light, and the speed of a horse.' Elbows up. Ambrosia down. Despite my anxiety, I decided to play it cool.

The Princess of Wales was her warm, old-world and welcoming self. An 'Alright?' from Tony, nods from dusty regulars, a cracked mirror, fraying carpet in the corner and the front page of the *New York Times* heralding the sinking of the *Titanic*. It was a sedate step back from the Palm Palace casino, and after the hyperactive drinks of the past few days it felt good to be back in the saddle of a Spitfire.

Walter was looking more lively than usual. His head seemed shinier, his moustache more pert and his eyes less marinated in whisky. Had Rhonda mentioned the return of his teaching wings, or was my eye compensating for the fact that for once I looked more dishevelled than my drinking partner?

After his toast, and in keeping with tradition, Walter pulled a random tome from the shelves in our triangular snug at the rear of the pub. As he held up the book to share its spiel, I saw the cover and quaked at the coincidence of his choice. *Opal Fever* by Nicholas Miles. Was it a random selection or was Walter on to me?

The orator sipped his Spitfire, donned half-glasses and waited while Claude curled up on the carpet. Walter loved a captive audience. Lonely men often do. Then he spoke with signature gravitas:

The ambush of an opal buyer on a remote road in the Australian interior is the starting point for this extraordinary novel. From that moment on the action never falters as the hunch-backed Chilla and his young companion Snow escape with a hundred and fifty thousand dollars worth of gems.

Walter paused for a sip. 'Chilla and Snow, eh?' he quipped. 'Cool customers, I'll bet.'

Burying the swag, they shack up in a mining settlement to wait for the hue and cry to blow over.

'Wonderful,' cried Walter, reinterring the book in its gap. 'The "hue and cry". You wouldn't see that in a back-cover blurb these days. Amazing how nouns change with the times.'

'Indeed.'

I often thought it best just to agree with Walter.

'What would a publisher choose nowadays?' he pondered. 'The fuss . . . the ado . . . the hullabaloo?'

But my mind was elsewhere.

'I wonder if Chilla and Snow get away with it?' I said.

He exhumed the book and tossed it my way.

'Only one way to find out.'

Walter rose and walked towards the bar, stepping over Claude's tail with well-rehearsed ease.

'Do you know,' he said, turning, 'that when I get up at night to go to the bathroom my feet automatically allow for your dog's appendage?'

'What are you saying?'

'That I've missed you, dear boy.' He drank his dregs. 'That I've missed you.'

I watched Walter perform his refuelling routine and it struck me that he was more a creature of habit than Claude. He walked past the bar, wriggled two fingers in Tony's direction, stepped outside for a smoke, ogled passing women, pushed the door, topped up Tony's coffers and then walked carefully towards our chairs, balancing the drinks the way a father might balance ice creams for his kids. Despite a shaky hand he never spilt a drop. He could have done it on a tightrope, and would if need be.

'I've got good news and bad news,' he said, sitting down. 'What would you like first?'

'I don't care.'

Walter pretended not to notice my sour mood.

'The bad news is that I've got to do a teacher-training session next week on the new twin-lamp, triple-lens overhead projectors and I haven't a Danny La Rue how the fuckers work.'

He pushed my drink in my direction.

'Don't worry – I'm sure Frank will step in and help out again.'

He opened the salted peanuts and spun the packet my way.

'But the good news is it will be my last IT exposé because Rhonda says I can start teaching again.'

I raised my glass.

'I'll drink to that.'

We sipped beyond the Plimsoll Line. The beer seemed colder and more refreshing than usual, though perhaps my mouth was drier.

'I've missed teaching desperately,' Walter continued. 'The mistakes mainly. I'd forgotten how poorly the Asians pronounce. I was chatting with a barely sentient boy from Beijing today who claimed there were six people in his *arsehole*.'

'What did he mean?'

'*Household*.'

Walter roared with laughter, stopping abruptly when he realised I hadn't joined in. He grabbed the nuts and tipped a handful to his mouth, washing them down with Spitfire. Then he combed the crumbs from his handlebar moustache, deliberately fastidious to emphasise my strange silence. His next move was uncharacteristically diplomatic.

'Something on your mind, dear boy?'

'Nothing out of the ordinary.'

'Bad day down the mines and yours?'

'Bog standard.'

Walter softened his voice.

'Fall asleep in your own lesson again?'

I strengthened mine.

'Who told you that?'

He scratched his neck. Contorted his face with reluctant delight.

'Ludmila.'

It was like finding the missing piece of the puzzle when cleaning behind the couch.

'Oh my god – the old Rover in her photos. It's yours!'

'She found it in the garage.'

'But it doesn't even go!'

'And don't you dare tell her. I'm stalling her, as it were.'

'You old rake. So you're the "English gentleman of dreams". A regular Don Juan DeWalter. Mind telling me how it happened?'

'Hardly Mills and Boon, I'm afraid. My lesson on rhyming slang was, if I may say so, a cracker, and she simply stayed behind after class for another.'

'Stayed after class or *strayed* after class?'

Walter nodded at two regulars as they opened the door, as though granting them permission to step through it.

'I tell you what, dear boy, my old Rover might not go, but Little Lud sure does.' He imitated her Ukrainian accent. 'More hard. More fast. More deep. She needs a lesson on comparatives. And, if I may say so, superlatives.'

Walter laughed at his own puerile erudition. I hadn't listened beyond his mention of the pet name.

'Little Lud?!'

'It's what I—'

'No!' I interrupted, raising both hands. 'Spare me, please.'

'She's not as sugary as she seems,' continued Walter. 'She's actually quite savoury when you get to know her.'

'At least you can bin the inflatable doll.'

'Just as well. She was so up and down.'

He sniggered. We sipped. To passers-by we must have looked as endangered as the fading photographs clinging to the walls.

'So did you buy her the Louis Vuitton handbag?'

Walter rolled his eyes.

'Guilty as charged. She deserved a present for putting up with my moustache. Just don't tell her it's a fake.'

'The moustache?'

'The bag.'

Our drinks were disappearing.

'Well,' he summarised, 'one thing's for sure: Rhonda couldn't complain about me not doing my bit for student rapport.'

By asking Walter to cover my lesson I had basically introduced the unconventional couple and would no doubt be asked to be best man at their wedding.

'I hope you know she's looking for a husband,' I warned him.

'And she's looking high and low,' he said. 'Must say I prefer low.'

Once again he laughed alone.

'I'd be careful if I were you.'

'Oh, don't worry, dear boy. I'm just going out with a bang, as it were. Doing my bit for foreign relations. Putting a salacious sword to my inner Eurosceptic.'

A police car blazed past. He waited for its siren to fade. I raised my pint. The coaster came with it.

'Is it Sarah?' he said abruptly, as though the siren had changed the subject.

'Is what Sarah?'

'The motive for your mood.'

'No. Nothing's really changed. She's given up on conceiving naturally and has her heart set on adoption. She believes the Credit Crunch was divine intervention and that she's meant to be a stay-at-home mum all of a sudden.'

Walter threw his hands in the air. 'Isn't that what you've always wanted?'

'Well, sort of. But not in such circumstances. And not adoption.'

'What's wrong with adoption?'

I sipped for composure.

'I don't deny there are plenty of children out there needing homes. I'm more than aware of that. I simply want to bring up my own child rather than someone else's. Glen said he loves it when people say Jack looks like him. If we adopt, that would never happen.'

Walter placed his pint on the table, rendering what he had to say more profound.

'I've never regarded you as vain, dear boy. A narcissist, upon reflection.'

'I'm not vain – I just want my son or daughter to resemble me.'

'It would resemble you in other ways.'

'Which other ways?'

'I don't know – character, personality . . . Perhaps it would inherit your distrust of the ambitious.'

'I have ambition.'

'To do what?'

'Right now, to give up teaching, if I'm not forced to give it up.'

For the first time that afternoon, Walter chuckled at something he himself hadn't said, although I wasn't trying to be funny.

'Well I hate to be the bearer of bad news, dear boy, but there's not much else you can do. The beauty of Sarah's profession is that she can turn to teaching if need be. We can't turn to business when the wind changes direction.'

'Am I a good teacher, Walter?'

'When you stay awake.'

'Am I a good man?'

'I'm afraid that's an oxymoron in my opinion. As Samuel Johnson said, "He who lives like a beast takes away the pain of being a man." But you're as good as they come, dear boy.'

Tony delivered two more drinks and a ham sandwich Walter had ordered. His tattooed forearm took the weight of the plate. I assumed the Roman numerals were his birthday but never thought to ask, nor did I have a chance as the brawny barman, all paunch and ponytail, rushed back to his waist-high wooden booth.

Afternoon was turning to evening and the bar was filling with professional people with professional thirsts. Two attractive young women sat down at the table near ours. Both were overdressed for the Princess, despite her being royalty, and were presumably on their way further afield. Their scents were strong, their faces painted, everything but their ring fingers appeared to have been prettied in some way. They resembled birds of paradise, flaunting rainbow wings.

'Anyway,' I continued, 'there's no point us discussing it because Sarah has already decided. She wants you to write me a character reference for the adoption agency, saying you've known me for a long time and that in your opinion I would make an excellent adoptive father.'

Walter smiled. His teeth were as yellow as Ludmila's. At least they had something in common.

'How can I write such a letter after what you've just told me?'

'Fine,' I replied childishly. 'I'll get Yoon Pong to write it for me.'

My turn to chuckle alone. It was a most unusual afternoon.

Walter had become self-conscious since the women arrived. He puffed his chest out, tweaked his whiskers, and when it came to stolen glances he was a kleptomaniac. Of the three of us at our table only Claude couldn't have cared less, and, to Walter's dismay, the dog got the admiring looks. Perhaps that's why he misplaced his patience.

'Oh, for fuck's sake,' he snapped, 'are you going to tell me or not?'

'Tell you what?'

'Why you're Sebastian Blue rather than Sebastian Pink?'

I sat back in my chair. Claude lifted his head while I changed position before returning it to the top of my foot. The only polish my shoes ever saw was the soft stroke of his snout.

'I'm worried about a student of mine.'

Walter narrowed his eyes and widened his interest.

'Lolita again?'

'Eva.'

'Go on.'

Our pints provided punctuation.

'She's done something of a runner to Prague.'

The furrows on Walter's brow converged like a low pressure cell on a weather map.

'So? Isn't she *from* Prague?'

'Yes, but . . .'

'But?'

I tossed him my *Times*. Tapped my finger on the article. For once Walter read quietly to himself while I waited on his verdict. It reminded me of when my second father used to read my school report cards, before asking my second mother why they were wasting so much money on private tuition. Both were accountants. Neither could spare the time to teach me mathematics. As a result, we had dramatically different interpretations of what it meant 'to count'.

Walter put the paper on the table theatrically and placed his glasses on it like a paperweight. Then he opened his sandwich, sprinkled salt on the ham, took a bite and spoke with his mouth full.

'Unlike you, dear boy, I'm no good at puzzles, so would you mind filling in the blanks for me?'

We both swallowed, though for different reasons.

'I'm worried the dead man might be Eva's boss.'

He took another bite.

'Why would it be Eva's boss?'

'Investment banker. Black Range Rover. Inner-city allotment.'

'There must be thousands of tossers who'd fit the bill.'

'Perhaps, but when I spoke to his wife yesterday she seemed anxious about his overdue absence.'

'Coincidence, dear boy. Coincidence. You've been reading too many thrillers.'

'My crossword says it was murder.'

'You've been doing too many crosswords.'

'You're the one who taught me to read into words. Eva means giver of life, you said.'

'Precisely – not taker of life.'

'Fact is stranger than fiction.'

'Not in this case.'

I changed tack.

'I found out Eva's father died shortly before she came to London.'

'That is tragic, but of no relevance.'

I leant towards Walter and stubbornly continued to press my theory.

'I told her to "kill time". Perhaps she thought I said "kill Tim".'

Walter washed down his mouthful with Spitfire.

'That's absurd. Why would she want to kill him?'

'Because you were right – he's the man in your vile joke, and she's the compromised au pair.'

'If that's true then I'm sorry to hear it. But why would you tell her to kill time?'

'Because when Rhonda gets back from holiday I was going to get her to intervene, to find Eva a new family.'

Walter thought aloud for a moment. Joined the dots of the disaster.

'So you told her to kill time. And she's gone and killed Tim?'

I nodded.

'Got yourself a *Misnomer* Murder there, dear boy.'

Walter laughed louder than he ever had before. So loud that Tony looked over from the bar.

'So what would you do in my position?'

'Quit talking bollocks and buy my friend Walter a drink.'

'But the banker's body was found at some allotments. I unwittingly told Eva that an allotment was the perfect place to dispose of a body.'

'Why in God's name would you tell her that?'

'I was referring to Bullseye.'

'And now you think you've hit one.'

His tongue probed a missing morsel.

'I even showed her my allotment.'

He glanced at the newspaper.

'You forgot to teach her the verb "to bury".'

Unlike the ham in his sandwich, Walter was on a roll.

'I'm serious, Walter. She's misinterpreted idioms in the past. I'm not saying she'd be foolish enough to think it a serious suggestion. But if she had been contemplating a drastic solution . . . revenge. And if he went too far – perhaps in the car . . .' I tapped the paper. 'In the Range Rover.'

'Good job you didn't tell her to "bite his head off".'

He grinned again.

'So you think all this is a joke and that I shouldn't investigate?'

'Investigate?! Blimey, if it is how you imagine it is, you'll be the one under investigation. I mean, you gave her the idea. You're practically an accomplice.' He took a bite and a sip and thought aloud. 'Bastard banker. Probably saw her as his bonus.'

Tony brought over two more Spitfires. Our table resembled a World War II airfield after a bombing raid. Then he somehow managed to weave his fingers like an octopus around our empties before picking them up and turning to head back to the bar.

We watched him leave. Then Walter raised his pint.

'To dogs' ears,' he declared, 'and the will o' the wisp; to keenness, and light, and the speed of a *hearse*.'

'A *hearse*?'

'Whoops,' jibed Walter. 'Sorry, burnt the toast.'

I reached for my newspaper and put *Opal Fever* back in its place.

'I'm pleased my predicament is providing you with entertainment. I'll work out my next move on my own.'

'Look, if Eva's killed her boss then I will personally misinterpret the idiom "eat my hat". But if you're really worried, why don't you take a leaf out of *Opal Fever* and sit tight and wait for the hue and cry to blow over?'

Walter giggled once again and stuffed his sandwich into his face.

'Or . . .' I thought aloud, finishing my drink and waking Claude.

'Or?' echoed Walter.

But my dog and I were on our way to the door.

■

The admissions officer was tidying her desk, preparing to head home for another BBC evening with her cat Crispin. 'Can I help you, Sebastian?' she snapped, as though that engagement were pressing.

'You look nice, Audrey.'

'Don't be ridiculous. What do you want?'

'Right, well, sorry to hold you up but I, er, was hoping to get the address of a student of mine.'

I tapped a paradiddle on her desk as though it was as simple as that. Audrey fingered the silver brooch on her blouse.

'I thought I told you . . .'

'It's a genuine emergency, Audrey. I promise.'

She sighed heavily, opened her filing cabinet and put her half-glasses back on.

'Name,' she barked.

'Er . . . Eva Kalivkova.'

She paused, frowned, looked at me.

'Has she moved since the last time I gave it to you?'

'That was her London address. Now I need her home address in the Czech Republic.'

Audrey lowered her head and raised her green eyes over her glasses.

'Do you know what you're doing, Sebastian?'

'Not really. I'm either about to save someone's life or make the biggest mistake of mine.'

'My, my,' she said. 'That *is* an emergency.'

She scribbled on a piece of paper and handed it to me while turning the other way in an attempt to confuse her conscience. I thanked the back of her head and ran for the door.

'Sebastian,' she called after me.

'Yes, Audrey?'

Her sad smile.

'Good luck.'

How she would have loved an emergency of her own.

■

Sarah was cooking when I got home, if 'cooking' is the right verb to describe cremating chicken, chasing brussels sprouts behind the microwave, slicing her finger, burning her wrist and bleeding onto Nigella's cover portrait on *How to Be a Domestic Goddess*.

'Mmm,' I said, sniffing the sacrifice. 'Smells delicious.'

'Oh, piss off, Sebastian. It's a disaster. This Lawson bitch makes it look a cinch.'

'You'll have to tone down that language when a little one arrives.'

'*If* a little one arrives.'

'*When.*'

We kissed politely like two hens pecking seed.

'I'm no good at this housewife thing,' lamented Sarah.

'You don't have to dish up haute cuisine. Meat and two veg will keep us ticking over.'

I stole a sip from her wineglass, which I doubted was part of the recipe.

'What's in the bag?' asked Sarah.

To my horror I realised that the Tesco bag containing the loot was poking out of my coat pocket. I had deemed it the safest place and carried it around all day, citing flu when my students asked why I wouldn't even take it off to teach.

'Oh, I, er, brought some baby carrots from the allotment.'

'Why don't we toss them in?' said Sarah, reaching for the bag.

'No!' I exclaimed, grabbing her arm. 'Let me wash them properly first. Strange pesticides at those allotments.'

Sarah opened a cupboard and grabbed the breadcrumbs, presumably to embalm the chicken, only the packet hadn't been properly closed and they scattered over the floor.

'That's it!' she cried, tossing the box in the sink. 'This just isn't me!'

'Hey,' I said, pulling her into my arms. 'It's just breadcrumbs. Claude will hoover them up in a heartbeat.'

Sarah sobbed like a child against my chest.

'I'll never be the woman you want. I'll never be a good mother.'

I stroked her hair.

'You *are* the woman I want and you *will* be a good mother. We'll both just need to learn new skills.'

Her chest heaved and shuddered. Tears flowed as though a dam had burst.

'Listen, Sarah, I've been thinking. Let's have that holiday after all. Maybe we need some time away to see if adoption's really for us.'

Her sobbing stopped.

'I thought you were busy at work.'

'To hell with work – let's have a second honeymoon. We'll drop everything and leave tomorrow.'

My wife freed herself from my embrace, wiped her eyes and looked into mine.

'Where would we go?'

I avoided her gaze.

'Oh, I don't know – wherever you want. Rome, Paris . . .' I cleared my throat. 'Prague.'

19

Second person plural

Sarah and I packed separate suitcases. She had too many shoes and I had to hide a small fortune among my socks; Her Majesty on all those banknotes would have to hold her nose. I sure hoped British Airways didn't lose my luggage.

After plumping for Prague – thanks to some gentle persuasion – Sarah had booked our entire trip online. I dropped Claude at Walter's, who said he didn't want to know what I was up to but that I could leave my hound with him as long as necessary because he was happy to have something to torture the squirrels with other than his slingshot. Ludmila was in the bath with a glass of wine when I called in.

The dawn flight was the cheapest. We were at Heathrow before the sun rose reluctantly above the horizon only to then disappear behind cloud. Sitting together in the departure lounge, I denied Sarah's search for my hand because my palms were sweaty. Like Claude awaiting his afternoon walk, my ears were trained on the tannoy, not for our flight to be called but fearing my name might be broadcast. If security inspected my suitcase I would be accused of smuggling money out of the country. Would a sane man risk gaol for someone who wouldn't bail him out?

To calm my nerves I had packed some light reading. Forget your Clive Cusslers, Danielle Steels and Dan Browns. My airport novel was penned by cult South Korean author Yoon Pong. What better way to kickstart a second honeymoon than by marking homework with your bride? I still hadn't read the critiques of English weather my students had written during the counselling session which ended so dramatically.

Beer Under Cherry Blossom
By Yoon Pong

In month of April, South Korean peoples have habit of pincic (picnic?) under cherry blossom. When I am student I play guitar in band. One day we get offer from beer company to play music at big stage cherry blossom party place. Of course, we accept, because reward would be lot of beer. Why not? We were teenagers. Beer most important thing.

The day out small show was success. We really enjoyed drinking during playing music, but I don't know if beer have good effect for quality of my guitar. Unfortunately we drink much because was weirdly strang don't care money. Suddenly one of my friends who is name Sung (I assumed he was the singer) fell down and froth at mouth. We called and shout his name but he couldn't answer. It was acute alcoholism. I never see before such strang station (a strange sensation?).

Eventually, Sung survive, because he had carried out lavage of his stomach. After that fear experience Sung don't stop drinking, but hasn't froth at mouth for five years.

PS Sorry Sebastian. I didn't write about England weather which was topic because you said no use swear word.

Sarah had saved enough flyer miles from her corporate days to earn us an upgrade; you can't blow *them* on a hedge fund. On boarding the plane Sarah peeled left while the unwashed masses and I filed right. Then I heard Sarah calling my name and realised I was supposed to have followed her.

The high-heeled hostess looked my jeans and faithful pullover up and down. Apparently you pay more for that pleasure. Sarah had the woman take her cashmere coat, ordered refreshments, then casually pressed some buttons to make her chair assume a yoga position. My wife was in her element, unrecognisable as the distraught woman I had scraped off the kitchen floor.

Sarah's father used to say that aeroplanes are coffins with wings which conveniently detach upon burial, and that if God had meant us to fly there would be a duty-free shop by the pearly gates. I shared his lack of faith in physics. I believe what goes up must come down, though not always when a person with stripes on their shoulders deems it the appropriate time. Launching through London cloud, which wisped over the wing like fairy-floss, I searched for a two-hour distraction. Recent digging at the allotment ruled out chewing my fingernails. Had we been flying with Ryanair I could have passed the time teaching the cabin crew English, though they probably would have charged *me* for the lessons. Instead I necked a Valium and watched Flightpath, wondering if the flame-coloured trail we were leaving across the Continent was cause for concern.

'It says here,' said Sarah, consulting her guidebook, 'that there's a bridge in Prague on the . . . *Certovka?* . . . canal where honey-mooners scratch their names onto a padlock which they then attach to the bridge's railings and toss the key into the canal as a sign of commitment.' She looked up at me. 'Should we do that, Seb?'

'I'm game if you are. We could use the padlocks from our suitcases.'

'Mine wouldn't be big enough to fit around the railings.'

'Don't worry,' I assured her. 'Mine is.'

Like Yoon Pong, Sarah had done her homework. She is nothing if not organised. Our hotel was perfectly situated – perched beneath Prague's castle and gazing across a Bohemian fairytale with menacing gothic touches. Soft autumn sun lit the constellation of gold orbs crowning 'the city of a thousand spires'. Imposing churches dwarfed quaint buildings which – with terracotta roofs, pastel facades and moustache-like awnings and windows – appeared to be made of gingerbread.

While Sarah freshened up after the flight, I went to the safe to store my stash along with her jewellery and our passports. The safe wasn't bolted to the wall but simply part of a chest of drawers small enough to be removed from the room by either thieves or underpaid housekeepers. I decided to put the Tesco bag in the bottom of my backpack and took it with us on our exploratory stroll.

'I'll meet you in the lobby!' I called to Sarah.

I showed Eva's address to the hotel receptionist, who pencilled the route on a complimentary map and said it was fifteen minutes from the city by tram. But I couldn't just conjure an excuse and wander off day-tripping on my own. I would have to choose my moment. That first day I didn't get it.

If Sarah did take up teaching she would be first pick for the social program. In one afternoon we managed to see most of the sights around Old Town Square, including the Mirror Chapel in the Klementinum, where Mozart played on a visit to Prague; the Jewish cemetery, whose higgledy-piggledy headstones reminded me of Walter's teeth; St Nicholas Church; Town Hall Tower; and, arguably Prague's biggest drawcard, the Astronomical Clock, which should be typed very carefully into Google in pre-trip planning.

On the hour, we stood among hordes of smartphone-wielding tourists as Christ led the twelve apostles on a procession and a hundred upturned nails stopped satanic pigeons pooping on the performance. A smiling skeleton then signalled time was up for Vanity, Greed and the Infidel. This star attraction offered little by way of distraction. With Eva's whereabouts and intentions unknown, reminders of death and time ticking away were the last thing I needed.

We found a café in a cobblestone lane and collapsed at an outdoor table; somehow even plastic chairs seem more charming on the Continent. As the waitress arrived to take our order I noticed her apron was longer than her skirt. Like Eva, though younger and visibly more self-confident, her beauty was natural, her hair blonde and her skin totally unblemished. Sarah's guidebook stopped short of listing the locals as an attraction, though it did suggest that Western men visited the city to satisfy devils as well as see saints.

The girl acknowledged us with a split-second smile and put her chewed pen to her order pad.

'What are you having, Seb?' asked Sarah, perusing her menu.

'*Pivo, prosím*,' I said to the waitress, handing back mine.

'What's that?' asked Sarah, looking up.

'Pint of lager.'

My wife rolled her eyes. 'Unadventurous as always.' Then she continued to browse the laminated sheet before curiosity got the better of her. 'Sebastian, how did you know the word for beer?'

I straightened a serviette.

'Oh, you know, you pick up linguistic morsels from your students. It's as close to perks as you get in language teaching.'

The waitress sighed impatiently and tapped her pen on her pad. Sarah tried to follow my lead.

'*Piv* . . . ?' she attempted.

'*Pivo, prosím*,' I said slowly.

'That's the one,' she said, giving up.

The waitress turned on her heel. Sarah moved our ashtray to the adjacent table and put her handbag on a spare chair. I anchored my backpack at my feet by threading a leg through its straps.

'So, what are your first impressions?' I asked, sounding as though I'd brought my work as placement officer on holiday, which in some ways I had.

'It's wonderful,' replied Sarah. 'Like a fairytale. Makes London feel rather dank and dirty.'

'Holiday eyes make any place look nicer than home.'

She placed her elbows on the table, folded her hands under her chin and stretched a dainty smile. 'Does that go for people too?'

'You are beautiful the world over,' I replied somewhat feebly.

We surveyed the cobblestone street: flowers in pots, a bicycle resting on a lamppost and postcard stands outside souvenir shops. Strange how silence was less conspicuous when we met than after we married.

'So,' said Sarah, breaking it, 'how are you getting on with that problem student of yours?'

Suddenly I preferred the silence.

'I, er, recruited Rhonda to take care of it.'

'Probably the best option. I'm proud of you, by the way.'

My smile was forced. My eyes evasive. I would have folded the serviette if I hadn't previously done so.

'Just doing my job.'

'Where was the student from again?'

The strap of my bag suddenly felt tight around my calf.

'Er, Hampstead.'

'I meant originally.'

'Oh, um, well . . . Prague, as a matter of fact.'

Sarah tilted her head to the left, like Claude when trying to decipher a command.

'Really? What a coincidence.'

I wished the beer would arrive so I would have something to do with my hands other than sit on them.

'Yes indeed, a coincidence.'

A car bumped along the street, which until then I thought was pedestrian-only. Its tyres seemed to make the cobblestones pop like bubble wrap.

'So,' I said, changing the subject, 'have you thought any more about the adoption?'

She fixed her hair in a ponytail with an elastic.

'Please don't ask me that, sweetheart.'

'Why not?'

'Let's talk about it over dinner. Somewhere romantic. Perhaps near the river with a Bohemian sunset.'

'Why can't we talk about it now?'

'I'd rather wait. It's not the right moment.'

'The right moment for what?'

Sarah leant forward. Took my hands in hers.

'To tell you.'

'To tell me what?'

'To tell you, Sebastian, that I'm . . .'

I nodded slightly, as I would have in class, to encourage the speaker to continue.

'That you're . . . ?'

She squeezed my hands and smiled.

'That I'm pregnant.'

I blinked as though momentarily blinded, perhaps by that Bohemian sunset. I was numb with mixed emotions: excitement, shock, fear, but above all, surprise. When words finally came they weren't the ones Sarah had expected.

'When did you find out?'

'Yesterday while you were at work.'

'So why the theatrics in the kitchen last night?'

'I wanted to see your reaction – to see if you really believed I would make a good mother.'

It didn't help the blinking.

'Strange way of going about it. Did I pass your little test?'

Her smile was genuine and contented.

'Perfectly.'

Sarah let go of my hands and sat back in her chair, putting her palms protectively on her belly. 'He or she is in there,' she said, glowing with pride.

'For how long have you been pregnant?'

It was like grading students, with a twist.

'Eight weeks.'

'Eight weeks?!'

'But, like I said, I only found out yesterday. I'd given up testing.' She leant towards me and whispered, 'Must have been that time before Walter's barbecue when I thought I wasn't ovulating.'

I sat back in my chair and digested the news.

'Your proficiency with numbers really has taken a battering lately.'

Sarah smiled.

'Perhaps, but I'll teach the little one maths if you don't mind. You can teach it English.'

We laughed together. It felt wonderful – food for an overdue future.

'I know we disagreed on how best to have a baby, Seb, but I would have eventually come round to trying IVF.'

'No you wouldn't. You would have adopted.'

She shook her head gently. Everything about her seemed more gentle suddenly. 'Wendy rang from the adoption agency. Said she couldn't proceed with our application.'

'Why not?'

She imitated Wendy's West Indian accent. "Your husband's heart isn't in it."'

Once again I had the perfect opportunity to tell my wife the truth about my parents. Once again I chose to ignore it. This was a moment to celebrate the future rather than dredge up the past.

'It's fitting we're in Prague,' I commented, 'because it was Kafka who said man's greatest achievement is to have a family.'

Sarah crossed her arms, shortening her sleeves and revealing the silver bracelet I had given her last Christmas.

'You really are a wealth of information on Czech language and culture.'

'Walter lent me a book called *Dearest Father* – Kafka's letter of lament to his insensitive dad. Given this news, I'll use it as a handbook for what not to do.'

Our beer arrived, as blonde as the girl who delivered it.

'I'm afraid we've changed our minds,' said Sarah. 'Could we have some champagne instead?'

The waitress frowned. There was clearly enough passing tourist trade not to worry about customer service.

'Don't worry,' I said, fishing my wallet from my pocket. 'My wife's not allowed to drink.'

Sarah smiled. I opened my wallet to pay and struggled to match the bill to the banknotes.

'Give it here,' said Sarah, leaning across and playfully snatching both.

'Sorry,' I said to the girl as my wife showed me up. 'I'm hopeless with numbers.'

'Probably soon we haf euro,' replied the waitress. 'Easier for everybody.'

'*Na zdraví*,' I said, raising my bottle. 'I'll drink to that.'

The waitress laughed, took the money and left.

'You make friends quickly,' commented Sarah, with a rising beer bubble of jealousy.

'It's called "building rapport" in the trade.'

'She's not your student.'

'She wouldn't need to be. Her English was excellent.'

'Well, I hope she's wrong,' said Sarah. 'The euro made cross-border transactions simpler but got rid of some beautiful banknotes. They were works of art. The Dutch guilder was my favourite because they were so big and colourful; like butterflies.'

'I'd be better with a barter system. My goat for your horse.'

'What would you charge for a lesson?'

'Two hares, an eel and a pheasant.'

Sarah laughed. I savoured the moment. Our relationship had suffered while trying for a baby but now that one had come along perhaps it was back on track.

'Speaking of banknotes,' she said, 'tomorrow we're going to the World Banknote Expo at the . . .' She turned to a dog-eared page of her guidebook. '. . . At the Náprstek Museum, or however you pronounce it.'

I took a sip of lightweight lager and wished it were Spitfire.

'Mind if I sit that one out?'

'Suit yourself. What will you do?'

I surveyed the ancient city.

'Oh, I don't know. Wander. Might call on Kafka, if he's in.'

The waitress brought my change, which I tried to savour for its artistic merits before placing it in my wallet.

Sarah sat up straight. Peered over her Pilsner.

'Have you still got my photograph in there?'

I took an enduring sip in the hope the question might be forgotten.

'Ah,' I announced, 'that's hit the spot.'

I licked the froth from my lip and read the logo on the glass.

'Sebastian Pink, I asked you a question: have you still got my photo in your wallet?'

'Um, well, no, as a matter of fact I haven't.'

Sarah sat up straighter than a meerkat.

'Why not? What happened to it?'

'I . . . er . . . lost it.'

'How could you lose the photo but not the wallet?'

'Do I have to answer that?'

'Yes.'

I recounted the story of my shy sperm sample and how her photo had relieved the blockage, only to then be forgotten on the cistern. Separated by a suppressed smile, Sarah's cheeks had reddened.

'So you wanked over my photo?!'

A young man at a nearby table turned his head. He didn't need English lessons either.

'Guilty, I'm afraid.'

Sarah reached across the table for my hand.

'Sweetheart,' she declared, 'I'm touched.'

20

The sentence

One river – the Vltava – flows under the Charles Bridge, while another river – of tourists – floods across it. Some of the artists who flank the half-kilometre crossing wait so patiently for a sale that they resemble the colonnade of Baroque statues standing with similar resolve behind them.

I watched Sarah cross the landmark bridge, light on her feet in flats rather than heels. Black tights, denim skirt, floral shirt. It was difficult to believe she was pregnant. I tried to imagine her with a baby bump. I tried to imagine the words my mother had used to tell my father all those years ago that I was on the way. Had she even bothered to tell him? Perhaps he'd already shot through.

Sarah turned to look at the castle on the hill, unaware that I was still watching her, unaware that my entrenched cynicism had turned to respect and admiration. In the few hours I had known she was pregnant she already seemed more like the Sarah I had fallen in love with. Her heart seemed as soft as her skin when we'd met all those years ago in *Flattery* — she in brand new business attire, me in my poorly ironed shirt. Perhaps it wasn't the predatory rungs on the career ladder that had hardened that heart; perhaps it was the fact she had been busy providing for her scarred yet self-indulgent husband, and for her dream of starting a family. Once again, Walter was right — she would never be as shallow as Margaret. She loved me and wanted to have my children. I was a lucky bastard after all.

My pregnant wife stopped briefly to admire a sketch by a local artist before being swept away with the current. I took a deep breath, turned slowly and set off on my mission, wondering if the World Banknote Expo boasted as many exhibits as I was carrying in my backpack.

■

Tram number 22 wasn't built for speed. I love trams (or 'blind trains' as Walter calls them) because they are slow, obedient and suggestive of sedate times; the perfect way to travel — any *other* day. I had three hours before I was due to meet Sarah at what had quickly become 'our café'. At the Malostranská station, conveniently located near Charles Bridge, I stepped aboard the slug and said, 'Vypich?' to the driver, who regarded me as though I'd asked if I could drive his tram. 'Vypich!' I repeated, in case he was hard of hearing. Passengers huffed as I reached for my map. '*Pomůžu Vám!*' barked an old man with a walking stick resting across his knees, for which I feared he may be about to improvise a use. I sat down in the disabled seat, which, linguistically speaking, seemed appropriate.

For a manacled means of transport our carriage twisted and turned as though unhinged, serpenting up the hill towards the castle then straightening once beyond. Cobblestones ceded to asphalt and soon the suburbs arrived, which were greener and more affluent-looking than I had expected. Houses were mostly modern and well maintained but some of the apartment blocks looked dreary and depressing. If the city were made of gingerbread, the suburbs were more savoury.

Břevnov, Prague 6, read Audrey's scribbled note. *Břevnov, Prague 6*, read the road sign. The butterflies in my stomach knew we were getting close and proved a better map than the one in my pocket. I tried to imagine Eva living in Prague 6: growing up, going to school, riding this very tram. I tried to picture her family, her friends, her sitting in a room somewhere getting nearer by the second, toying with the idea of moving to London, to Hampstead, to Primrose Hill, to The Future Perfect . . . Were I her father, would I have let her go? The further the tram travelled from Prague the more arbitrary I deemed Eva's place in my class. While treading them, life's paths seem frustratingly ungovernable. When looking back they seem as pre-destined as tram tracks.

'Vypich!' called a vague voice from behind me. I turned to see the old man with the cane across his knees who had shouted at me when I boarded. 'Vypich!' he said again, raising his stick and pointing out the window, narrowly avoiding the startled woman sitting opposite. I pressed the STOP button and nodded my thanks. His return smile was toothless.

I stepped off the tram into the middle of a main road. When the traffic eased I crossed the street and showed Audrey's scrap of paper to a passer-by who frowned and shook her head. It dawned on me how poorly prepared I was. Guidebooks abound for those visiting Prague's historic highlights, but there is no manual for those delivering casino spoils to its suburbs. Not even an appendix. Hadn't anyone else ever found themselves in this mess?

The next passer-by – a well-dressed man carrying an umbrella despite the clear sky – was more helpful. I hadn't a clue what he said but he pointed the umbrella towards a nearby set of traffic lights and then indicated a right turn. I obeyed his instructions to find myself staring down a residential avenue with front gardens on either side.

I was aware of my heart beating as I walked along it.

The next passer-by – a woman holding her young daughter's hand – spoke some English and said, 'One street more left,' which wouldn't have got her into an advanced class but was proficient in the circumstances. I came to the end of a row of houses and a view down the valley towards Prague. The wind was fresh but the sun warmed the vista of orange roofs and golden spires. I felt hope, anxiety, sadness, excitement . . . and a very long way from Chalk Farm.

Then I saw it – Na Probuzení – the street on Audrey's note. A surge of nerves shot through me. I needed number forty-seven. A three-legged ginger cat had been sleeping on the footpath and reluctantly limped away as I approached. I retraced my steps when I saw fifty-five. The poor cat had just resettled. A white-haired woman watched me from her window. The driver of a passing car slowed and stared. I must have looked out of place and was aware my presence wasn't going unnoticed. Did they have Neighbourhood Watch in Prague 6?

Like most of the surrounding houses, number forty-seven was brick and two-storey. With skylights in the roof and a paved driveway on the side leading to a lock-up garage, it appeared the archetypal suburban residence which Zeus might have drawn if asked to sketch a house. I had imagined something rustic and rundown. This was modern and mundane. An unlocked gate led to four concrete steps, which I climbed as silently as possible to give me the option of changing my mind at the top of them. I slipped the address in my pocket and combed my hair with my hands. My finger was shaking visibly as it inched towards the white button on the doorframe.

Ding-dong!

At least the doorbell spoke English.

A boy on a bicycle saw me, stopped suddenly, then turned and rode back whence he'd come. I imagined Sarah at the banknote museum. Suddenly I wished I'd gone with her.

A minute passed.

Ding-dong!

I peeped in the front windows, fleetingly, not wanting to attract further attention. The rooms were sun-filled, spacious and silent, the furniture seemed new and unused, and on the mantelpiece above the fireplace was a lone photo of two children laughing and embracing. I didn't dare risk dallying to analyse the photo, but assumed it to be of Eva and her brother. For the first time the thought crossed my mind that they could have been twins, which might have made his passing more difficult for her to bear. Anything was possible. All I knew about Eva had been pieced together via hearsay or her own awkward instalments.

After a circumspect scan of the street, which made me feel sinister despite my good intentions, I snuck around the side of the house. Every window was closed. Every view obscured by curtains. A wooden gate led to a back garden, which I was preparing to scale, my foot on the handle, when I heard the soft sound of music, not from a stereo but from an instrument. I cocked my ear and froze as though caught in a searchlight while attempting a prison break.

Was it a violin?

Like a hunter on a scent I scaled the gate, jumped to the ground as quietly as possible and let my ears lead the way. The garden was smart yet simple – a lawn ringed by shrubs but no flowers other than a few scattered clumps of dandelions. Stepping stones in the far right-hand corner led the way to a wooden shed. As I approached the house, buzzing with nervous adrenaline, startled sparrows fluttered from a seed tray suspended from the branch of a tree. Eva's house felt like a home. A home from which, like the sparrows, she had fled.

Despite the sunshine a light illuminated a back room whose open French doors gave onto the garden. The music grew in volume as I neared them, sponge lawn allowing me to do so in silence. I recognised the tune but couldn't name it, unlike the adult girl whose eyes were closed and who swayed like a surging tide as she played. Eva's skilful hand rose and fell, as though sewing the refrain into fabric. Her jaw was clenched. Her face stern. The instrument nibbled at her neck.

What a fool I had been.

I didn't dare knock, didn't dare interrupt the sound of Eva's honesty and my stupidity. Instead, overcome by a joy similar to that of waking up and realising it was all a bad dream, I lay on the lawn and stole the sonata. The uncut grass cushioned and consumed me; it seemed more lush than London ryegrass. Unaware of her audience, Eva played with assurance and passion. At times she appeared to overpower the instrument, at others it appeared to have the upper hand. It seemed an intimate relationship, a tempestuous relationship, but the result was more than beautiful.

I closed my eyes. I can't remember for how long . . .

'*Have you buy ticket?*'

The music in my dream continued. The music in my life had stopped.

'Have you buy ticket?'

I opened my eyes and blinked at blue sky and blinding sun filtering through blonde hair and a familiar foreign face. Scattered marshmallow clouds seemed as soft as the ground on which I would have slept happily ever after. I felt groggy but strangely elated, as though I had woken from somewhere deeper and more recuperative than sleep.

'I can't believe,' continued the voice. 'I can't believe. Was much frightened. Was to telephone police before see Teacher's old shoes.'

I had gone back to the old faithfuls for my holiday. The new ones would have given me blisters.

'I'm sorry,' I said, closing my eyes again and savouring the sun on my face.

'Of?' inquired the voice above.

'*For* or *about*. Sorry *for* or *about*.'

Her soft laughter.

'Much travel to teach lesson,' she said.

'I think you've taught me one,' I replied.

Eva sat down beside me and plucked a single strand of grass, which squeaked as it left the earth. Perhaps in protest.

'Vy sorry?' she asked.

'For not believing you when you said that mark on your neck was from a violin.'

Eva chose not to respond, though I knew she'd understood. Then she plucked another strand of grass, which lost its life with the same shrill lament.

'You play beautifully. I don't think I've ever heard the violin played so beautifully.' Eva said nothing. I trod as warily with my words as I had done with my feet upon entering her garden. 'Who taught you to play the violin so beautifully?'

Another strand of grass left the earth, pulled more forcefully this time. Plucked.

'Farzer,' she replied, surrendering her softness all of a sudden.

I remembered Eva talking about her father at the casino and on Parliament Hill. Time couldn't heal all wounds, she'd said, though it was hard to imagine what he could have done that was so wrong, so horrible, if he was capable of teaching his daughter to play the violin with such tender touch.

'Whatever mistakes your father made, Eva, he has turned you into a remarkable person. You are gifted and wise. I hope I do as good a job with my child as your father did with you.'

She sighed in frustration.

'I no understand.'

I raised my head and regarded her briefly, shielding my eyes with my hand.

'Your slippers worked, Eva – I'm going to be a father.'

'Vot?!'

'I'm going to be a father.'

She grabbed my arm and shook me as though frantically trying to wake me.

'Congratulations! Is amazing. I happy you.'

She plucked another strand of grass and was silent for a few seconds. How long had it been since the sun found my face?

'Can I ask qvestion?' she said.

'You can ask me anything.'

I realised I was speaking to Eva as though stretched on the psychologist's couch.

'Vy you in my garden?'

I propped myself up on my elbows and looked at Eva properly for the first time since trespassing. She was barefoot and dressed in a white Mind the Gap T-shirt and a blue ankle-length skirt with a white floral pattern around the hem. She seemed partly at home and partly elsewhere, like all those who have fled.

'I was worried about you.'

'About *me*?'

'Yes – I thought you might have done something silly.'

'Something . . . ?'

'Angelique said you wanted to be close to your brother and I didn't know how to interpret that, given that you said your brother is . . .'

The whites of Eva's eyes.

'You speak Angelique?!'

'I dropped by to give you the money we won at the casino and she said you'd rushed back to Prague to see your brother. I worried that meant—'

'No right you speak Angelique!'

I shuffled up straighter on my elbows, as though my motive would make more sense to her if delivered from height.

'I was worried about you. Why did you say you wanted to be with your brother?'

Her mood darkened. She scratched her neck.

'Would be birsday tomorrow,' she said. 'Is good I here to my muzzer.'

I lay back down and closed my eyes, sparing her my scrutiny.

'I'm so sorry, Eva. You and he look so happy in the photo.'

I had forgotten to measure my words. The sun was warming my face, the grass was tickling my ears. It reminded me of when I was a child playing football at the local park, perhaps savouring a goal someone else had kicked. I wasn't an attacker. Never have been.

Eva's response was delayed. I imagined her confused expression, the one I had seen in class so many times.

'Vich photo?'

'The one in your living room.'

Another pause as she figured out how I might have seen the photo. Nothing I said seemed to spook her, despite the invasion of privacy.

'Photo long time . . . before . . . *všechny problémy*.'

'Before . . . ?'

'Is better you no understand.'

She plucked another blade of grass.

'At least you had a father, Eva.'

'Vot means?'

I took a deep breath before delivering words I had never before uttered in that order.

'I was abandoned by my birth parents and adopted by a couple who were more interested in making money than in making me their son.' Eva made it feel easy to free the prisoner I had kept captive for so long. 'Nobody fucking wanted me, Eva, neither by nature nor to nurture. And all I've ever wanted was to call someone special my father.'

The sweet sound of birds chirping. Eva hadn't understood. Couldn't possibly have understood. I didn't understand it myself. Or did she know the best psychologists simply listen and let the patient release the burden?

Eva's attention was diverted by something inside the house, by movement rather than sound. She stood without hesitation, hitching her long skirt slightly as she stepped through the surrendering grass, up the step and into the house. I raised my head and, through the same French doors I had watched her play the violin, I now saw her stand on tiptoes and reach for something near the ceiling, invisible to me yet visible to her. She reached again and again, persistent, never giving up; her movement slightly clumsy like a child's first attempts to catch a ball. Then she snared it, whatever it was, cupped her hands together, ran into the garden and threw her arms to the heavens. A butterfly fluttered free, hovering above her head for a moment as if to thank her. Then, light as a feather, it disappeared over the fence.

Rescue complete, Eva returned to my side and sat down.

'I'm so sorry, Eva.'

'*For* or *about*?'

I smiled to myself. She was such a good student.

'For making assumptions about you.'

'Vot means?'

'As I said – I thought Tim was your violin.'

'I not understand vy you sink zis?'

I hesitated. She plucked another strand of grass.

'Because I was standing at the window of my classroom and I saw him give you the opal in his car.'

Eva tilted her head and pondered what I'd said, then she slapped my chest – though she didn't detect the Tesco bag concealed under my faithful blue pullover.

'You are stupid man. Opal from bruzzer. Zeus to break. Tim to fix.'

It couldn't possibly be that innocent.

'But you refused it initially.'

'Vot?'

'At first you didn't want the box, the opal.'

She thought for a moment. Cast her mind back to an exchange the supposed victim remembered less clearly than the witness.

'Ven box close I ref . . . ref . . . ?'

'*Refuse.*'

'Ven box open and see opal say yes.'

I had misread the clues.

'So where's Tim now?'

'In London.'

Solved nothing other than the puzzle in my paper.

'Are you sure?'

'I talk him zis morning to say no come back London next week.'

My fucking paper.

'Vy you to ask?'

I took another deep breath – the smell of grass was wonderful. Then I looked sheepishly at Eva.

'I thought . . . well, it seems silly, but I thought perhaps he was dead.'

The whites of Eva's eyes again.

'Vy you sink zis?'

'Actually, I thought you might possibly have . . .' I lowered my voice to a whisper. 'I thought you might have killed him.'

It sounded ridiculous, having just witnessed Eva save the life of a butterfly.

'Kill?!' She put two pistol fingers to her temple to ensure she'd understood the verb.

'Yes.'

Her brow furrowed. For the first time I noticed her pendulous earrings were treble clefs.

'Vy kill Tim?'

'Because I thought he was . . . well, you know, and after you ran from the allotment I worried that you might have done something drastic.'

'But I say you no haf problem Tim.'

'No you didn't. At the allotment you asked me to stop—'

'Yes,' interrupted Eva. 'To stop!'

Shame surged. My mouth fell open. Realisation was a trance. I had misinterpreted my own language, the one thing in the world I was good at. I remembered Eva's call from the darkness: *Sebastian no understand language he teach.*

The sound of sparrows returning to the seed tray. When was the last time I'd heard a bird's wings flap?

'Forgive me, Eva, but the evidence suggested otherwise. Why did you say he touches you?'

'He buy for me flowers ven I sad for family, for home far, for bruzzer memory. He *touch* me. Emotion, no physic . . . physic . . .'

'*Physical.*'

It appeared I was the beginner. Tim did indeed have a heart. English teachers pride themselves on their knowledge of secondary, even tertiary dictionary definitions of words. As I found out the hard way, it is a mistake to assume students only know the primary meaning.

I sat up and looked at her, relieved I was wrong but for some reason clinging to being right.

'So why did you cry and run from the allotment when I told you I wanted to help you?'

She averted her eyes, bit her lip, shook her head. Whatever the reason, it was weighing her down.

'I hate that you . . .' She looked at the sky as if for inspiration, for the courage to speak. 'I hate that you see wrong but . . .'

'But?'

She closed her eyes.

'But still see truth.'

How can a heart pound so loudly at the same time it skips a beat?

'The truth? What truth?'

A cloud obscured the sun. The temperature dropped instantly. Goosebumps. Eva bowed her head as her expression too became downcast. She was once more the shy girl of her placement interview, the girl in whom I had sensed suffering, the girl I had sensed needed help. Tears rushed to her eyes. Tears of sadness. No doubt about it. Tears of secret sadness all along.

'The truth I can't never to lose.' Her chest heaved. 'Ever, never.' Her body shook. 'All my life.'

I put my hand gently on her shoulder.

'What truth, Eva?'

Her face was in her hands.

Some men no ask, just take.

'Is stupid life,' she said, wiping her eyes, bravely finding her voice. 'You vont farzer – and I vish I no haf.'

Every ounce of the happiness I had known on the grass, the fleeting happiness, was irretrievably lost.

'You don't have to say any more, Eva.'

Her tears were flowing freely, staining her flawless cheeks like dirty footprints in snow.

'Sebastian no understand language he teach,' she said, 'but . . .' Her entire body shuddered with the volcanic pain of what she had to say, of what she had to say to someone, of what fate had decided she'd say to me. She looked at the sky, at its vastness, at the tiny cloud in front of the sun that could somehow throw the entire world into shadow. She grasped at a breath, at the power to share her secret. I gave her time. All the time she could need. 'Sebastian understand more zan language.' I closed my eyes as I realised I had followed the right trail to the wrong man. 'No Tim violin, but farzer.'

I hated the birds for singing. They had no right to sing, while the girl who fed them sobbed softly, head bowed, hands in lap.

The torture of time stopped. Not knowing what to say said it all. Though paralysed on the grass, I searched for words that might comfort her in some way.

'I'm sorry, Eva. I'm so terribly sorry.'

She smiled through her tears, the most courageous smile.

I tilted my head to make eye contact.

'Did your brother find out, Eva?'

Her reluctant nod dislodged a tear. I wanted to wipe its stain from her face but thought better of it and withdrew my hand.

'Is that why he . . . ?'

Another gentle yet perceptible nod that unmasked her father's guilt with such innocence.

I lay back down on the grass, lost in the agony of it all. My secret was infinitesimal in comparison.

'How can you play the violin after what you've just told me?'

Eva lifted her head. Took in the sky again. Her voice seemed more assured.

'For memory of bruzzer.'

If I hadn't arrived at school precisely as the Range Rover pulled up, Eva's and my lives would have been different. So different. And yet the same.

After minutes of sorrowful silence, broken only by the oblivious birds, Eva placed something light on my chest. I raised my head to see a Woodstock souvenir: a necklace woven from blades of grass interwoven with dandelion flowers.

I took the necklace in one hand and held it up to the sun.

'Thank you,' I said. 'It's sweet. And I have something for you too.'

'For me?'

I pulled the Tesco bag from under my pullover. Eva recognised it instantly and raised her palms in polite refusal, as she had initially refused the opal. I tossed it on the grass beside her. Tears drying, she regarded it as though it had fallen from the sky.

'I'm not leaving here with the money,' I said. 'You won it and you keep it. I thought perhaps you might use it to pay the fees to study architecture in London. If you keep studying English you'll soon be good enough to get a place at university. But foreign students pay more.'

She smiled briefly, almost begrudgingly, perhaps embarrassed to be touched by the thought.

'You vill to be good farzer.'

The sun shone again, though I resented its warmth and what it had illuminated. Now I understood her clothes, her shyness, her fondness for the opal. I hadn't misread the clues; I had used them to fill the wrong grid. Now only one clue remained – or was it a clue I had already solved? I stared at the sun, challenging its strength, refusing to let it blind me.

'Can I ask you one final question, Eva?'

'You must,' she replied. 'Obligation.'

'Did your father die in a car accident?'

My Czech student leant in front of the sun and looked deeply into my eyes, forever scarred for looking at what they shouldn't have seen. She raised her hand and moved two outstretched fingers slowly towards my face as though attempting to hypnotise an animal. Her fingertips were cool on my eyelids. Ever so gently, she closed my eyes.

I had seen enough of the mystery.

That final, unfilled piece of the puzzle. There is always one. Often the easiest. Gnawing away. Bedevilling your day. Though perhaps some puzzles are best left unsolved.

Every now and then, even today, when I think I had the right answer for *Committed by crude Mr Rude (6)* that morning on Primrose Hill, I shake my head in shame and remember her freeing the butterfly. My old friend Eva was a gem. No way was she capable of murdering anything other than the English language.

Eyes closed, I listened to Eva unwrapping the plastic parcel on her back lawn in Břevnov. The spongy grass, the intoxicating sun . . . I could have slept in the sadness. Perhaps I did for a second or two.

'Um, Teacher . . .'

I ignored the voice.

'Sebastian?'

She shook me awake. I forced open my eyes and reluctantly raised my head.

'What is it?'

Eva held open the Tesco bag so I could see inside without getting up.

'Cup of tea?' she offered.

■

Whoever had stolen the money and replaced it with tea bags had fortunately done so with my favourite variety, Lapsang Souchong, which overpowered the smell of sauerkraut in Eva's spacious but simple kitchen. Had I checked the contents of the bag when I'd dug it up I would probably have suspected Eva of the theft, but in light of recent events I decided not to pursue that line of inquiry. The last thing I needed was another mystery. It must have been some lucky random thief who was after my carrots but had to settle for cash.

On the two occasions that Eva and I drank together we chose refreshments that one of us found obnoxious. In my case – Cannabis Vodka. In hers – Lapsang Souchong; it was as exotic as I got. I had persisted with her concoction but one sip of mine sufficed for her to contort her face like a child chewing veggies and toss the remainder down the sink.

The house was so quiet I could hear the hum of the refrigerator and the tick of the kitchen clock. I imagined Eva's mother must be lonely here on her own.

'Where is your mother?' I asked.

'Shop,' she replied. 'Special dinner for bruzzer birsday.'

'What's she cooking?'

Colour rushed to her cheeks. I was pleased to see its return.

'She to try England recip . . . recip . . .'

'*Recipe.*'

'Yes – toad in hole.'

My laughter surprised me. Just a few minutes ago in the garden I thought I might never laugh again.

I indicated the front of the house.

'Is that you and your brother in the photo in the living room?'

She nodded.

'How old would he have been?'

'Twenty-four.'

I smiled plaintively but could think of nothing comforting to say. Her pain, her mother's pain, could never find comfort in words. I stepped towards the window and put my mug on the kitchen bench.

'Well, I hope you enjoy your dinner.'

'Oh, yes. Thank you. I am sure.'

Eva took a tea towel from its unusual perch – a music stand – and wiped the sink where her tea had splashed. When she then hung it back on the stand I noticed that the towel was decorated with a London tube map – a souvenir for her mother, no doubt.

I pointed to the tea towel.

'Will you be back in London?'

She shrugged her shoulders.

'Perhaps. I not know.'

I looked at my watch, thought of Sarah, of the life that had to go on. It had all seemed so mundane, so meaningless. Now, in light of Eva's tragedy, I realised how precious it was.

'Well, I should go. I'm meeting my wife for lunch.'

Eva appeared surprised.

'She is outside?'

'No, she's in town, visiting some museums.'

'She like Prague?'

'Londoners like anywhere it's not raining.'

We both laughed somewhat nervously. I think we were sensing that it was time for goodbye, that after showing each other the hidden parts of ourselves we would never see one another again.

'Can I ask qvestion?' said Eva.

I opened my arms. 'Anything you want.'

'You never say me why two is lucky number.'

I smiled. Remembered the casino.

'Two is the number of children my meeting and spending time with you made me realise I need to have.'

She smiled and blinked back tears.

'I haf for you prissent,' she said, pointing upstairs. 'Please to vait.'

'Another one?' I protested.

But, as in Hampstead, she was already out the door.

I stood alone in Eva's linoleum kitchen. The noise of the fridge and the clock somehow amplified the silence. I imagined the trauma the walls around me had witnessed: the slammed doors, the raised voices, all so at odds with the velvet music that Eva and her brother must have played. It choked my throat, the tragedies that people could contrive simply by living, by being alive. I may not hitherto have been in favour of adopting, but, without the slightest hesitation, I would have adopted Eva as my daughter.

Carpeted yet creaky, the staircase announced her return. Once again she hitched her long skirt slightly to descend the stairs, before smiling briefly and handing me a slender paperback book.

'Is Kafka,' she explained, as I turned the short but significant read over in my hands. '*Metamorphosis*. Have you read?'

'Ah . . . no. No I haven't. Thank you, Eva. I'll treasure it.'

'Is in English,' she continued, as though she needed to justify the gift. 'I buy to improve because know of heart in Czech.'

'*By* heart.'

Eva grinned.

'*By* heart.'

The clock ticked away awkward time. Neither of us seemed prepared to say the words we knew needed to be said. I stepped towards her, placed my hands on her upper arms and moved to kiss her forehead before hesitating and stepping back.

Eva grabbed my arm. Pulled me towards her. 'Is okay,' she whispered, bowing her head.

'Look after yourself,' I said, before turning in the direction of the hallway.

'God pickle you,' she replied.

I turned back to face her.

'God what?'

Eva blushed.

'*Pickle* you?' she repeated more cautiously.

I stared at her, blankly at first then with a slight smile.

'Vait,' she said, running from the room.

I walked to the kitchen window and watched the garden where my sprawled imprint lay in the grass. The stairs creaked again as Eva returned with her English dictionary and searched frantically for the relevant page.

'Pickle,' she repeated, more assured this time and passing me the book with her finger on the entry.

I took it from her and read:

Pickle *n. & v.* *n.* **1** (often in *pl.*) food, esp. vegetables, preserved in brine, vinegar, mustard, etc. and used as a relish. **2** *colloq.* a plight *(a fine pickle we are in!)*. *v.* keep. preserve.

I didn't bother to correct her. It seemed a fitting farewell.

21

Telling stories

Sarah ordered the goulash with dumplings, saying she was eating for two. I got a double gin and tonic, saying – since she couldn't have alcohol – that I was drinking for two. Why is it that British travellers venture far afield only to then pick a favourite bar or restaurant and patronise it for the duration of the trip? We even sat at the same table, though in our defence, and so as not to be labelled unadventurous, we summoned a different waitress.

'You okay, sweetheart?' asked Sarah, moving our ashtray to an adjacent table as usual. 'You look pale.'

'I'm fine. Just a bit overwhelmed by the news.'

Sarah rubbed her belly. Smiled a sunbeam.

'I know,' she said. 'Exciting, isn't it?'

The waitress brought my gin and Sarah's water so quickly that, once out of earshot, Sarah suggested she was the owner of the café.

'So,' my wife inquired, 'what did you get up to this morning?'

My gin went down the wrong way, though I coughed for longer than it actually took to recover in an attempt to conceive a response. In my haste to get back to the city on time I had forgotten to devise an alibi for my morning's excursion to the suburbs. Lying on the table, now splashed with gin, Eva's parting gift caught my eye.

'I, er, popped into a bookshop . . .' I noticed a crinkle down the spine. 'I popped into a second-hand bookshop and, er, spent the morning sitting by the river reading Kafka.'

'Really?' said Sarah, leaning over and picking up the book. 'What's it about?'

I hadn't a clue, though I knew with Sarah I could say what I liked. She would never read it while they were still churning out *Property Week*.

'Well, it's . . . it's complex, and I'm not even halfway, but essentially it's about a boy driven to death by the actions of his father, and a girl from Prague who played the violin too beautifully.'

Sarah frowned.

'Sounds harrowing,' she said, reaching over and snatching the book. 'I'll read it on the flight home.'

I tried to snatch it back.

'Don't be silly, darling. Here, give it back.'

She pushed away my outstretched hand.

'What's wrong with you, Seb? You've been trying to convince me to read more for years. Now I'm not working I'll have time.' She contemplated the cover. 'And I might as well start with the greats.'

Sarah smiled and stowed the book in her handbag.

As the waitress passed our table, I ordered another double G&T.

∎

For the first time in my life I sat on a plane thinking a crash would be the best option. As our return flight approached the English Channel, Sarah approached the end of *Metamorphosis*. I had spent the duration of the journey preparing for the accusatory glance she would cast me on turning the final page and questioning my incorrect summary. I would simply come clean. Say I hadn't spent the morning reading the book by the river but had told her Eva's story instead.

I had never seen Sarah read so attentively, brow creased, bottom lip twitching ever so slightly. She didn't even raise her head from the page to reach for her unsalted cashews and watered-down orange juice. The title of the book seemed appropriate in more ways than one. When she closed the cover and took a deep breath, as though it were her first since the start, I closed my eyes and waited for the question: Why had I lied about reading the book? Instead her hand found mine, followed by her head on my shoulder.

'That was some story,' she said. 'Terrible that a boy could fear his father to that extent. But I liked the – what would Kafka call it? – "unknown nourishment" he received from his sister's violin playing.'

As though in slow motion I opened my eyes and reached for the book, conscious that my hand was shaking.

'You're right, Sebastian,' continued Sarah, as I beheld Eva's mysterious gift. 'The lives of people are in books.' I moved my hand across the cover as though dusting off treasure. 'Do you think that was a true story?' asked Sarah, unaware of the alarming inference.

I opened my mouth to speak but words simply wouldn't arrive. My throat felt dryer than it had ever felt. My tongue a dead weight. Did I think it was all a true story? In many respects, I hoped so. In many others, I hoped not.

Sarah sat forward. Eyed me with genuine concern.

'Whatever's the matter, sweetheart?'

'F-fear of flying,' I replied.

'Goodness me,' she said, sitting back in her chair and tightening her seatbelt for descent. 'You sound like Fer-Frank.'

■

'Perhaps we should stop for bread and milk,' said Sarah, as our taxi approached Chalk Farm.

I nodded indifferently. The subject of food was not one that interested me and my stomach, which was still upside down.

'There's a mini-mart coming up on the left,' announced the driver. 'Would you like me to stop there?'

'Lovely, thanks!' shouted Sarah.

Suddenly I forgot my condition. Looked at my wife, then at the driver.

'I thought his listening hatch was closed,' I whispered.

'They can still hear what you're saying,' she replied. 'There's an induction loop. Or a microphone. I can't remember.'

I had told Eva where we could bury the money while in the cab on the way to the allotment.

My stomach churned again.

'Tell me something,' I shouted to the driver, whose eyes promptly appeared in his rear-view mirror. 'Do you drink Lapsang Souchong?'

I felt Sarah's perplexed gaze on me.

'Er, prefer English Breakfast, guv.'

He was off the hook.

22

Ellipsis

Nine months . . .

23

Substitution

'Welcome to The Future Perfect. My name's Sebastian. Is this your first visit to London?'

'*Ja* . . . er, yes,' replied Johann, twenty-four, from Munich, hair shaved militarily short.

'And what are your first impressions?'

'Vot are my . . . ?'

'Do you like London?'

'*Ja* . . . er, yes.'

I yawned. Sipped cold coffee. Looked across the street to Yeats' house and contemplated his poem 'When You Are Old'.

'What do you like about London, Johann?'

He shrugged his shoulders. Raindrops on his jacket.

'London *gut*. Is *gut*.'

'Okay.'

I flipped his student card and was amazed to see that he was working as an au pair. Must have been a mistake. Audrey was making more and more errors since a middle-aged shoe salesman from Leeds had swept her off her size-seven moccasins and excited her into heels.

'It says here that you have a job. What job do you have, Johann?'

'I au pair.'

Sorry, Audrey.

'I thought only women did that job.'

'I man.'

'Indeed you are.'

'Excuse me?'

'I agree that you are a man.'

He looked confused. I didn't blame him. I detected the start of a linguistic labyrinth through which I had lumbered countless times without yet locating the exit.

'Is *gut*.'

'To be a man?'

'To be au pair,' he corrected.

I looked out the window at the grey spitting sky that seemed to have descended to ground level.

'How many children do you look after?'

'One. A boy.'

'Okay.'

His answers appeared arrogant and terse, but I knew he was more agreeable than language allowed.

'You haf?' he asked without intonation.

'Yes, twin boys – Phineas and Cadmus.'

His shaved scalp shifted forward, explaining his confusion better than his tongue subsequently did.

'Not name England?'

'No, they're Greek names. They mean "oracle" and "from the East". What's your boy called?'

'Brian.'

I rolled my eyes at modest, traditional parents.

'Is *gut*,' I said, amusing myself.

Johann's mobile phone rang. He reacted as though it had delivered an electric shock and rushed to turn it off, rummaging through the pocket of his coat. I pulled my newspaper from my own pocket and filled a square in the grid.

Johann's scalp moved again.

'Vot you do?' he asked.

'Sudoku.'

'Vy?'

'Well, it keeps the mind active and is far less dangerous than a crossword.'

That scalp of his needed a seatbelt.

'Vot means?'

'It means, Johann, that from tomorrow you will be in room five. Next!'

■

Phineas and Cadmus were on their bottles when I got home as soon as the school bell rang the working day's neck. I no longer went to the Princess with Walter. My friend and father figure would no doubt have missed me had he not had his hands full with Ludmila. They were yet to settle on a name for their unborn baby but still had a month to wait. It was wonderful to think that Walter's house would soon be bursting with life other than squirrels. The pair were planning a summer wedding at which I would be best man. The sly Ukrainian had finally got what she wanted. So too the lonely Londoner. The only aspect of their relationship that was slow in starting was the Rover, though Walter said the baby had most likely been conceived on its back seat.

Most of my students had passed their exam, except for Jean-Paul who, despite overconfidence, still wasn't ready for 'upper intermediately' and had skulked off home to his 'liar' of a father and 'arse' of a mother with his tail *entre* his legs. I was happy to see him go but still wished him /awl th̪ə best/. Agnes had fled to Sweden to study theology; Giovanni had returned home to Italy to admire his own reflection; Fernanda had gone back to Brazil to finish her degree in beauty therapy; while the rest of the Gobbledygook Gang had come with me to upper intermediate, apart from Sibylla, who went straight to advanced because she scored one hundred per cent on the test and even corrected one of the questions.

We'd had a classroom party to see the leavers off, at which Yoon Pong strummed a banjo while Doughnut and Kazuki did the vocal equivalent of scratching their fingernails down the board by trying to sing along to his plucking. I hadn't heard from Eva and assumed she had either stayed in Prague or was busy with Zeus.

Marking their exams had been as entertaining as ever. Referring to a restaurant dinner she had shouted for a friend, Doughnut wrote: *I went out with Ting Mae and some chickens were on me.* Proud of her compatriots, Kazuki wrote: *Japanese pleople are warmed and hospital.* And bragging about a ski trip that was obviously exciting enough to keep her awake, Mercedes wrote: *I had lovely holiday on the slurps of Chamonix.*

Student numbers, as usual, had dropped during the winter and The Future Perfect was busy but not breakneck. Rhonda had kept her promise and eased Walter back into teaching, giving him a pre-intermediate class to help him re-find his feet. She didn't have him replaced as head of IT and, strangely enough, most of the machines started purring. Otherwise it was business as usual, apart from the arrival of an Australian teacher gone walkabout from Wagga Wagga with whom Cynthia squabbled over the pronunciation of Maldives and vitamins.

Dressed in a grey tracksuit with milk and puke stains on the shoulders, Sarah was watching *Letters and Numbers* when I walked in, beating the contestants and Carol Vorderman to the solution of the mathematical equations. Claude dozed by the coffee table and the sucklers were in Sarah's lap, one on each thigh, gorging themselves on Boots baby powder and growing visibly almost by the day. As a mother Sarah was getting the hang of things, though she had upset the midwife by having the babies on the bottle rather than the breast in a matter of hours.

I went into the bedroom to throw my jacket on the bed and noticed two of Sarah's business suits on her side of the mattress. Then I made two cups of Lapsang Souchong (I still had plenty), sat down on the couch beside my family and stared at the screen in the corner of the room. The sound of a clock ticking and two hunched contestants eyeing the jumbled letters: U, S, T, E, X, H, D, A, E.

'Exhausted,' I said, yawning.

'So am I,' added Sarah.

'No,' I said, pointing at the telly, 'I mean the answer to the conundrum – *exhausted*.'

Sarah turned her head to look at me. The boys stopped sucking for a second.

'That's spooky!' she declared.

'Nah,' I replied, 'pure coincidence.'

Sarah shifted Phineas slightly and put her hand lovingly on my leg.

'You've still got it, sweetheart.'

I kissed her pale cheek.

'So have you.'

I sipped my tea and sighed with pleasure, certain we would live happily ever after. Sarah gazed out the window.

'I think it's going to rain.'

'I'll put the bin out early. Then I'll fix us some tea.'

'No need, there's leftovers in the fridge.'

The clock ticked again as we pondered P, A, E, S, S, N, P, I, H.

'I, er, noticed some old business suits on the bed, Sarah. You taking them to Cancer Research?' My wife shifted on the couch. Phineas stopped sucking and started crying. Cadmus soon joined the chorus. I plucked him out of Sarah's lap, sat him straight on mine and gently rubbed his back. Sarah did the same with his twin brother. 'I can take the suits for you on my way to work tomorrow,' I shouted over the din.

Sarah grabbed the remote and turned the telly down, before turning towards me with a hangdog expression more suited to Claude.

'I'm not taking the suits to Cancer Research, darling. I'm taking them to be dry-cleaned.'

'Why?'

Claude raised his head.

'Margaret's offered me a job.'

Cadmus burped.

'What did she say when you declined?'

Phineas echoed his brother's emission. Their behaviour was identical, even if they weren't.

'I didn't decline it, Seb.'

Claude lowered his head as I turned mine in the direction of my wife.

'What – you accepted her offer?!' Cadmus started crying again, or wailing would better describe it. 'But you promised, Sarah. What about the boys?'

'We'll get an au pair.'

The wailing grew more cacophonous.

'But you promised!'

'Don't be a baby, Seb. And don't frighten them either.'

I lowered my voice and comforted Cadmus by rocking him.

'Part time?'

'Full time, I'm afraid. At least until I get some seniority. Margaret's been amazing. I told you, Seb – it's all networking.'

I looked at my boys, my baby boys; they had their mother's eyes. I thought of Kafka, or Eva, of controlling, overbearing fathers.

'Sarah, sweetheart, it is of course your right to work, and I know you're only doing it for us. When they're a bit older, perhaps I could take a break from work and stay home with them for a while. But they're so young. Couldn't you at least wait until they're six months? Don't *you* need a break as well?'

'The longer I leave it the less employable I will be. And I may not get another offer like this. I'd be walking into this job at Margaret's company at a time when many people are getting laid off.'

'But you did say you'd stay home for a while if we had a baby.'

'That was when we had savings. And I never expected two for the price of one. Twins cost double.'

I slumped back on the couch. Claude raised his head again, perhaps hoping for an afternoon walk.

'I'm sorry, Seb,' continued Sarah, 'but it's for the best. I've already put an ad on au pair world dot com.'

I bounced Cadmus on my knee.

'Don't advertise there. Walter will turn up for the job.'

Claude realised he was out of luck and placed his snout back on the floor. Sarah reached for Phineas's dummy and placed it in his mouth.

'And my mother can help out if need be.'

I looked at the telly. The jumbled letters spelt *Happiness*. No wonder I couldn't see it.

24

The future continuous

The boys were dressed in jump suits as brand new as their bodies inside. Sarah insisted they look their best for the interview, as though they were the applicants rather than the au pair. I hadn't helped Sarah's search but hadn't hindered it either. In three weeks of looking, five Poles, two Hungarians and four Scandinavians had been rejected on the grounds they didn't have enough experience and that ours would be their first London placement. Girls from Krakow to Copenhagen were vying to bring up my boys in Chalk Farm. So when an au pair who claimed to have worked in the area applied for the position, Sarah insisted I be home for the interview, saying she had a positive feeling.

It was a Saturday morning in summer, though a stiff wind and drizzle suggested a less agreeable season. Despite the weather I had walked Claude, planted turnips at the allotment and bought the morning paper on my way home.

'Could you clean your fingernails?' asked Sarah.

Oh, and cleaned my fingernails.

When the doorbell rang Claude raised his head abruptly and barked, something he'd never done before. He was no guard dog, unless I didn't want anyone to steal the shoes across which he snoozed most of the day.

Sarah buzzed the candidate into the building and went to open the door, as quietly as possible since the boys had fallen asleep moments earlier. I stayed in the living room with Claude. The girl would no doubt be nervous and crowding her at the door would only make her more so.

'Hiya, come in,' I heard my wife say, no doubt offering her hand in a businesslike manner. 'I'm Sarah.'

'Happy to meet you,' said the au pair.

Her 'h' was rough, like summoned spit.

I stood as they approached the lounge room and tossed my paper on the coffee table. To be continued, perhaps in front of the cricket.

'This is my husband, Sebastian,' said Sarah, leading the applicant in.

She was wearing the opal. An old friend is a gem.

Head bowed, hesitant yet true to his instincts, my labrador sidled up to Eva and gently flapped his tail. Between his eyes, ears and tail, it struck me that Claude was the best communicator of us all.

Acknowledgments

Although this is a work of fiction, you wouldn't be reading it without the assistance of some truly great and greatly true people.

Sincere thanks to Fran Moore, for finding this book a home and for making me feel as though I've found one at Curtis Brown. To Louise Thurtell at Allen & Unwin, who went into bat for this book as only someone who loves cricket can. To Isobel Dixon, for planting the seed that grew into this project and for her time spent reading the first draft and improving the second.

Thanks to Juliet Rogers, current friend and former publisher. To Ali Lavau for her wise eye. To Ann Lennox for her patient ear and diligent hand. To Brooke Clark for her precise pencil. And to everyone at Allen & Unwin who laboured and believed.

Thanks to Richard Stokes for curious conversations, for Gin Sarnies, for reading and listening, and for leading me by chance to Kafka, Donne and Byron, all of whom are paid tribute here.

Thanks to the wacky genius of John Bevan for the cryptic crossword clues. They are all his doing. He supplied them on demand. Between you and me, I think he enjoyed the experience.

Thanks to Martina Stima and Nikol for checking my Czech. To Eun Woo and Keiko for allowing the dog to eat their homework. To John Geraghty, who understands the struggle and who lent me his family home for the final edit. To Marion McMahon for also providing me and the book with lodgings in our hour(s) of need.

Last and foremost, thanks to my family. To my mother and father for their unflagging faith in the risk of writing. To my children for the smiles that creep through the study door. And, above all, to my wife Daniela – I love you more than all the words I have ever written, and I couldn't have written them without you.

God pickle you all.